THE RIVALS

THE FINISH LINE SERIES
BOOK 1

HOLLY ROSE

The Rivals
Copyright © 2024 by Holly Rose
All rights reserved.

No part of this book may be reproduced in any form or by an electronic or mechanical means, including information storage and retrieval, without the written permission from the author, except for the use of brief quotations in a book review.

This is a work of fiction. All names, characters, places and incidents portrayed in this production are fictitious. No identification with actual persons (living or deceased), places, buildings, and products is intended or should be inferred.

No generative artificial intelligence (AI) was used in the writing of this book or the artwork. Without in any way limiting the author's exclusive rights under copyright, any use of this publication to "train" generative artificial intelligence (AI) technologies to generate text, pictures, or video is expressly prohibited. The author reserves all rights to license uses of this work for generative AI training and development of machine learning language models.

[ISBN]
Cover design by Holly Rose
Edited by Lindsey Clarke
Proofread by Sophie Claypole

For the fangirls

CONTENT WARNINGS
AND A NOTE ABOUT MOTORSPORT

Content Warnings

The Rivals is an adult romance novel that contains strong language, explicit sexual content (on page, all consensual), and some content readers might find triggering. This includes discussions about mental health, therapy and anxiety. There are themes of misogyny and sexism. Loss of a parent and bereavement is mentioned. There is an on page car collision and discussions of past serious car accidents.

A Note About Motorsport

The Rivals depicts a fictional version of motorsport and is inspired by the real world sport of Formula One. However, this fictional version is different from the real life sport and if you're a big fan of F1 please be aware a lot of aspects of the sport have been changed. If you are new to motorsport, I have a small glossary of terms at the back of the book.

PLAYLIST

Radioactive | Imagine Dragons
Porsche | Charlie XCX feat. MØ
Wherever I Go | OneRepublic
Starboy | The Weeknd feat. Daft Punk
Super Rich Kids | Frank Ocean feat. Earl Sweatshirt
Monte Carlo | Remi Wolf
INDUSTRY BABY | Lil Nas X & Jack Harlow
Stargirl Interlude | The Weeknd feat. Lana Del Rey
Delicate | Taylor Swift
21 | Gracie Abrams
I Like Me Better | Lauv
Fast Car | Jonas Blue feat. Dakota
I Know Places (Taylor's Version) | Taylor Swift
Safety net | Ariana Grande feat. Ty Dolla $ign
Cannonball | The Sweeplings
The Chain | Fleetwood Mac
The Alchemy | Taylor Swift
Diet Pepsi | Addison Rae

ONE

GREAT BRITAIN

A WEEKEND AT HOME

THE COLLISION ENDED IN SECONDS. Two Formula One cars came together and spun off the track into the gravel. Dust flew up into the air as stones flicked over the shiny cars. One broken suspension. One damaged front wing. Both cars beached in deep gravel while the race continued without them.

And I would give anything to be seated in either of those wrecked cars. Instead, I watched from the armchair in my parents' living room.

"Come on!" both my parents shouted at the TV, Mum on the edge of the sofa, Dad beside her, tapping his foot.

The dust settled and the two drivers scrambled out of their seats. Philippe, a driver known for his fiery temper, threw his steering wheel on the ground before climbing out and pointing at his teammate. Stefan Brudes stood before his ruined car and threw his arms out like he was shouting "*What?*".

Before joining the Torrin team, Stefan had a reputation for staying cool, calm, and calculated, but his rivalry with his team-mate had brought out an ugly side of him. Everyone had watched their relationship deteriorate this season, with near-

1

misses and snarky comments in interviews, and finally, here they were, shouting at each other beside two broken cars.

It was one way to end the racing season.

A marshal ran over to Philippe and tried to guide him to the barriers, but he pushed the guy away. He headed straight for Stefan, his eyes wide and his finger still pointing. The cameras zoomed in on them both. They exchanged words, but no microphones were at the side of the track. Suddenly, Stefan shoved Philippe. Philippe retaliated, swinging his arm back and aiming a punch.

"Bloody Hell! Stefan's still got his helmet on. Philippe will end up with a broken wrist!" Dad said to the TV while I rolled my eyes at the display.

"Stefan is the one who should be throwing the punches. He's lost a chance at the Championship," Mum replied.

"Those two were trouble from the start. The Torrin team never should have signed Stefan." Dad shook his head as their fight progressed. The commentators discussed the drivers' unprofessional behaviour and began speculating about what their team would do with them.

I rolled my eyes. These guys were F1 drivers. Elites. At the top of all motorsports. And they were brawling like a couple of drunks at the pub. Neither of them knew how lucky they were.

Five stewards ran over and separated the drivers, dragging them off.

"There's no way the two of them can stay on the same team now. Torrin has a decision to make," one of the commentators said.

"They both have contracts for next season," the other interjected.

"Contracts be damned! It's over for those teammates!"

The commentators continued their discussion while the cameras returned to the real action: the race.

My phone buzzed and I picked it up from where it sat against the armrest. My ex's name flashed in a notification, informing me that he'd posted an update to his Insta story. I should have unfollowed him when we broke up. Part of me was tempted to look, but I knew better. I cleared the screen of notifications and leaned forward to place my phone on the coffee table, further from my reach. Mum eyed me but didn't comment on my actions. That woman never missed anything.

"My bet's on Philippe to leave the team and Stefan to stay," Mum suggested, continuing the teammate discussion.

"Really? But Philippe is a Champion," Dad replied.

"Former Champion. He hasn't won in years. He's nearing retirement. Stefan is young and hungry. They'll keep him. But they'll need someone with the right temperament to replace Philippe. Someone the team can control easily. Probably a rookie." Mum knew everything about F1, from the politics to the mechanical side. If someone asked her who won the 1974 Spanish GP, she'd answer right away.

"It will have to be a rookie. Everyone else has signed contracts for next year."

I frowned at the TV as the race continued. Aiden Sterling went down the main straight, comfortably in the lead, and now his only challenger for the world title was out. That was his third Championship in the bag. The man was unstoppable at this point.

At the last W race, Sofie asked me if I thought anyone could beat him. Would Sterling continue to dominate for years to come, with no one coming close? I told her he's not unbeatable. He just needed the right challenger. Someone he wouldn't expect.

"You surprise everyone," Sofie had said.

I'd smiled and told her, "Only if the F1 glass ceiling breaks."

"You did a test for Montagne last year!"

"A publicity stunt."

I'd lost hope that I'd ever reach F1. It didn't seem to matter how many seasons I'd won in other racing series, how well I raced in the W series, or how dedicated I was. The window of opportunity had closed long ago.

I glanced at the glass cabinet my parents kept in the living room. All my winner's trophies, cups, and runner-up plates were displayed in a neat line along the shelves. Mum kept the cabinet spotless and always directed any guests to this room first so she could answer their inevitable questions once they spotted the display. The cabinet showed my journey from a little girl in a go-kart to a woman who'd stalled in her racing career.

I looked down at my phone on the table, my ex's words ringing in my head. *It's not working for me anymore. You're always away at races, you spend more time with your car than me, and for what? You're not moving forward. No one would be disappointed in you if you called it quits. Not every driver makes it to F1.* That's why I wouldn't look at his fucking Insta update. I might not be strong enough to unfollow him, but I would not view his stories.

In the middle of the glass cabinet sat my Championship trophy for this season's W series. The last race ended weeks ago and I'd felt restless ever since. I was a winner, a Champion, but there was still this part of me that wanted more.

Recently, I'd started to wonder if I'd wasted my childhood in dirty, oily go-karts. Maybe I should have focused on my education, gone to university like my brother, like everyone else. Spent my weekends with friends, dated more, and had a life. Or perhaps I was letting my ex's words get to me.

Sterling went over the finish line. Another Championship

won. Another race year over. More of the same to come next year.

"Can't say it was an exciting end to the season. I think the fight was probably the highlight," Dad said, slapping a knee and getting to his feet. "Tea?" he asked Mum and me.

I shook my head.

"No... Wait, what's this?" Mum asked, her eyes still fixed on the screen.

The cameras were in the pits, watching Philippe arguing with his team principal. He stormed off and disappeared back into the garage. The cameras tried to follow but couldn't get close enough.

"I think your mum's right: Philippe is out. Give me a shout if you change your mind and want a drink." Dad left for the kitchen and I heard the click of the kettle.

"Maybe I should retire too," I said.

"Don't be ridiculous! You're twenty-nine and at the peak of your game!" Mum snapped.

"I'm not at the peak, though. Peak would be F_1." I sighed. Some drivers entered F_1 in their teens.

"You're not giving up!"

Dad returned with a steaming mug and we continued to watch the coverage. Sterling celebrated on the podium, spraying champagne over the crowd below. What must it feel like to know you're the best in the world?

The coverage switched to the pundits for the post-race discussion.

"*I think we're going to see so much more from Sterling next year...*"

Blah, blah, blah...

"*A big update! I'm hearing news from the Torrin team. Philippe has left. They have an empty seat for next season.*"

"Wow, now everyone will be wondering who will replace him. What do you think?"

The pundits went on to discuss all the possible options. They grew increasingly elaborate, suggesting that other teams might offer a driver swap or how drivers from less successful teams might find imaginable ways to get out of their signed contracts and take the free spot. They suggested drivers from Formula 2 and even wondered if Degrassi might come out of retirement.

Eventually, the discussion ended, and they went on to interviews before the show wound up. Another F1 season over. Dad switched the TV off and silence filled the living room. Outside, a bright autumn light shone and birds sang in the bushes in the front garden.

My phone vibrated against the coffee table, making Mum jump.

My manager's name flashed. I grabbed it and stared at the screen. She usually didn't call much after the racing season ended and I'd signed all my contracts for next year.

"Answer it then!" Mum said.

I hit the green button.

"Hey Jean, what's up?"

"Winter, Torrin want you! They're offering you the seat for next season. You're in Formula One!"

TWO

AUSTRALIA

WEDNESDAY EVENING - FOUR MONTHS LATER

He didn't think he had another Championship season in him,
but that was a secret he'd never share with anyone.

"PLEASE, please come. Don't make me go to my first event alone," I begged Gem, kneeling on the edge of her bed in her hotel room.

"I'm not risking it with this ankle," she said, leaning against the headboard, her phone in one hand, her right ankle propped up on a pillow with an ice pack on top. She'd twisted it on our run this morning.

"It's probably nothing. You just twisted it," I argued.

"Are you my personal trainer now?" She shifted on the bed and leaned forward to tie up her short blonde hair. It was just long enough to form a tiny ponytail; a few strands fell out as soon as she leaned back. "I have an old injury in that foot. I need to be at my best so I can help you be on your best form this season. I'm not risking it. You don't need me there. You'll

7

be fine. It's no different from any other event you've attended before."

I sighed. "I know."

"You'll be great, and if you're not, stay for the bare minimum and come back to the hotel. No one will question you leaving early when your first race is in a few days." She stared at me, her hazel eyes boring into mine to make her point.

"Fine. You're right." I slid off her bed and stood. Gem was like the big sister I'd always wanted. Excellent fitness training and she gave good advice, too. She'd been my personal trainer for the past three years and we'd grown pretty close in that time.

"Show me the dress before you leave!" She waved me off as her phone started buzzing and she answered the call.

I hurried out of her room, the door closing slowly, and I caught the sound of Gem laughing. It had to be her girlfriend on the phone. The door shut with a click and her happy voice disappeared. I took a long breath, wondering what it was like to be in a long-term, supportive relationship. Gem and her girlfriend made long-distance look easy. While Gem worked away travelling with the race season, they'd phone, video chat regularly, and visit between races.

Returning to my hotel room, I changed out of my T-shirt and shorts and shimmied into a black dress. It hugged my toned body but didn't show too much skin. The skirt fell just above the knee and the neckline was not too low-cut. A perfectly suitable dress. I'd prefer to wear something a bit more adventurous or colourful, but since this was my first official preseason event, it was better to play it safe. I left my hair down for a change. Usually, I always had it tied up. Mum kept telling me to get it cut short as it would make life easier getting in and out of all my racing gear.

With only a few minutes to spare, I grabbed a small black

bag, threw my room key and phone inside, and slipped on a pair of black heels.

MY NEW TEAMMATE, Stefan Brudes, stood beside our team's PR manager in the hotel lobby. My heels clicked against the shiny marble floor as I rushed to them.

"Winter, you're two minutes late," Reyna said, looking up from her phone. She wore a formal navy dress with low heels. Her makeup was simple, the bronzed lip colour complementing her light brown skin. In the short time I'd known Reyna, she always looked immaculate, polished but professional, with never a hair out of place or a chipped nail in sight.

"Sorry," I said, stopping beside her.

"Michael and the others have already left, but I wanted the three of us to have a quick chat before we join them." Since joining the team, I'd learnt Reyna was a big fan of "quick chats".

Stefan stood in brooding silence, his dark suit tailored to perfection and his dirty blond hair swept over to one side. He hardly registered my appearance apart from a tiny nod.

"So, this event is held every year at the first race by F1's tyre supplier, Donna. Every team attends and everyone involved with the sport is usually invited. The press will be there, so I expect both of you to be on your best behaviour." She paused to glance at Stefan. He nodded and she continued. "When we get to the event we will get photographs first, then I'll direct you to certain journalists, and then you're free to mingle. Please remember you aren't just Torrin drivers: you are ambassadors for the team and our brand. Now, Winter, you'll probably get asked the same questions about—"

"The first female F1 driver in over forty-five years," I interrupted, and Reyna frowned.

"Yes, and we went over how you need to respond. No sarcastic remarks, please."

"I know. I was only joking in our practice interview." I wasn't.

"And Stefan, you'll get questions about what happened last season. You are to direct the conversation towards the new season, a fresh start. You're focused and excited about the new car. This will be your year. If any journalist insists on a comment about the incident, tell them about your winter break at a secluded retreat learning mindfulness and how to refocus for the new season." Translation: he had to take an anger management course after brawling with his ex-teammate on the side of the racetrack. Reyna only ever referred to the punch-up as "the incident", and I had to stop myself from sniggering every time she mentioned it. "Okay?"

Stefan grunted in reply. I'd only heard him speak a handful of times. Maybe he did too much mindfulness in the mountain retreat and now, he'd forgotten how to talk.

"Let's go."

Reyna marched to the glass-fronted door. Stefan gave me another curt nod before following her. I glanced at the lift, wishing Gem hadn't twisted her ankle.

THREE

AUSTRALIA

WEDNESDAY EVENING

He spotted her at the bar.

A CAR DROPPED us off at a different hotel in the city and Reyna took us into a large event room that overlooked the bay. Guests gathered in different groups around the dimly lit space. A curved bar wrapped around one end of the room while a small screen was set up at the other end. I took a step forward, my eyes drawn to the wall of windows. Melbourne's city lights reflected off the sea, glittering in the night, but I didn't have a chance to take in the beauty as Reyna placed her hand on my back and directed me away from the view.

We entered a side room where bright lights blinded me for a few seconds.

"Photos first, remember," Reyna whispered in my ear as she positioned me next to Stefan before a big banner with the Donna logo plastered all over it.

"Don't forget to smile," Reyna said as she stepped away from us and the cameras began to flash and click.

Once they'd taken enough photos of us, Reyna took us back into the hall and guided us to different members of the press. After answering their questions, I was grateful for Reyna's advice and practice interviews. Eventually, the press grew tired of me and I was able to make my escape. I spent some time with our team principal, Michael, as he introduced me to different people, their names quickly forgotten. There was a real mix of guests, sponsors, ex-racers, a few local celebrities and business representatives from Australia. I spotted a few familiar faces. I'd been a part of the motorsport world since I started karting as a kid, but this evening, I found no one I'd feel comfortable walking up to and starting a conversation with.

After greeting more people than I could count, I needed a drink. I made my way over to the bar and picked up a small glass of champagne. Scanning the room, I spotted Stefan with a bunch of Torrin sponsors. One glance at his miserable face made me turn back to the bar. No way was I heading over there.

I sipped my champagne. One glass wouldn't hurt. I didn't drink during the race season, but technically, it was still preseason with five days until the first race. Nerves began to creep up my spine, but I glanced over my shoulder and decided I'd rather face an utterly humiliating crash on my first race than join the small talk with Stefan.

"Hey," came a voice from beside me.

I turned to find Aiden Sterling, the current Formula One World Champion, standing beside me. For a second, I was starstruck. He'd won three World Championships and won his last two back-to-back. He was the only Black racing driver to win a world title and was far from finished with his career. Even people who didn't watch motorsport knew of him and what he'd achieved in one of the most competitive sports on the planet. It was only months ago that I watched him on TV winning his third title, and now, here he was, standing next to me, his newest competitor.

He looked different in a suit and tie. My eyes scanned from his shiny shoes, up his powerful thighs, over his white shirt, and up to his cocky smile.

"You're almost empty," he said, tilting his head to my glass.

I stared back at him. We'd never met before. We'd been at the same motorsport events a handful of times, but we'd never been introduced, and I'd never seen him up close like this. I hadn't noticed how attractive he was before. He was taller than I expected, too, which could be a disadvantage for F1 drivers. My gaze tracked along his chiselled jaw, up his straight nose and settled on his brown eyes.

As British drivers, our paths should have crossed before now, but he was older than me, so we'd never raced against each other in the lower Formulas as kids. He'd always been a few years ahead in the game.

His dark eyes dipped to my lips and I realised he had no idea who I was.

How could he not know who I was?

I was the newest F1 driver.

Over the winter break, my signing with the Torrin team became headline news. My story broke into mainstream news, not just the sports section or the latest racing blog posts. I should have been offended and thrown what remained of my drink in his face. But that would be petty, and Reyna wouldn't be happy if I caused a scene.

Sterling was my rival and he didn't even know it.

But perhaps that gave me an opportunity.

Winning races wasn't only about what happened on the track; mind games and politics off-track played a part. I opened my mouth to ask him what he thought of his Championship rivals, but a guy in a smart suit carrying a tablet came up to him and whispered in his ear.

"Sorry, I'll be right back," he said, giving me a polite smile.

He placed his glass down on the bar and followed the guy. I watched his back disappear into the crowd.

Suddenly, the room went quiet, the music faded, guests stopped talking, and the lights dimmed. The screen at the other side of the room came to life with the Donna tyre logo in the centre. A film began playing: a flashy silver sports car drove along winding clifftop roads. It was the latest sports model of the Silvers's road car. Silvers manufactured high-end sportscars and ran an F1 team. The film zoomed in on the tyres and then on the driver inside the car: Sterling. The advert ended by showing the Silvers and Donna logos on the screen, a collaboration of car and tyre.

Guests clapped when the film finished, and the lights brightened again. The managing director of Donna and the Silvers's team principal stepped before the screen. Sterling joined them, the three men shook hands, and more guests clapped. I glanced over at where I'd last seen my own team principal. Michael frowned at them while Stefan stood beside him, with the same bored look on his face.

I listened to their Q&A, but my gaze drifted from the big screen towards the wall of windows. At one end, there was an open doorway leading out onto a balcony. A woman in a long red dress walked back inside and joined the crowd around the screen.

A warm evening breeze blew in and brushed against my skin, calling me outside. I took one last look around the room. While everyone listened to the Silvers's team principal chat about their new sports car, I stepped outside.

The balcony curved around the whole building, with a set

of steps going down to a lower deck and more steps down to a viewing platform that looked out over the marina. Palm trees and bushy plants decorated the balcony, hiding a few guests from view. A couple stood close to each other, but I could only see two elbows sticking out from behind a plant and catch bits of their whispered conversation.

Not wanting to disturb them, I took the stairs to the lower level and continued until I reached the lowest deck. I leaned against the rail and stared out at the bay. Lights reflected on the still water. Boats were tucked away for the night. A low hum of music came from a venue across the bay. I took it all in, closing my eyes and soaking up the tranquil atmosphere. I would think of this moment when I was in the car waiting for the red lights to go out, to centre myself, the calm before the racing storm.

I had to do well this weekend. It was the first race of the season and I had to make the right first impression. I had a contract with Torrin for only one race season, one year, so continuing in F1 depended on how I performed. Every race would count. Preseason testing had gone okay; the car felt good, but there were still balance improvements to make. I tried to push the thoughts out of my head before they could spiral. Instead, I focused on the sound of the water in the bay.

"Hey!"

My eyes flew open and I jumped back from the rail.

"Sorry, I didn't mean to make you jump," Sterling said, one hand on the rail, a concerned look on his face.

My heart raced, but I took a steadying breath.

"My own fault for standing here with my eyes closed."

He placed his other hand on the rail and leaned forward, looking out at the water as I had moments ago.

"I love it here," he said, moving to face me again.

"Really?" I turned to him and raised an eyebrow. "What's your favourite part? The weather? The track? The fact that it's the start of a new race season?" The questions spilt out of my mouth too quickly, but this was my chance to get an advantage. If I could get him talking about his car, then I might learn a detail that would help with my own car's set-up for the race.

He still had no idea who I was, but he'd expect me to know him.

"All of it. I love the people here. The atmosphere," he replied, not really answering any of my questions.

"Are you ready for the start of the new season? Ready to defend your title?"

He smiled. "Ready as I'll ever be. The car felt good in testing, but you never really know where you stand against your competitors until race day." He shrugged and glanced out at the view again.

"Really? You must have some idea about who your biggest competition will be."

"All the usual suspects—Cavallo, maybe the Stewart team, Torrin—will probably be up there too, but as I said, I'll have to wait until Qualifying to see whose car can perform, and I don't really want to talk shop right now. Who are you here with? The press? A local business? One of the teams?" He turned to face me and grinned.

Damn it, he'd caught me. Maybe I'd been too obvious with my questions. If he thought I was with the press, then he'd stick to his team's approved lines. If he thought I belonged to another team, then our conversation would end.

"Hang on a minute. A racing driver who doesn't want to talk about racing?" I feigned shock, placing a hand over my heart.

He laughed. "I have other interests."

"I don't believe you. I know racing drivers and all they talk about is brake temperatures, tyre pressures and track limits."

He laughed and moved ever-so-slightly closer, looking right

at me. His eyes roamed my face. "So, you know racing drivers? You're not here with a local business then, and you're probably not press either, so that leaves... a team."

Shoot. I'd slipped up again.

He moved closer, still searching my face, trying to place me.

A breeze picked up from the bay and blew across the deck. It brushed my auburn hair across my face.

"Who are you?" he asked, leaning in and gently catching a loose lock of hair in his fingers.

I took in a deep breath. His scent was woody, earthy, with a light hint of something citrusy. He brushed my hair behind my ear, his fingers lingering, slowly trailing behind my ear and down my neck. My gaze dipped from his dark brown eyes down to his full lips. It would be so easy to close the distance and press my lips to his. To kiss him.

No.

What was I doing?

His fingers began to trail along my jaw. I reached out and grabbed his wrist, stopping him. We stared at each other, both breathing heavily, neither of us moving apart.

Eventually, I stepped back, letting his wrist go and breaking the tension. Panic surged within me. I shouldn't want to kiss him. I was meant to get information about his car or team, not kiss him or fall for his charms. I'm not sure what scared me more: the fact I'd wanted to kiss my rival or the fact I hadn't wanted to kiss anyone since my ex.

"I'm sorry, I shouldn't—"

"It's okay. I'm going to get another drink." The words tumbled out of my mouth, cutting him off. I didn't wait for him to reply. Instead, I rushed back up the deck.

"Hey! I didn't get your name!" he called after me, but I kept going, heading back inside and into the crowd.

I found Reyna with Stefan.

"I think I'm going to go back to the hotel. I want an early night," I announced.

"Sure. Stefan, are you coming too?" Reyna asked him.

He nodded and the three of us left together. As we walked out, I spotted Sterling on the other side of the room, searching for someone.

FOUR

AUSTRALIA

FRIDAY

Most F1 drivers were cocky, arrogant show-offs, and he'd played right into that stereotype. Fucking promotional events! Now, he had a new reason to dislike them. Way to start the season by embarrassing himself in front of a gorgeous stranger. At least he could get his head back in the game before the first race—or that's what he thought.

"YOU'RE LATE!" Reyna met me in the corridor, her tablet clutched against her chest. She wore our team's navy shirt and a tailored pencil skirt. Even flustered, she looked smart. She'd tied her dark hair back into a high ponytail.

"I'm sorry. I was held up talking to my engineer." Ash wanted to discuss the car's set-up for Qualifying tomorrow. The first and second practices had gone okay, but we still had plenty to discuss and data to go through.

"Come on." Reyna turned around and I followed her along

the corridor. Voices filtered out of an open doorway. "While I waited for you, Mateo started talking to me."

"Who?"

"One of Cavallo's PR guys, the arrogant Italian, and because you were late, I had to speak to him."

We both paused in the doorway to the press room. At one end were banners and six chairs, all but one occupied. Cameras and journalists filled the rest of the room, with team members like Reyna standing at the back. A man with olive skin and dark hair, wearing Cavallo red, winked at Reyna. She gave him a polite smile and whispered in my ear, "See? Arrogant."

I tried not to laugh. "He doesn't seem so bad."

She rolled her eyes. "Go on, they're waiting for you." She nodded towards the last empty seat.

A press conference took place before every race weekend. Six drivers were selected to take part. They chose different drivers each time, but Championship contenders were usually picked the most. Since we were at the first race weekend, it made sense for them to pick me, as I was the new rookie.

I looked up at the five drivers already seated, waiting for the questions to start. My teammate Stefan sat in the middle of the front row, his expression blank. On either side of him sat the Cavallo drivers. Matias da Silveira, the only Brazilian driver, adjusted his red cap, making sure he had it centred perfectly on his head. His French teammate, Théo Laurent, played with his thumbs, a look of growing impatience lining his forehead. Behind Laurent sat Heikki Koskinen, the other Silvers driver. He sat up straight, his blue eyes forward, scanning the crowd of reporters.

And in the middle of the back row, next to the remaining empty seat, was Aiden Sterling. His gaze focused on me as I walked up to the last chair and sat down. His eyes went wide, staring at the Torrin logo on my top. His mouth fell open as if he wanted to say something, but no words came out.

I smiled.

"Now that everyone's here, we can begin," one of the organisers announced.

I focused on the cameras and ignored Sterling's stare.

One by one, the journalists asked us questions.

They started with Stefan and I watched the back of his head. His shoulders stiffened every time the press asked him about the fight at the end of last season. He gave short answers and spoke so quietly that two reporters had to ask him to repeat himself.

"Do you think your relationship with your new teammate will be better than the last?" one person asked.

"Yes," Stefan replied.

The journalist looked at me. "Winter, what do you think?"

"I think we're getting on well, and I'm learning a lot from him, even if he's not the most talkative teammate." I smiled and received a few polite laughs from the small crowd.

The press moved on, asking the Cavallo drivers about their chances this season and Koskinen about his summer training. They came to me and the inevitable question about being the only female driver came up. I answered them the way I had at the event, exactly as Reyna had coached me. After my last answer, I spotted Reyna at the back of the room. She gave me a quick thumbs-up.

Eventually, they came to Sterling. They all asked variations of the same question and it all boiled down to whether he could win a fourth World Championship title. He gave his answers with smooth ease. I watched him carefully. The man I'd met at the party vanished. His answers were prepared and rehearsed but delivered in a natural manner. He smiled at the right moment; he gestured occasionally with his hands and made eye contact with different people in the crowd. He even laughed at a joke that, in my opinion, wasn't that funny. He became a well-timed show. I'd sounded robotic compared to him.

AS SOON AS the conference finished, I jumped to my feet. Reyna waited for Stefan and me near the door, and we filed out into the corridor with everyone else. The press left at one end of the corridor while we continued further into the building, heading back towards the paddock where the team motorhomes were.

"You both did great, but perhaps we can work on your technique, Stefan. Next time, maybe try to build up more of a rapport with the journalists," Reyna said as we walked.

Stefan made a non-committal noise in reply.

"Winter, you were great!" she cheered, but I wasn't that good—not perfect like Sterling with his charm. "A really good first impression. I'm thinking we should follow up with—"

"Hey, Winter! Can I have a word?"

The three of us all turned around at the same time to find Sterling jogging to catch up to us. Stefan gave him a nod and continued towards the glass doors, out into the bright sunlight.

"Sure. I'll be two minutes," I said, turning to Reyna.

"Michael wants us back," she said, looking from me to Sterling and back again.

"One minute?"

She sighed and followed Stefan out into the paddock, the doors sliding shut behind her.

I faced Sterling, waiting for him to start. I folded my arms.

"Look, about the other night." He rubbed the back of his head.

"The night when you didn't realise who I was?"

"Sorry about that. I spent the winter break away. I knew you were joining F1, but I didn't recognise you without the race suit or team colours."

"Right." Apparently, I had something in common with Superman: all it took was ordinary civilian clothes and my hair down.

"It was unprofessional. I'm sorry."

"Are you sorry for not recognising me or sorry for trying to kiss me?" I asked.

His posture tensed and I enjoyed watching him sweat under my scrutiny, but he suddenly relaxed and grinned at me.

"I remember it the other way around. You tried to kiss me."

"What? No, I didn't!"

"I think you protest too much."

I could feel heat creeping up my neck and into my face.

"Listen, I didn't try to kiss you. I'm here to race and win. I simply saw an opportunity to ask you a few questions about your car and strategy."

He looked so amused, like he didn't see me as a threat to his Championship plans.

"Stick to racing. You'd make a terrible spy."

"I'll see you on the track," I said, turning. I made my escape through the double doors, but he followed me. Outside, I squinted into the bright Melbourne sun for a fraction of a second before walking towards the Torrin motorhome. At least he couldn't follow me inside there.

"You need to work on your temper. It's not good to get this worked up before Qualifying and you don't want the other drivers finding out how easily you get annoyed," he said, trailing me.

I stopped suddenly and he almost walked into me.

"I didn't ask for your advice."

"That was a freebie. A little tip for the rookie." He winked, still smirking.

"Stop smiling at me like that and I don't need your tips. I can beat you fine without them, thanks."

I started walking again. This time he didn't follow, but I could hear his low chuckle.

"See you on track, Rookie! I look forward to seeing the Torrin car in my mirrors!" he called after me.

My hands curled into fists. Infuriating man.

FIVE

AUSTRALIA

SATURDAY - QUALIFYING

She was the last person he'd expected to sit down next to him in the drivers' briefing. The woman he'd almost kissed. He might have embarrassed himself, and she might have taken him by surprise, but at least he'd gotten under her skin. She was far too easy to tease. Maybe this race season would be a little more interesting than the last.

WHEN I RETURNED to the Torrin base, Reyna asked me what Sterling wanted. I brushed her off, telling her he wanted to welcome me to F1. She didn't look convinced, but she dropped her questions anyway. We had a meeting where Michael asked for a full report on first and second practice and made plans for the race weekend.

The next day, Qualifying arrived and the stands were packed with spectators. I could feel the excitement in the air, an atmosphere of anticipation for the first race weekend of the season. My first ever Qualifying in F1.

When I arrived, the crew was already in the pits, working on the cars. Cables, laptops, and equipment surrounded both Torrin cars, like they were on life support.

This was the worst part of the day: the waiting. I hated waiting. Nerves began to build and I couldn't stay still for very long. I wanted to jump in the car and get going, set a time, and get my name down on the board. Gem joined me and offered a few words of encouragement along with some stretches to do before I got in the car. My engineer, Ash, kept feeding me data on lap times but none of it sunk in. The numbers jumbled up in my mind.

Eventually, the time came to get in the car. I glanced at the number nineteen on the front nose: my racing number, my number on an F1 car. With my gloves on, the steering wheel in place, and a last thumbs-up from Gem, it was time. Other teams started releasing their cars into the pits and they began to line up, waiting to go out and set a time. My teammate went first and then they signalled for me to go. With one deep breath, I pulled out of the garage and went for it.

Qualifying Report
Pole – Aiden Sterling
2nd – Stefan Brudes
3rd – Matias da Silveira
4th – Winter Jones

FOURTH ON THE grid for race day and I wanted to scream. One of the Cavallo drivers, Matias da Silveira, beat me by a fraction of a second. He was being interviewed along with my teammate and Sterling, as the top three.

"Don't worry," Ash said as I got out of the car. "The Cavallo car is good for Quali, but we have the race pace."

"How do you know that? We haven't raced against them yet."

"Trust me, I know these things. I can tell by looking at their car." He gave me a light pat on the shoulder before returning to his computer screen as the pit crew surrounded my car, plugging in cables, cooling down the brakes and checking it over.

I looked up at one of the TVs in our pits. Sterling's face filled the screen as he answered questions and waved to the fans. He barely looked like he'd broken a sweat and he'd had his hair cut since I'd last seen him. How was it possible to look so good, so at ease, after wearing a tight fireproof balaclava and helmet for over an hour? Stefan looked a mess compared to Sterling. His blond hair stuck up all over the place, but he seemed unbothered by it. Sweat covered Matias's forehead, but he beamed, smiling wide at the cameras.

Tomorrow was a new day, and I'd make sure I wasn't in Sterling's mirrors.

Race Points

$1^{st} - 25$

$2^{nd} - 18$

$3^{rd} - 15$

$4^{th} - 12$

$5^{th} - 10$

$6^{th} - 8$

$7^{th} - 6$

$8^{th} - 4$

$9^{th} - 2$

$10^{th} - 1$

SIX

AUSTRALIA

SUNDAY - RACE DAY

During the drivers' parade, his gaze kept lingering on a newly familiar head of red hair. She had it tied up in a high ponytail today. All the drivers piled onto an open-top trailer so the fans could spot and wave to their favourite racer as they drove around the track. He found himself at one end of the trailer, and she stood at the other end, her back to him. It was probably for the best. She was too distracting.

IN THE MORNING, Mum phoned me three times to give me a detailed breakdown of my Qualifying lap times and where I could have made improvements. She went on to my race strategy. I half-listened while getting ready in my hotel room before heading to the racetrack. I wanted to tell her I had a whole group of strategists, engineers and mechanics to advise me, but her non-stop chatter kept my nerves at bay. If I listened to her, I wouldn't think about how this was my F1 debut and that I couldn't mess it up.

At the track, I found myself waiting to get started again. This wasn't the same as Qualifying. The routine was different, but I still had to play a waiting game, and nervous energy started building.

I sat on the edge of the racetrack, on a patch of grass leaning against the wall, watching the pre-race build-up. It was a chaotic circus. Each team continued to work on their cars on the track, with all the cars lined up in their starting grid positions. Lead engineers and strategists gathered in little groups, discussing race plans in hushed words. VIP guests drifted up and down the grid, taking in the atmosphere. The tension built with the chatter of the crowd in the stands, the heat coming off the tarmac, and the faint scent of oil. Camera crews and TV pundits darted around, trying to grab a last-minute word with a driver. I watched Reyna with Stefan on the other side of the track. She was trying to convince him to do an interview with a German TV crew.

Luckily, only one TV crew interviewed me: the British production team. They asked me a few questions about how I was feeling and my strategy. I gave them simple replies and they moved on. Perhaps Stefan was rubbing off on me. Next time, I would give one-word answers.

I watched the camera crew move up the grid to Sterling, but he refused to speak to them, waved them off and kept his head down, talking to someone from the Silvers team. His refusal surprised me, especially after his performance during the press conference.

"Hey, Winter?" I looked away from Sterling to find Matias da Silveira standing before me. I should have seen him coming from a mile off in his bright red Cavallo race suit. "I wanted to come over and give you a proper welcome to the sport." He held his hand out to me.

I jumped to my feet and we shook hands.

I'd forgotten about his accident, but as I gripped his hand in mine, I remembered the crash. Scar tissue covered his dark brown skin over his fingers and across his knuckles. This sport still had a deadly side. Two years ago, his car crashed, flipped, and then burst into flames. He couldn't get out quickly enough. The marshals rushed in with fire extinguishers, but the fire took hold. Matias fought to get out. He managed to unclip his belt and clambered out while inhaling searing smoke. His race suit's fire-resistant layer had saved his life, but he didn't escape completely unscathed. He spent the rest of the season in recovery, having skin grafts and reconstruction on his hands. He was lucky to be back in F1: lucky to be alive. When our hands parted, I kept my eyes on his face.

"Thanks," I said.

"There's another reason I wanted to speak to you. My wife is a big fan and she'd really like to meet you."

"Yes, of course! I'm a big fan of hers too! Who wouldn't be?" His wife was an Olympic Gold-winning cyclist.

"She won't be at a race until Europe."

"That's okay. Tell her she is always welcome on my side of the Torrin garage."

He chuckled. "Not sure how my team will react to my wife in a rival team's pit garage, but I'll let her know anyway." He smiled and walked back over to his car.

I returned to my spot, leaning against the wall. A mix of emotions swirled inside me. Fear of the dangers of this sport collided with the high of a world-renowned athlete knowing who I was and wanting to meet me. I tapped my fingers on the ground, one finger at a time, a slow, repetitive action.

Gem joined me, sitting down on the grassy edge beside me.

"You okay?" she asked.

"I'm taking it all in," I replied, looking from one end of the grid to the other.

"It's okay if you're nervous."

"I know."

She nodded and we sat together in silence. There was never any pressure to fill the quiet with Gem. She wouldn't force conversation, either, or try to talk me through my nerves. She let me be, and I knew she would be there if I wanted to talk.

My mind drifted to the race, the car set-up, the possibilities, and all the things that could go wrong. I shook my head and tried to forget all my doubts and fears. I spotted Sterling walking with his engineer and our eyes met. He gave me a nod, and it was the reminder I needed, a reminder to focus on the here and now. He had pole position and he was my target.

"Winter?" Gem nudged me and I turned to her. "I think they're getting ready for the national anthem."

I got to my feet and followed the others to the top of the grid. All the drivers gathered in a line on a strip of red carpet. I stood beside Stefan, who didn't even acknowledge me, but I was getting used to his cold side. Race officials stood in front of us, a big band behind us, and the national anthem began.

When the music ended, the crowd cheered. The VIPs and camera crews left the grid. The teams made last-minute adjustments to the cars and began to gather up any equipment. I put the rest of my gear on. Gem helped me with my helmet and I finally got into my car. After all the waiting, time began to speed up. The warm-up lap became a blur, and I was back in my fourth position at the starting line. The car vibrated around me like a living beast. My hands gripped the steering ready to take control. I stared up at the five red lights until they went out.

I HAD one of the best starts of my life. I aimed for the racing line and followed Sterling's car. He had a great start, too. I managed to pass Matias da Silveira's Cavallo on the first bend, and for a split second, I thought I could get past my teammate, too, but Stefan had the advantage and kept me at bay.

The rest of the race went smoothly for Torrin and me. I pushed and pushed but couldn't catch Stefan. He remained in front, but the Cavallo drivers stayed behind me. Ash was right: the Cavallo cars didn't have the pace. There were a few accidents, nothing major, and four cars retired from the race.

When the chequered flag waved and I crossed the line, I slowed down, making my way to the pits. I came third. The top three lined their cars up below the winner's balcony, each car behind a sign with a big number on it. I parked before the number three.

When I finally got out of the car, Sterling was already celebrating. He ran up to his team. They gathered behind a barrier and cheered him on. He'd won the first race of the new season, securing twenty-five Championship points. Stefan took longer to get out of his car and nodded in my direction. I nodded back. Our teammates crowded behind the barriers, too. I put on a smile and went to celebrate with them, but I couldn't help feeling disappointed. I'd wanted more than third place. But I also knew how petty I'd sound if I voiced my disappointment out loud. I should be happy; this was only my first race, and most F1 drivers never finished on the podium in their first race. Most rookies didn't score a seat in a top team with such a fast car, either. Somehow, I'd managed both, yet I still felt deflated.

As Sterling celebrated with his team, he flipped up the visor of his helmet and winked at me. Smug bastard. I turned away from him, keeping my own visor in place so he couldn't see my irritation or disappointment.

Next time, I'd do better. I'd wipe that smile off Sterling's face.

Mum: Congratulations, darling! Third place is a great start to the season. I do have some feedback and I think your pit crew could make improvements to their stop times. Your Dad is super proud, too. I'll call you later. Lots of love xx
Winter: Thanks, Mum. Tell Dad I say hi. Please do not say anything to the pit crew when you're at the Italian GP. Xx

Sofie: Ahhh!!! You did amazing! xx
Winter: Thanks, Sofie! Hope you're doing okay xx
Sofie: Yeah. Just waiting for the new W series to start. With you gone the Championship is mine! Xx

Autumn: Hey, sis! Congrats on the first race!
Winter: Since when do you call me "sis", bro? Are you high on paint fumes again?
Winter: I bet Mum told you to send that.
Message Unread

SEVEN

RACE REPORTS

United States

1st – Stefan Brudes

2nd – Aiden Sterling

3rd – Winter Jones

Canada

1st – Stefan Brudes

2nd – Matias da Silveira

3rd –Heikki Koskinen

4th – Winter Jones

Did Not Finish (Engine Failure) – Aiden Sterling

Italy

1st – Heikki Koskinen

2nd – Aiden Sterling

3rd – Stefan Brudes

4th – Winter Jones

Championship Driver Standings

Stefan Brudes – 83
Aiden Sterling – 61
Winter Jones - 54

He shouldn't have told her that. He'd given away a little strategy to the Rookie, but he couldn't help himself. When he stared at her face, he forgot who he was talking to. She had a smattering of freckles across her nose and cheeks. He wanted to trace his fingers over them. When she looked at him with her hazel eyes, it felt like she really saw him, the real him. There would be no hiding from Winter Jones.

I PACED my tiny room in the team's motorhome. The small box room provided a space to change into my race suit and a place to collect my thoughts before heading out on the track. Gem perched on the chair in front of my desk. She searched the Official F1 YouTube channel on her tablet and started playing a clip from the last race in Italy. She propped the tablet up against a fruit bowl on the desk while I paced back and forth behind her.

"What is he doing that I'm not?" I asked.

"You're putting too much pressure on yourself," Gem replied. She leaned back in the chair and crossed her ankles.

"Can you up my training?"

"I've already adjusted your routine once. You can't do any more. You do need to sleep, you know!"

"I need to up my game!"

"Winter, you're doing really well. It's only round five. You've got the whole season to go. You've finished in the top five at every race. You need to stop putting so much pressure on yourself. If you keep this up, you'll burn out before we even get to the summer break."

"Ugh! I just don't understand why I can't beat Stefan. We're in the same car! If I can't beat my teammate, then what's the point? If I can't get past Stefan, then I don't stand a chance of beating Sterling!" And I really wanted to wipe that perfect smile off Sterling's face.

A knock sounded and Reyna opened the door.

"Sorry, am I interrupting? I can come back later."

Gem started to answer, but I spoke over her.

"No! Come in! You're the person I need to speak to!"

"Really? Me?"

I pulled her inside and shut the door behind her.

"Yes, what can you tell me about Stefan's car? Is he setting it up differently from mine?"

Reyna frowned. "You know I'm PR, Marketing and Communications? I'm not an engineer or strategist."

"Ignore her," Gem said, sitting up straight in her chair. "She's having a stress out."

"About what?" Reyna frowned in concern.

"I'm not winning. Obviously. Reyna, has anyone from Stefan's side of the garage said anything to you about the car? Or Stefan? Ash tells me the same thing every time I ask—that the cars are set up for each driver, and he's doing everything he can to make improvements for me."

"Again, you're talking to the wrong person, and Stefan barely speaks to anyone. This morning's press conference was painful. He's a nightmare off-track, and it's meant to be my job to make him more media-friendly!" Reyna threw her hands up into the air and slumped down onto the little couch squashed into the back of the room.

"Has this become some sort of pity party? Guys, snap out of it! Reyna, Stefan is Stefan. He'll never be an easy interviewee, but that's part of his charm, and a lot of the fans love him for it. Try to work with what you've got. Swim with the current, not against it," Gem said.

"Yeah, that makes sense," Reyna replied, looking thoughtful.

"And Winter, you need to relax. You're getting too stressed, putting too much pressure on yourself, and I reckon it's having a negative effect on your driving. Take a step back. Remember where you were this time last year and look at where you are now. You will win a race. I don't believe it; I know it. You just need to stop worrying. It will happen."

I took a slow breath. "Okay. Fine, you're right."

"I should start charging for these motivational sessions." Gem leaned forward, grabbed an apple out of the fruit bowl and took a bite out of it.

At that moment, her screen showed an interview with Sterling. Taylor Macintosh, a well-liked and respected motorsport journalist, was interviewing him. Her questions focused on his racing, but she asked him one about his dating life. He deflected with a joke about spending most of his free time with his personal trainer and never answered the question properly. Taylor laughed at his comment and didn't push for a real answer.

"You know, if you did start winning races, it would make my job much easier because the press would want to talk to you instead of Stefan. It would solve both of our problems," Reyna said.

Gem turned and glared at Reyna.

"At least my mum won't be at this week's race, so that's some pressure lifted. I don't have to worry about her doing anything embarrassing or hounding the pit crew." I glanced at my phone on the table, knowing there were at least two unread messages from her.

"She's not coming? I love your mum. She knows so much about F1 and she's a dream in front of the camera, too. Did you see the interview she did at the Italian GP?" Reyna asked.

How could I avoid the interview my mum did? The British TV crew caught her in the paddock and asked her questions about how I was coping now that I was racing in F1. She went into too much detail and even started talking about my sleep routine.

"Everyone saw the interview," Gem replied, returning to her screen. She switched to a video on neck-strengthening exercises.

"I love my mum. She's always been my biggest supporter, but sometimes she can be a lot, and I want to focus without worrying about her or dealing with her disappointment."

"I understand," Reyna said.

"Hey, what did you come in here to say?" I asked her.

"A documentary crew are filming all the cars and drivers. You and Stefan are required after lunch today. Hopefully, it won't take longer than an hour."

EVERY CAR LINED up on the Circuit de Barcelona-Catalunya on Thursday afternoon. They positioned the cars down the main straight. Silvers won the Championship last year, so they went at the front. Torrin came second, Cavallo third, and so on. Each driver had to stand next to their car and look towards the camera as the crew took long, sweeping shots down the line of cars. It was painfully boring as they re-filmed at different angles. There was a strange atmosphere to the track, with empty spectator stands and no running engines. The sun shone high in the sky and my eyes started watering from trying not to squint or blink while the camera focused on me.

Eventually, they finished the big shots and moved their equipment further down the track. The TV production company wanted to take close-up clips of each driver individually.

"Ugh! It's over," I muttered.

"Total waste of time," Stefan grumbled.

Four words: it was probably the most he'd ever spoken to me. He pulled his baseball cap off, brushed a hand through his hair, shrugged, and slouched off towards a shady spot by the barriers.

At least they hadn't asked us to wear our race suits. We all wore our team polos, baseball caps, and team-approved shorts.

The other drivers started moving from their cars, talking to one another. I glanced down the long straight and spotted Sterling with the crew. They filmed him looking wistfully off into the distance, the sun on one side of his face highlighting his cheekbones and razor-sharp jawline. He had pretty boy looks with a rugged masculine edge. No wonder the camera crew looked so pleased to be filming him.

I rolled my eyes.

"Hey!"

I jumped. Satoru Hayashi, one of the Stewart drivers, stood right in front of me, smiling.

"Hey," I replied, glancing up and down the grid again.

"Do you remember we met at the Motorsport Awards last year?"

"Um..."

"I was at the table next to yours."

Hayashi was currently the youngest F1 driver at twenty, having entered the sport last year at only nineteen.

"Don't worry if you can't remember; it was a busy night." He bounced on the balls of his feet. "So glad you made it to F1! The Torrin car is so fast this year. Stewart car is catching yours, though." He continued to chat about his team and car. He didn't stop to take a breath and I had a hard time keeping up with him. "What do you think?" he asked and looked at me expectantly.

"Um... Probably best if we don't discuss our cars. I wouldn't want to accidentally give away Torrin secrets."

He chuckled.

"Causing trouble, Hayashi?" Sterling approached us. "They want Stefan next," he told me, looking back at the camera crew.

"He's over there. Feel free to go get him." I pointed to where Stefan stood in the shade by himself.

Sterling shouted over to him and gestured towards the production team. Stefan made his way over to them.

"He looks to be in a good mood today," Sterling said, and Hayashi laughed.

"Shh... He'll hear you laughing," I hushed.

Hayashi went quiet and peered over his shoulder to where Stefan stood with the film crew.

"Stefan won't care," Sterling said.

Hayashi's teammate called his name and waved for him to join a group of the drivers further down the grid.

"See you around, Winter!" He ran off towards the group.

"So, you and Stefan are getting on well, it seems? Real teammate bonding."

I ignored the comment and folded my arms. Stefan did his own thing, and it wasn't like he was close with any of the other drivers, either. I planned on beating him on the track, not befriending him off-track.

"Have I touched a nerve?"

I glared at him. "Isn't there someone else for you to annoy? Like your own teammate, since you're so keen on close teammate relationships."

"Heikki and I have a professional relationship."

"And by professional, you mean he knows his place, and that's the number two spot behind you."

"He has the same car and the same opportunities as I do. But he's nearing retirement anyway. He's just enjoying his last years in F1."

"Right." I looked away from him.

"I'm guessing you're frustrated you haven't beaten your teammate yet." He inched closer to me and lowered his voice.

"And what makes you think that?"

"Your emotions are written all over your face. Looking at you, I can see it all," he said, moving to stand in front of me so I couldn't avoid him. His eyes roamed over me; I could almost feel his gaze trailing along my skin, a feather-light touch. I had no choice but to stare back at him, up into his dark eyes.

"Listen." He spoke in a hushed voice. "Stefan is fast; he's got a natural talent for speed, but he has plenty of weaknesses. His driving style is sloppy at times, especially mid-race. He gets complacent. Your team is pitting him on the later side. Ask to be pitted first, before Stefan, and then make sure to put in your best laps afterwards. You'll undercut him, and then when he pits, he'll come out behind you."

"Why are you telling me this?" I asked, moving closer to him. My attention flicked to his lips for a fraction of a second.

"I'm bored of racing Stefan. Maybe I want a real challenge," he said, and I stared back at him, waiting for him to turn his confession into a joke or try to make fun of me. But he didn't. He simply returned my stare.

"See you later, Rookie." He winked and strolled off towards his car.

NINE

SPAIN

SUNDAY - RACE DAY

He sprayed her with champagne and got lost in her joy and that smile. That damn smile. Her happiness was contagious, and he enjoyed seeing Stefan's sullen expression more than he had expected. He'd forgotten how much he disliked Stefan Brudes.

CHAMPAGNE SPRAYED EVERYWHERE. I squeezed my eyes shut as Sterling aimed the fizzing liquid in my face. I turned my own bottle on him, chasing him down to the very edge of the platform. He leaned over the railings to spray his team. They stood below, cheering his win. I looked down at my own Torrin crew as they celebrated with me.

I'd finished in second place, and most importantly, I'd finished in front of Stefan. The adrenalin still buzzed through me and I felt a heady joy of excitement and relief.

I looked over my shoulder at the podium. Our three trophies were placed on each step. Stefan sat down beside his third-place trophy after barely celebrating with his champagne.

Instead, he sipped it straight from the bottle. He'd pulled his cap low on his head, but it didn't hide his disappointed expression. Noticing my attention, he paused, lifted the bottle to me in an acknowledging gesture, and then took another sip.

Not about to let his mood lower mine, I marched up to the podium, put my bottle down, and picked up my second-place trophy. The weight of it felt good in my hands. I returned to the balcony edge and raised it into the air. My team cheered and the crowd in the stands joined. The noise boomed around me. Sterling stood next to me, lifting his trophy in the air, too. The crowd responded even louder. The noise was almost deafening. We both lowered our trophies at the same time. I leaned into Sterling, catching his scent, a blend of sweat with his woody, earthy aftershave and champagne.

"I'm coming for you, Sterling," I shouted over the noise of the crowd.

"Looking forward to it," he replied.

<hr>

LATER THAT NIGHT, the whole team piled onto our chartered jet. I still held onto my second-place trophy as I followed Gem to two seats a couple of rows in. Ash sat on the other side of the aisle from us.

"You might have to let go of that eventually." He nodded at the trophy in my lap. My hands gripped around its metal middle. "They might not let us take off until you put it in the overhead locker."

Gem laughed, pulling out a sleep mask from her little travel backpack before securing her seatbelt.

The last of the team entered the plane and the flight attendants started closing the door.

"Hey, where's Stefan?" I asked, looking down at the back of

the plane. It didn't seem as full as the flight in. Stefan wasn't the only one missing, either.

One of the pit crew sitting behind me leaned forward.

"Didn't you hear? He's got his own private jet now," the guy said.

"He also invited some of his technicians to fly with him," the guy next to him joined in. "Maybe if you start winning races, you'll be able to get your own jet." He leaned back in his seat.

"And offer us a ride, too," the first guy added.

I didn't reply and turned back around.

I bet Sterling had his own private jet, too. With three Championships behind him and loads of sponsorship deals, he could travel to each race however he liked.

"Ignore them," Ash said, taking a book out of his travel bag. From the title and monochrome cover, it had to be either a murder mystery or a thriller.

Michael sat right at the front of the plane. Reyna was across the aisle from him. He already had his laptop out and was typing away on it.

"Does he ever stop working?" I asked Ash, nodding towards Michael.

Ash shook his head. "He stops when he's won or when the season is over."

"Excuse me, miss. You need to put that away." A flight attendant stood over me, pointing down at the second-place trophy in my lap.

Gem started laughing.

MONACO

WEDNESDAY

Even at a party with over a thousand guests, he found her.

"COME ON!" Gem shouted, cycling ahead up the hill. Her bright pink sports top clashed with the red bicycle she'd rented. Mine was silver and Reyna's bike was pale blue.

I cycled after her, pushing my legs to go faster.

"Slow down!" Reyna called from behind us.

I kept pushing, following Gem, the wind rushing past my face. The sea crashed against the cliffs below and the sun warmed my skin—perfect weather for a cycle.

Gem rounded the corner, reaching the top of the climb. She slowed down, coming to a stop at a viewing point. She put a foot out to steady herself and I joined her, stopping my bike next to hers. We both stared out at the view.

The sea sparkled under a perfect blue sky. Yachts sailed through the waves while smaller boats bobbed along. Monaco gleamed in the sunshine, a mass of buildings cut into the cliffs. Tall glass structures towered over clusters of red rooftops.

"Beautiful," I said, my voice breathy from the exercise.

"I could get used to this." Gem turned to me and grinned.

"Guys!" Reyna shouted, just making it up to the viewing point. "You know I'm not an athlete, right? Did you have to go so fast? And uphill, too!" She slowly wheeled her bike to us. "Wow!" She stared out at the view.

"See? Totally worth the steep climb," Gem said.

"It's stunning. I can't believe I've never been up here before." Reyna continued to take it all in, rubbing the back of her hand across her forehead. "Wait a second!" She got off her bike and rested it on the ground. She took out her phone from a hidden pocket in her cycle shorts. "We need a photo for socials." She stepped back and took a few pictures of Gem and me. "Perfect! Got the view in the background, too."

"Okay, we'll give you a minute to recover and then we race back down," Gem said.

"What?" Reyna quickly put her phone away and grabbed her bike.

"I'm good to go now," I said, my fingers tightening around the handlebars.

"We only just got here!" Reyna got back on her bike.

Gem moved her bike and glanced at me with a wicked grin. She was the best trainer I'd ever had because she knew how to have fun. It wasn't all stretches and nutritional advice. I moved towards Gem, lining up next to her like we were on a starting grid.

"Three, two, one..." I began.

"Go!" Gem shouted, and we both launched ourselves back down the hill.

"I hate you both!" Reyna shouted after us, her voice carried on the wind.

WE DROPPED the bikes off and walked back to the hotel. On the short walk back, a few girls stopped us for photographs. They were in the city for the race weekend. Reyna took pictures of us with each girl's phone. Eventually, we made it back, turning off the main street and into the hotel's front courtyard. A woman in a floral summer dress perched on the edge of the low wall surrounding the fountain. She stared down at her phone but looked up as we approached.

"Emily?" Gem paused mid-step.

The woman jumped to her feet, her curly hair bouncing with the movement, and launched herself at Gem, throwing her arms around her. Gem hugged her back, both of them laughing.

"What are you doing here?" Gem asked as the two of them pulled back but kept hold of each other's hands.

"Surprise! Are you surprised?" Emily asked.

"Yes!"

They embraced again and kissed. It was like something out of a movie. The two of them stood before a bubbling fountain, the sun shining down on them, in one of the most glamorous cities in the world.

"Come on," Reyna nudged me and we entered the hotel, leaving Gem and Emily alone. "I helped Emily organise the surprise. She messaged me saying she had time off work and wanted to visit Gem. I arranged the flights."

"Is that why you suggested the three of us go out this morning?"

"Yes, but next time, I'll be sure to pick the activity. I'm not cycling anywhere with you two ever again. My muscles already feel stiff."

I glanced over my shoulder and peeked at Gem and Emily through the windows. They looked so happy together.

As we entered the lift, I let out a sigh. There'd been a time when I'd had a relationship like Gem and Emily's, or I thought I did. My ex used to visit me on race weekends. He'd be there before the start, cheer me on from the sidelines during the race, and then greet me after I got out of the car. As the months and years went by, he came to fewer races. He didn't come to any of my W races last year. Then, we broke up halfway through the season, and I focused all my energy on my racing career instead. I hadn't realised I missed having that kind of support.

<hr>

EVERY YEAR, the King of Monaco hosted a big event before the race weekend and everyone in F1 attended. Nerves built as the evening grew closer. I'd picked out a dress weeks ago. It had to be special, a dress fit for an event hosted by a king. My black evening gown had a slit down one side and a low back, with criss-crossing straps. Stylish, sophisticated, and a little sexy too.

Gem wasn't going with us tonight. She had dinner plans with Emily instead. I wished she was coming, but I didn't complain; she deserved to spend time with her girlfriend. She hung out with me in my hotel room while Emily took a shower in their room. She lounged on my bed, reading the latest copy of *Lights Out* magazine while I got ready, putting the finishing touches on my makeup. I went for dark eyes and a classic red lip. I'd put my hair into those chunky curlers earlier and now I had to let them down and hope they'd hold for the entire evening.

"He's got another interview in *Lights Out*," Gem commented, turning the page. She leaned on her side, propped up on one elbow with the magazine in front of her.

"Who?" I pulled my hair free from the curlers and abandoned the mirror to see who she was talking about. She pushed the magazine in my direction.

I snatched it off the bed to find Sterling's face staring back at me. Dressed in a gorgeous, tailored suit with a crisp white shirt and open collar, he looked less like an F1 driver and more like a Hollywood movie star.

"*With no one to stop him, Sterling believes this season could be his fourth World Championship title,*" I quoted the article and flicked the page to reveal more photos. He'd taken the suit jacket off in the next photo. His eyes looked down, a small smile on his lips, like he'd shared a secret with the reader, with me. I glanced at the intimate photo one more time before chucking it back on the bed with a groan. "No one to stop him! Who does he think he is, saying that? Stefan is literally right behind him in points, and I'm not far off either!"

"Ignore it. You know these writers spin interviews to make them more punchy." Gem picked up her magazine again and flicked through to a different write-up.

I went back to the mirror and finished my hair. The curls fell in big ringlets down my back with a hint of 1940s glamour.

A knock sounded on the door and Reyna stepped inside. She looked stunning in a pink dress with a slit up one side. She'd straightened her dark hair, so it fell pin-straight down her back. Golden bangles glinted on her wrists, matching the gold earrings. Sleek and sophisticated as always, but tonight, she'd gone all out. Gem gave Reyna a low whistle.

"Stop it," Reyna hushed, but a hint of colour flushed her cheeks. "Are you ready? The cars will be here soon."

"I need my bag." I grabbed a small black bag to hold my phone and room key.

We left together, Gem going back to her own room while Reyna and I made our way down to the lobby. Michael and our technical director, Leo Winstone, stood waiting near the doors when three classic Rolls-Royce cars pulled up outside: a Silver Shadow, a Silver Cloud, and a Phantom. They were all painted in the Torrin colours—midnight navy with a dark red stripe edged in gold. Anywhere else in the world, paintwork like that would be tacky, but somehow, it worked in Monaco.

"We're going to the event in these?" I asked, my mouth agape as I stared at the three classic cars.

"Yes," Michael replied. "Welcome to Monaco. We don't do things by halves this weekend." He stepped through the door to be greeted by the driver of the first car. The rest of the team followed, but I stayed rooted to the spot.

"Come on." Reyna reached for my fingertips, taking my hand and leading me outside in a half-daze. We got into the last car, the Silver Cloud, the leather cool against my skin as I leaned back into my seat. Reyna slid in next to me. With everyone in their cars, we left, rolling down the twisting, winding streets. The city lights dazzled in the dusk, the sky awash in warm pinks and oranges as the sun sunk beneath the horizon.

ELEVEN

MONACO

WEDNESDAY

One dance wouldn't hurt him. He knew he was lying to himself,
but he'd happily stay in denial for now.

OUR CAR PULLED up outside the red carpet. Photographers lined the barriers, their cameras already flashing. I'd been to plenty of events during my time in the world of motorsport, but none of them were like this. Reyna glanced at me, a silent question in her eyes. I nodded. I was ready.

A man opened our door and we both slid out of the car and into another world. The flashing lights became a frenzy. They blinded me for a moment and the shouting rang in my ears. The short walk to the entrance became a total assault on the senses. It passed me in a blur until I stepped inside the building and the doors shut behind us. The sound of clinking glasses and low chatter replaced the chaotic din outside. My eyes slowly adjusted to the low lighting.

We were guided from the entrance hall into a grand room.

Pink marble columns held up a magnificent high ceiling decorated with classical paintings and gold moulding. Rich red drapes hung around the arched windows and my heels sunk into the plush crimson carpet. Every inch of the room dripped in lavish décor. Guests wore long gowns and sharp black tuxedos. Waiters carried trays of fizzing champagne. The decadence overwhelmed me, and I didn't know where to look or what to do first.

Luckily, I had Reyna by my side. She navigated the party like a pro, introducing me to different guests. I had no idea how she managed to remember so many names and faces. After meeting too many people to count, Reyna and I slipped away to the bar. While waiting to be served, I spotted Stefan in the crowd. He sipped his drink, nodding along to the woman standing beside him.

"How come Stefan didn't come with us in the cars?" I asked. She turned from the bar to look at Stefan on the other side of the room.

"He's staying on a friend's yacht. Apparently, it's huge and brand new."

"Is that why he looks less grumpy than usual?"

"That won't last." Reyna laughed and turned back to the bar to grab our drinks.

She passed me my glass of a fizzy, non-alcoholic drink I'd picked at random and took a sip of her white wine.

"Reyna!" Leo, our technical director, emerged from behind a small group. "Michael needs you," he said.

"Sure, where is he?"

Leo pointed in the vague direction, and Reyna disappeared in a blink. I was tempted to chase after her as I wasn't sure how I'd navigate the party without her guidance. For a few minutes, I made small talk with Leo until he bumped into someone he knew from a different team, and suddenly, they were in an intense discussion about a possible technical regulation change for next season. It was all based on rumours, but that didn't stop their speculation. I took another sip of my drink and left them to their chat.

I wandered through the hall, weaving around glamorous women and well-dressed men. Music from a live orchestra played, the sound thrumming through my body as I headed outside onto a busy terrace.

Night had settled over the city and lights twinkled over the sea. I made my way through the crowded space, squeezed by round tables full of laughing groups, until I could get a better look at the view. Finding a quieter spot, I leaned against the wall surrounding the terrace and looked out at the sea. I'd never tire of how beautiful it was here.

"I'm starting to wonder if you have a thing for terrace views." Sterling came up beside me and leaned against the wall. His tailored suit looked to be the same one he wore in the *Lights Out* magazine interview. He even wore it the same: open collar, no tie.

"And you don't?" I asked.

"Fair. Is this view better than the Melbourne one?" he asked.

I considered his question and scanned the view again. "They're both beautiful in their own way. Company could be better."

"Haha. There's still time for you to run off like you did last time." He smiled, a challenge in his eyes.

"Depends. Don't try to kiss me again."

He put a hand over his heart. "I promise I won't try to kiss you ever again." He paused and let his hand fall to his side. "Unless you ask me to."

I shook my head. "Are you drunk?"

"No. I don't drink during the race season."

"Yeah, right."

"I'm serious. I like to keep a clear head."

"Then you have no excuse for that terrible line. Maybe I should run off again." I glanced back at the crowded tables, pretending to look for an exit route.

"Don't go now; we've got a lot to catch up on, like how my tip on Stefan worked well for you last race." He shifted so he was leaning one arm against the wall, facing me with his whole body.

"Are you after something in return? Because you won't get any insider Torrin strategy from me." I took another sip of my drink.

"A 'thank you', perhaps."

I snorted, almost choking on the fizzy liquid.

"At least now that you've beaten him once, it should be easier to do it again."

I took another sip, refusing to talk race tactics with him.

He opened his mouth to say something, but he was cut off by a sudden burst of loud laughter. Hayashi came stumbling through the crowd with a beautiful woman on his arm. They both laughed, arms around each other as they stumbled towards the wall a few metres from us. Hayashi didn't notice Sterling or me; he only had eyes for the woman in his arms. He pushed her against the wall and they started to kiss. For a few seconds, we both watched them, transfixed by their drunken giggling and kissing. I glanced at Sterling.

"Jealous?" I asked him, his gaze moving from the couple back to me.

"No. I don't date or fuck around during the Championship season. That's why I've won three titles and Hayashi over there has none."

I laughed at his arrogance. "Really?" I said, raising my

eyebrows and reminding him of our almost-kiss at the start of the season.

"That was preseason. It doesn't count."

"You don't drink and you don't fuck, so what do you do?"

"Win races," he replied seriously.

I shook my head. Did he ever stop with the whole "perfect athlete" routine?

"Are you jealous of them?" He grinned, his eyes twinkling with mischief.

"No. I'm staying focused; like you say, I've got a Championship to win. I'll be the first rookie World Champion." I gave him my sweetest smile.

"Ha. Please! No one wins the Championship in their first year."

"No one has yet. You blew your chance, but I won't blow mine."

"And you think I'm arrogant and overconfident?"

"If I am to beat you, I must become so much worse than you and all the other drivers put together."

He laughed, not mockingly: a genuine, carefree laugh. I'd never heard this sound from him before. It wasn't his press conference laugh. This was a real laugh. It lit something within me and I wanted to hear it again. Not just to hear it, but to be the one to make that sound leave his lips. "You're probably right," he said.

We both looked out at the view again. A silent moment passed between us.

"Have you seen the ballroom yet?" he asked.

"No."

"I'll show you."

He held out his hand to me. I nodded, abandoned my drink on the wall, and placed my hand in his. His fingers tightened around mine and he took me through the crowded terrace and back inside.

<hr>

CHANDELIERS OF DIAMOND glass hung from a vast vaulted ceiling. Low lights shone over maroon-panelled walls and a live band played from one end of the ballroom. The music echoed through the vast space, the melody mixing with the sound of guests talking and laughing.

I stood beside Sterling at the edge of the room, watching people dance. A woman in a flouncy pink dress whirled past us with her partner, both of them smiling with a carefree air.

"You want to join them?" he asked, pointing to the couple as they disappeared into the packed crowd on the dancefloor.

"Huh?"

"Do you want to dance?" He tilted his head towards the dance floor.

I laughed. "I don't think so."

"Come on, I can tell you want to. I meant it when I said I wouldn't kiss you again."

I rolled my eyes.

"But I guess I can't promise you won't try to kiss me," he said.

"You're being ridiculous. I'm not dancing with you."

"Probably for the best. You clearly can't trust yourself around me, Rookie." He gave me a teasing grin with a challenging look in his eyes. A dare.

Fine. I took off into the crowd, pushing past dancers, not stopping for anyone. I paused in the middle of the ballroom and turned to find him right behind me, a triumphant smile on his face.

"Don't complain if I stomp on your toes." I held my arms

out for him and he stepped closer. He took my hand and laced our fingers while he wrapped his other arm around my back. Our bodies brushed together. He leaned even closer and his lips brushed against my ear.

"I wouldn't dare," he whispered, and then he took the lead, moving us to the beat of the music.

"I didn't know you could dance," I said as we continued to step in smooth circles.

"I told you I had other interests, remember, Rookie?"

"Hmmm…"

"You don't like it when I call you that?" He raised a brow.

"I'm hardly a rookie."

"It's your first season in F1, which makes you a rookie, right?"

I sighed. "Technically, yes, but I'm an experienced driver who's raced in plenty of other competitive series. I've won the last three W series titles and I'm twenty-nine; I'm hardly some fresh-faced teen driver."

"Fair point. Do you want me to stop with the nickname?" he asked.

Yes, no, maybe, I couldn't reply, so I ignored his question and focused on dancing.

He gently took us into a slow spin and I stared up at him. His warm brown eyes stayed on me. The crowd and noise blurred around us. We could have been the only ones there. His hand on my back slipped ever so slightly, and despite the warmth of the night, a shiver ran down my spine. The music began building into a crescendo and then slowly tailed off. Sterling brought us to a slow stop and his head dipped towards mine. His lips almost brushed against my jaw and his breath tickled my ear.

"Sterling," I whispered, and he leaned back to look at me. His gaze dipped to my lips.

"Winter," he said as the band began to play a new song. He unlaced our fingers and dropped his arm from my back. "Thanks for the dance." He gave me a nod and walked off through the crowd.

As I watched him go, I lifted my hand to my chest. My heart raced and my mind began to spin. I shouldn't have danced with him.

Qualifying Report
Pole – Winter Jones
2nd – Aiden Sterling
3rd – Stefan Brudes

MONACO

SUNDAY - RACE DAY

He'd gone and fucked up his race. That's what happened when he got too twisted up in his own thoughts, going over past failures. Now, he could add this race to the list. He wished there was a button for switching off spinning thoughts.

IN MONACO, Qualifying was everything. The tight street circuit made overtaking almost impossible. Whoever secured pole position had the advantage. I had pole position. My first pole in F1. Now, Sterling would be in my mirrors.

In the interviews after Qualifying, I tried to hide my smug smile, but I'm not sure I did a great job of concealing it. Sterling avoided my eyeline at all times. There wasn't much time to celebrate my Qualifying triumph as race day approached.

Once the glamourous Monaco events and dazzling fanfare ended, it was finally down to business. I lined my car up in the first-place grid spot and waited. In the corner of my eye, I could see Sterling's car in second place. My car vibrated with life and

I kept my hands secured on the steering. My eyes focused on the five red lights. One by one, the lights switched on. Then, all five went out.

I launched my car into action. Following the racing line, I had a great start. Sterling was right behind me, trying to line his car up beside mine, but I made it to the corner first and pulled ahead as I exited the tight turn. Now, all I had to do was stay ahead of him for seventy-eight laps.

Lap by lap, I increased the gap between Sterling and myself. He remained in my mirrors, becoming smaller with every turn of the track. I couldn't get cocky this early on. The Monaco GP had a reputation for playing tricks on drivers. With every lap, you'd begin to relax, get into the rhythm of every bump and curve in the road, and slowly, it lulled you into a false sense that you had control of this twisty street circuit. This was the effect of Monaco, a cruel trick that fooled drivers into pushing the limits. One tiny mistake, or concentration slip, and it was race over.

Staying focused, I kept my pace and followed my race strategy. My pit stops went to plan, and for a time, it felt like everything had come together. I was completely absorbed. Nothing else mattered. Everyone else disappeared. It was just me, my car, and the track.

It wasn't until I crossed the finish line that I came out of this racing haze. I pulled up on the track before the number one sign, and it took me a few moments to realise I'd won.

I'd won. I'd won my first race. I'd beaten my teammate again. I'd beaten Sterling.

Once I was out of my car, the celebrations became wild. The Torrin team roared and the crowds in the stands cheered. My body hummed with adrenalin, my heart pounded, and the world around me became a distortion of colour, noise and excitement.

While spraying champagne at my team, I glanced down the busy track as people gathered near the podium. Sterling lingered at the back of the crowd. He hadn't finished in the top three, and I had no idea why or what had happened to him. During the early stages of the race, he'd been right behind me. Then he'd vanished from my mirrors, and I'd been too focused on my own race to worry about what had gone on behind me.

Our gazes stayed locked for a second. He nodded his head, an acknowledgement of my win, and then he turned away, walking back up the track and into the pits.

Mum: 6 Missed Calls
Mum: Congratulations, darling! We're so proud. I knew we should have come to the Monaco GP, but we'll see you next week. I have some thoughts on how best to tackle Qualifying at Silverstone. Lots of love. Xx
Winter: Thanks, Mum!
Winter: See you and Dad soon! Xx

Sofie: Woo!!! FIRST F1 WIN!!!
Sofie: And at Monaco, too!
Winter: Thanks, Sofie! I don't think it's sunk in yet.

Championship Driver Standings

Stefan Brudes – 100

Winter Jones – 97

Aiden Sterling – 90

THIRTEEN

GREAT BRITAIN

THURSDAY

Sometimes, he couldn't face interviews. Being a three-time World Champion meant everyone wanted to chat to him, and some days, he found it difficult. But being a three-time World Champion also meant he could simply refuse an interview, and nobody would question why.

CELEBRATING my first win was short-lived because the British Grand Prix followed Monaco, and everyone wanted a piece of the British drivers. Interviews, fan signings, charity events, media sessions. It started from the moment I arrived back in the UK, and Reyna worked extra hard to organise everything alongside my usual racing and training commitments. She created a spreadsheet for the whole week and weekend.

The downside of the home race weekend was spending more time with the other British drivers. It shouldn't be a negative. I didn't mind spending time with Benjamin Knight, who raced for the Lawrence team. He was friendly and easy to get on with during interviews and events.

Then there was Sterling.

We hadn't spoken properly since our dance in Monaco, apart from when he congratulated me on my first win during a press event. That didn't count since we were surrounded by other people and on-camera. It wasn't like I wanted to speak to him alone anyway. I made sure to keep my distance as much as I could.

Thursday morning, we had a fan signing session at the Silverstone media centre. Racing fans lined up through the building and out the door to get their T-shirts, caps, and photos signed by the three British drivers.

Reyna accompanied me into the signing room. Sterling and his team's PR consultant were already there. Sterling sat at one end of a table. His PR guy stood beside him, handing him a stack of photographs to sign. There were two empty seats alongside Sterling and pens were scattered over the table.

"We have an hour here and then we'll head back to the hotel," Reyna read from her tablet while we walked to the table. I hesitated before taking the seat furthest from Sterling. He gave me a nod and then went back to signing his photo cards.

"Hey guys! Guess I'm in the middle." Benjamin Knight strode into the room. He took the last chair between Sterling and me. It creaked as he shuffled closer to the table. "Did you see the line outside? Do you think an hour will be long enough?" He turned to look at Lawrence's PR woman. She shrugged.

"Are we ready?" a burly security guard at the doors asked.

"Yes." Benjamin picked up one of the pens on the table and held it out. I nodded and Sterling carried on signing his cards like no one had spoken.

The security guard opened the door. Excited chatter came

from the hallway. A girl at the front of the line squealed when she saw Sterling. He'd be the main draw at this signing. He had the biggest profile between us and he'd won three world titles. It made sense that fans wanted to see him the most, but I still had to resist the urge to roll my eyes.

Reyna pulled out a stack of photographs from her bag. They were of me standing in front of the Torrin car. They'd taken them during the car's launch before the season started. I was in my brand new Torrin race suit and stood to the left of the car with my arms crossed. It wasn't the most flattering picture of me. Someone had cropped the photo. The original shot had both Stefan and me in it. He'd stood to the right of the car, with me on the left.

I groaned.

"I know," Reyna whispered in my ear.

"Surely there are better pictures?"

"Michael insisted on using official team photographs. I'll have to arrange a proper shoot when we have time."

I frowned at the pictures and then glanced over at Sterling. He raised his eyebrows at my photographs before turning away. Of course, his photocards used a picture of him looking hand-some in his race suit leaning against a wall. I opened my mouth to tell him to mind his own damn business, but the first fan approached our table. She looked to be in her early twenties, wearing a Silvers T-shirt with a denim jacket on top. When she turned slightly to hold out a Silvers cap to Sterling, I spotted the embroidery on the back of her jacket. A stitched design of Sterling's car racing alongside my teammate's car. The stitching was so fine and detailed. This wasn't ordinary merch: she'd made it herself. It must have taken her hours, days, possibly weeks. Sterling signed her cap and she giggled when he passed it back to her. Fans began to line up in front of his side of the table.

This was going to be a long signing session.

"COULD WE GET A PICTURE, TOO?" the woman asked as I signed a Torrin cap for her daughter. The girl looked to be around eight. She hadn't spoken a word as I signed her cap, but she smiled shyly at me.

"Sure." I handed the cap back to the girl. Her eyes went wide as she examined my squiggly signature. I pushed my chair back and stood to the side of the table. The mum got her phone out and pushed her daughter towards me. I crouched in front of the girl, gently took the cap from her hand, and placed it on her head. I stood behind her and we both smiled at her mum. After she'd taken at least five pictures, the girl turned to face me.

"Thank you," she said in a small voice and ran back to her mum.

As I returned to my seat, my gaze locked with Sterling's for a fraction of a second. He smiled and went back to the fan standing before him, a man in his thirties with six different photographs for Sterling to sign.

"Excuse me, bathroom break!" Benjamin pushed his chair back and left the room.

Mine and Sterling's eyes met once again, but we quickly looked away.

A woman with her two daughters approached me with loads of photos and a few magazine articles they wanted signed. Luckily, all those photos were more flattering than my team-approved one. I started signing them, but when I got to the last one, my pen ran out. I shook it, but the ink had run dry. I reached across to a pen in front of Benjamin's seat. My fingers brushed against soft skin and I flinched. Sterling had gone for the same pen at the same time as me.

"Sorry," he said.

"No worries."

"You take it." He picked the pen up and held it out to me.

I took it from him and our fingers brushed. I tried to ignore the sparks that flew through my body at his touch. Instead, I focused on signing the last picture for the woman. I ended up handing her the neatest signature I'd ever written.

A girl in her teens, around thirteen or fourteen, came up to our table wearing a Silvers T-shirt and holding a stack of photos in her arms. She placed the pictures down before Sterling and he started to sign them, with that charming smile that hadn't slipped once since we'd begun the event.

"Can I get a photo with both of you?" she asked Sterling and then looked over at me.

"With both of us?" he asked, pointing his pen to his chest.

"Together? In the same photo?" I added.

"Yes, please!" She bounced on the balls of her feet and clutched her signed photographs to her chest.

"Okay," I said, sounding unsure.

Sterling slid out of his seat.

"Thank you!"

I followed Sterling and the girl to the end of the table. She held her phone out, looking for someone to take the picture for her.

Reyna stepped forward and offered to take the photo. She gestured to the three of us, getting the girl to stand in the middle while Sterling and I stood awkwardly behind her.

"Closer!" Reyna instructed, and I shuffled a step towards Sterling. He did the same. Reyna took a step back, trying to fit us all in the frame. "Move in closer: otherwise, I can't get you all in. Put your arms around each other and smile." Reyna gave me a pointed look and I did as she instructed.

Sterling moved in, placing his left arm over my shoulder

while I tucked my right arm around his middle. My hand brushed his broad, toned back. I breathed in his familiar scent: woody, earthy, with a hint of something citrusy. Our eyes met and for a fraction of a second, I was back in the Monaco ballroom, wrapped up in his arms, dancing together.

"Ready!" The daydream shattered.

I quickly focused on the phone in Reyna's hands and smiled.

"Lovely," Reyna said, holding the phone out to the girl.

She thanked Reyna and we returned to the table to find Benjamin back from the bathroom.

"Did I miss anything?" he asked.

Sterling and I both shook our heads.

AFTER LUNCH, I had an interview with a women's sports magazine, and then, mid-afternoon, I went back to the Silverstone track. The British TV crew wanted to record a special piece with the three British drivers. They'd organised three BMW Minis and wanted us to drive one of the presenters around the track. The presenters would do a casual interview with us while we drove and talked them through the different corners and challenges of Silverstone. They planned to show the recorded interviews before the race on Sunday. Driving a Mini around the track sounded pretty fun. Out of everything on Reyna's spreadsheet, I'd looked forward to this event the most.

Benjamin was already there when I arrived. He stood on the track with the three presenters and camera crew. The Mini Coopers lined up behind them: one in red, one in white, and one in blue.

We made small talk while waiting for Sterling. Minutes

ticked by with no sign of him. One of the producers whispered in the ear of one of the presenters. The producer walked off to the side of the track with her phone. She came back a few minutes later.

"Looks like it's just the two of you," she said to Benjamin and me.

I frowned. "Where's Sterling?"

"He can't make it." She slid her phone into her back pocket.

"That's a shame," Benjamin said, polite as ever.

"Why not?" I asked, less politely.

The producer shrugged. "His manager said something about a mix-up, but we can still proceed without him. It won't change our plans too much."

"A mix-up? He was with us earlier at the signing. He didn't mention he wasn't coming this afternoon." But would he have told me he wasn't coming?

"Which colour do you want?" she asked, pointing to the red, white, and blue cars.

No one else seemed bothered by Sterling's absence, but it irritated me. If Benjamin and I had to be here, then so should he. He shouldn't get special treatment or be let off the hook because he was the current World Champion.

"Would you mind if I took the blue one?" Benjamin asked me.

"Yeah, whatever, I'll take red," I replied.

"Thanks, Winter!" Benjamin's face lit up while I'd lost all my enthusiasm.

GREAT BRITAIN

SATURDAY – QUALIFYING

He did nothing wrong.

THEY SAY the crowds at your home race are worth an extra second a lap. It's as if the electrifying support from the fans turbo-charges your car. That's exactly how it felt racing around Silverstone during Qualifying. It was one of the fastest tracks of the season and it felt even better with the fan support.

We were about to enter the last Qualifying session. In the first round, I'd posted the fastest lap time, and in the second session, Sterling got the quickest time with only a fraction of a second between us. For the last part of Qualifying, all the remaining cars were on the track, each driver trying to set their best time. I could hear the crowd cheer, even with my helmet on and the noise of my engine. I went around the track twice, trying to find enough space to pull a fast lap. If I got too close to the car in front of me or came up behind a car slowing to return to the pits, it would impact my time. I needed the perfect lap to beat Sterling and to secure pole for tomorrow's race.

I crossed the start line and began a fast lap. I took every corner perfectly and hit my fastest times down the straights. Silverstone had to be one of my favourite race circuits. I'd raced here as a kid and knew every inch of the circuit off by heart. I could close my eyes and know exactly where I was, based on the feel of the tarmac under my tyres.

I'd almost finished the perfect lap when I came up to a slow car.

"Damn it," I hissed, catching up to the silver car. It was either Sterling or his teammate. I continued to gain on them. They weren't doing a hot lap, but I was and wasn't about to ruin my time for them. As I got closer, I could see the red and blue of Sterling's helmet. He should move aside. That's how it went in Qualifying: cars on fast laps were given space and cars on slow laps would move aside to let them through. If the race stewards thought a driver actively impeded or blocked another driver's lap time, they'd face a penalty. Sterling had to know I was on a fast lap. I was close enough now that he'd have seen me gaining in his mirrors.

As I caught him, we both turned into the last corner. He took the racing line instead of moving out of my way. I avoided his car by millimetres, and then, as I exited the corner, I went wide. Avoiding him cost me time.

"Bastard!" I screamed as I crossed the finish line.

Sterling pulled off on the straight and disappeared, probably going for his own fast lap.

"Box, box, box!" Ash said over the radio, calling me back to the pits.

"Did you see that? He ruined my best lap!"

"If you pit now, we'll have time for one last hot lap. You got this." Ash sounded so cool over the radio. He always kept a level head while I raged. That had been my best lap and Sterling had ruined it.

I followed Ash's instructions, making my way into the pits. The crew put on a fresh set of tyres and I returned to the track. This was my final chance. Once over the start line, I put everything into my last try.

The lap was going well, maybe even better than my previous attempt, but I came across Sterling once again. This time, I caught up to him about halfway around, but he was on a fast lap, too. He must have made a mistake for me to catch him. I followed closely behind him, taking advantage of the slipstream his car created. As we approached the next corner, I had more speed than him and went for the overtake. He tried to out brake me as we headed into the bend, but I had the advantage. He tried to come back at me. We both went wide; my tyres crossed the white lines on the track, but I managed to stay in front and pulled ahead of him on the straight.

Overtaking rarely happened in Qualifying because fighting for track position meant losing time. Qualifying was all about getting the fastest time, putting together the perfect lap. I still felt like I had a good lap time and pushed for the finish line.

"Yes!" I shouted down the radio as I crossed the line.

"Head back to the garage," Ash replied, no excitement in his voice.

"What's wrong?"

"Head back. We'll talk once you're out of the car."

"No, tell me now!"

The radio went silent for a few seconds. "The stewards deleted your last lap time. You exceeded track limits." He was right. I'd gone wide battling with Sterling and crossed over the white lines that marked the track limits. If all four wheels of the car went over the lines, then the stewards would delete the lap time. This was a bit of a grey area in the rules in my opinion. At some racetracks, the stewards didn't keep a close eye on cars going over track limits; sometimes, they'd give out warnings first, and for a lot of racetracks, going over the lines would cost time, which was a form of punishment on its own.

I swore. "What does this mean?" I demanded, even though I'd almost made it back to the pits.

"You're starting in tenth position."

"What?! This is Sterling's fault. He pushed me wide and he impeded my fast lap earlier. Where's he starting?"

"He's ninth. He was given a five-place grid penalty."

"So he fucks up my fastest lap and still starts higher than me?" I pulled into the garage and the crew swarmed around my car.

"We'll talk out of the car," Ash said, ending the radio conversation.

THE INTERVIEWS after Qualifying became a nightmare. I might have let my anger and frustration get the better of me. I was asked a couple of stupid questions, which only intensified my dark mood. Luckily, Sterling was nowhere to be seen during the interviews, but this only irritated me further as he'd once again managed to get out of something the rest of us were required to attend. The press sessions were mandatory.

At least Stefan was on pole. If any other driver had secured pole position, they'd be unbearably happy and smug, but Stefan was his usual quiet, brooding self. Reyna had a challenge getting him to answer questions with more than one-word answers, while she glared at me every time I got too heated answering questions about Sterling.

Michael was furious with the Qualifying results and launched an appeal with the stewards to reinstate my fastest time. At least my team had my back, but Michael didn't seem as annoyed as I was about Sterling blocking me.

"He's been given a five-place penalty," was all he had to say on the matter and that was the end of our discussion.

After an early dinner in the team's motorhome, I travelled back to the hotel with Gem. I looked forward to getting back to my room and putting this day behind me. I had to find a way to calm down and refocus for the race tomorrow. Gem suggested taking a long bath, but I wouldn't be able to sit still for long enough. Adrenalin still pumped through my body and every time I closed my eyes, my fastest lap replayed in my mind. My hands on the steering wheel, the noise of the crowd, and Sterling getting in my way.

As we travelled to the hotel, I got my phone out and started scrolling. This only riled me up further. I couldn't help looking at everyone's reaction.

"They're saying I've ruined the British Grand Prix for the British fans!" I said as I read a post on the *Lights Out* app.

"Stop doom scrolling," Gem replied, looking out the window at the campsites in the distance. Most fans camped over the race weekend. There weren't many hotels near the track.

"*With no British drivers on the front row for the race, fans are facing a disappointing start to the weekend, and they're not hiding their opinions on the disastrous Qualifying session, with some voicing their anger over Winter Jones's aggressive tactics,*" I quoted the article. "Aggressive! What the hell?!"

"Ignore it. You know what these sports bloggers are like. They can turn anything into a story."

"Fine." I closed the *Lights Out* app and opened up a social media app instead. Big mistake. "Hysterical! I wasn't hysterical in the interviews!"

"That's it. Give me your phone." Gem held her hand out to me, giving me a stern look.

"I'll stop! Look, I'm stopping!" I closed all my apps down.

"No, give it here. You can have it back tomorrow after the race."

"Really? You sound like my mum."

She didn't reply but kept her hand out to me. I sighed and placed my phone in her palm. She took it and put it away in her bag.

We sat in silence for a few moments.

"Talking about your mum, isn't she coming to the race?" Gem asked.

"My parents are coming tomorrow. I convinced them to only come for the race day. Good job I did. Otherwise, I'd be getting a lecture from her on my poor performance."

"Tomorrow is a new day. You can fight your way up. It's not impossible."

"I know." I sighed, trying to let go of the anger and frustration. As usual, Gem was right. Anything could happen during tomorrow's race.

FIFTEEN

GREAT BRITAIN

SATURDAY - AFTER QUALIFYING

He thought she'd never ask him to kiss her.

AT THE HOTEL, Gem left me in the lobby and went back to her room. I waited at the reception desk to pick up my room key. A few guests came through the hallway as I waited, and I recognised some of the faces and team logos on their shirts. Multiple F1 teams were staying at the same hotel. There weren't many other places to stay in the rural area. Reyna told me that Stefan had brought his own motorhome with him and I wondered if he bought it to avoid being around other people. This morning at breakfast, I'd bumped into Hayashi and he'd invited himself to eat with me. I'd nodded along to his energetic conservation with bleary eyes, wishing I'd taken my breakfast up to my room or eaten at the team motorhome instead.

The hotel had that quaint, typically British vibe, with patterned carpets, panelled walls, and framed paintings of countryside scenery. It was nothing like the decadent glamour of Monaco or the flashy modern hotels in the USA. I stood next to the dark wooden reception desk. It even had a big brass bell on top with a tiny handwritten note that read, *"Ring for assistance."*

I dinged the bell and a young woman came rushing down the hall. The reception desk was in a big hallway with a grand staircase going up either side. Three different corridors were going off in opposing directions. The building was a warren of winding corridors, and it was easy to get lost, as I'd learnt when we first checked in.

"Can I help?" she asked.

"I handed in my room key this morning: room thirty-three."

"Sure!" She turned to a big wooden cabinet with little cubby holes for all the different room keys. She scanned the numbers until she got to thirty-three, then handed me the big, old-fashioned key.

"Thanks." I turned and headed for the corridor at the end of the lobby, under the staircase.

Waiting in reception had helped to calm me. I didn't feel as hyped-up as I had in the car on the way back. The adrenalin of Qualifying was slowly leaving my system. Maybe I'd try to take a bath like Gem suggested. I'd need something to occupy my evening without my phone.

I entered the narrow corridor, mentally recalling the way: turn left, then take the stairs to the big glass atrium. Movement caught my attention. I glanced to the right and all of my anger returned.

Sterling was making his way down the corridor with his back to me. He must have walked right by me while I stood at the reception desk. He didn't even have the guts to speak to me face to face and apologise for messing up my lap time.

My fingers tightened around my room key, the metal biting into my skin. I wasn't about to let him get away with it.

I marched down the corridor after him.

"Hey! Sterling!"

He looked up from turning the key in his door.

"I'm not getting into this now," he replied. His door clicked open.

"Yes, you are!" I said, reaching his door. "You blocked my fastest lap, and you haven't got anything to say about it?" I stared at him, waiting. The adrenalin buzzed around my body again. So much for cooling down.

He opened his door and went to step inside. I reached for his arm. His bare skin was warm against my fingertips.

"Seriously? Not even a 'sorry'?"

"I didn't realise you were on a hot lap, okay?" He pulled away from me and stepped inside. He left the door open, so I followed him into his room, letting the door click shut behind me.

I scoffed. "It was obvious I was on a fast lap!"

"I was focused on my own car. I wasn't keeping tabs on yours." He unclipped the watch on his wrist and placed it down on his bedside table.

"Come on! You knew! Otherwise, they wouldn't have given you a penalty." I placed a hand on my hip.

"I've had plenty of mistaken penalties before. The stewards got it wrong."

"That's bullshit! You didn't want me to secure another pole position and another win after Monaco!" My breathing quickened.

He marched back over to me and leaned a hand on the doorframe behind me. I fought the urge to back away from him. I wouldn't let him intimidate me.

"Why would I give you a tip on your teammate to block you a few weeks later? I don't play dirty on the track, and if anyone is owed an apology, it's me!"

"What?"

"For overtaking me while I was on my hot lap. We both lost time, messing around, fighting for track position."

"It's not my fault you messed up your fastest lap. I shouldn't have been able to catch you, but I did, which means you made a mistake! That's on you, not me!"

"You're unbelievable," he replied, his voice low, his breathing heavy. He leaned in closer to me.

I stared into his eyes, refusing to back down. We were so close I could see flecks of gold in his brown irises, beautifully framed by dark eyelashes.

He leaned in even closer; his breath heated my cheek. I moved closer to him. My gaze dipped to his lips. They looked soft, and he parted them ever-so-slightly as if he knew what I was thinking.

He moved towards me like he was about to kiss me, his hand reaching for the back of my neck, but he stopped millimetres from me. Time seemed to stand still in that moment. I wanted this. I wanted him to kiss me.

"Kiss me," I whispered.

He responded instantly, closing the gap between us.

SIXTEEN

GREAT BRITAIN

SATURDAY - AFTER QUALIFYING

She never called him by his name. Never Aiden, always Sterling. Sterling, Sterling, Sterling... When she called him Aiden, it threw him. And he knew there was no going back from this moment.

OUR LIPS MET in a rush and his hand tightened around the back of my head, his fingers in my hair. I dropped my room key, which hit the floor with a dull thud. Reaching my arms up, I wrapped my hands behind his neck. His lips were softer than I'd expected, but fierce and demanding at the same time. I parted my lips for him, our kiss deepened, and my body melted against his.

He pushed me against the door; my back hit it with a light thump, but neither of us broke apart or slowed the pace. His hands slid down my back and I arched into him. His lips left my mouth and began to trail down my jaw to my neck. I gasped as his teeth grazed my skin.

He leaned back, his lips swollen, his dark eyes on me. His gaze rolled over me and a shiver ran down my spine when he gave me a satisfied smile. I looked him over, too. He still wore his Silvers T-shirt and shorts, the fabric stretching across his broad shoulders. I was in my Torrin polo and shorts, too.

His hands moved from around me and he brought his thumb up to my lips. He traced my bottom lip and then paused in the middle, pulling my lip down slightly. I drew his thumb into my mouth and gently bit down. He grinned.

How we'd gone from arguing to this, I didn't know, but I knew for sure that I didn't want to stop. I placed my hand flat against his chest and pushed him away from me. In a wild move, I switched us around, pushing him up against the door instead.

Placing my lips to his ear, I whispered, "That's better."

He kissed me frantically in response like he couldn't get enough. His stubble brushed against my skin as I trailed kisses over his jaw. His hands moved over my body, tracing every curve and dip. Every place he touched felt electrified. I wanted more.

Clothes landed on the floor. Everything became a frenzied rush: hands roamed, lips explored, and we found ourselves naked, tangled up on his bed.

I swore I'd been on top of him, but now he leaned over me, my back pressed into the mattress, his lips on mine and his hand between my legs. I gasped as he pressed down on my clit.

"Aiden," I moaned. "Aiden, please."

He stilled, broke the kiss and moved back so his forehead leaned against mine. We both breathed heavily.

"You stopped?" I whined. His hand remained between my legs. His fingers were right there, right at the edge of pleasure, but he'd paused, leaving me on a precipice. I wanted more than anything to topple right over the edge and fall into pure bliss.

"You said... This... We..." For a split second, that cocky overconfidence of his vanished. He was right to have doubts or a second of clarity. I should feel the same. I should ask what the hell we were doing together naked in his bed. I should stop this. I should...

"Do you overthink like this in the middle of a race?" I asked, knowing how my question would play out.

Our eyes met and his widened. I trailed my hand from the tops of his shoulders down his chest, down to his hard erection. He took a sharp breath as I wrapped my fingers around him and gave a gentle squeeze.

I put my lips to his ear.

"Is that why you made a mistake today? You made a mistake and then fucked up my hot lap in turn," I suggested, provoking him further.

He half-groaned, half-growled. His other hand fisted in my hair.

"I didn't—" He started to argue, but I squeezed him again and his words cut off.

"Why don't you fuck me hard and fast, like you fucked me on the track today?"

He moved even further back and I let go of him. The hand in my hair loosened and his fingers slipped down my thigh, leaving a trail of wetness as they went.

I'd gone too far, pushed him too much, but then his lips quirked into that cocky smile of his. The arrogant version of Aiden Sterling was back.

He sat back on his heels, kneeling beside me.

"If that's how the Rookie wants to play," he said, pulling the top drawer of his nightstand open. He took out a foil packet. "You sure you want to play this game with me?" he asked, and I watched as he tore open the packet and rolled the condom on.

I propped myself up onto my elbows and let my eyes roam

over him before answering. I stared at the way he knelt on the bed and the way his hand moved up and down his cock while his heated gaze stayed on me. I'd been so unprepared for this version of Sterling. Sure, he looked handsome and polished in all the magazine photoshoots, and he always looked fit in his race suit, but seeing him like this, so exposed and yet so sure of himself, was something else entirely.

"I want you to fuck me, Sterling."

Suddenly, he was back on me; his lips captured mine in a rushed kiss. My arms wrapped around his shoulders as his hips settled between my thighs, his arms on either side of me, holding his weight. He placed himself at my entrance, moving up and down as if testing to see how ready I was. I wrapped my legs around him and pressed my heels into his backside, wanting more, wanting him.

"So impatient."

I groaned and dug my nails into his back.

He chuckled against my neck. I arched my hips, feeling him right there, right where I needed him.

"The Rookie can have it her way this time," he whispered and thrust all the way in.

I cried out and arched my back even further.

He pulled out, only to push back in. A jumble of words passed my lips. The pressure felt good. He felt so good. I rolled my hips, feeling every inch of him.

"Fuck," he gasped and kissed me.

I moved my hips to meet every one of his thrusts. My hands clawed his back, my thighs clenched around his hips, and my heels pressed against him, urging him to go faster, harder.

The bed started creaking under us, but I could hardly hear it over my own ragged breathing.

Our movements became faster, but I wanted more, needed more. He adjusted his angle, grabbed one of my legs and hooked his arm over. He felt so much deeper in this new position, hitting just the right spot.

"Oh my God! Yes!" I was close; a coil tightened within me.

"Stay with me," he said, his voice husky.

I couldn't help it: the demand in his voice had my eyes meeting his, and I watched as his control snapped and he pounded into me. Pleasure exploded. He released my leg from his hold and his weight shifted forward as he chased his own release. My orgasm left me in waves and I shuddered against him. We were both breathing heavily as we came down from the high, our bodies slick with sweat. A few seconds passed before he slid out of me and slumped back on the bed beside me.

"Fuck," he said with an exhale.

"Yeah," I agreed as it hit me: what we'd done.

I'd just fucked my rival and enjoyed it.

SEVENTEEN

GREAT BRITAIN

SATURDAY - AFTER QUALIFYING

If she wanted to pretend that nothing had happened between them, then fine. But he couldn't pretend and he planned to have a lot of fun reminding her of their time together. He knew this wasn't just about sex.

I HAD no idea how long I hid in Sterling's bathroom. Once he disposed of the condom, I grabbed my underwear from the floor and locked myself in there. I cleaned myself up, tried to untangle my hair, and then I put the lid down on the toilet and sat there for minutes.

I tapped my fingers on the edge of the seat while I stared at the products on the shelf above the sink. They were all lined up in a neat line. He had a big pot of moisturiser at one end and a little container of oil at the other, and his toothbrush was placed in a glass by the tap. He'd unpacked his stuff and everything had a place. Folded towels rested over a rail and a dressing gown hung on the back of the door. I hadn't bothered to unpack any of my bathroom stuff. My hotel room was a mess compared with his, with a half-unpacked suitcase on the floor, clothes flung across my bed, and a pair of dirty socks on my bathroom floor.

In bed with Sterling, I'd told him exactly what I'd wanted, demanded it from him, and now I was hiding in his bathroom. What had I been thinking? I put my head in my hands. I'd have to leave this room and face him eventually.

A gentle knock sounded on the door.

"Hey, are you okay in there?" he asked, his voice a little rough. The sound sent me back to when he'd been inside me and I'd moaned for him to give me more.

"Winter?" he asked, waiting for an answer.

This was stupid. I shouldn't be embarrassed. It was just sex.

I stood up and tried one last time to detangle my hair before opening the door.

He stepped back at my sudden appearance. He wore only a pair of boxers. I averted my eyes, not trusting myself to even glance at him.

"This never happened," I said, moving past him to find my shorts. They were on the floor on the other side of the room. I picked them up and shimmied into them.

"So that's how you want to handle this?" He crossed his arms over his chest and smirked at me. The muscles in his arms tightened as he folded them. I focused on finding my shirt instead.

My navy Torrin top was tangled up with his Silvers top near the door. I had to pass him to get to it.

"You beg me to fuck you and now you're pretending I'm not even here," he said, and I could hear the cocky smile in his voice. He was enjoying this far too much.

"We never speak of this ever again," I said, grabbing my

shirt and pulling it over my head. Once back in my clothes, I faced him.

"Right." He grinned at me.

"This isn't a joke. I'm serious! And you can't tell anyone about this!" I motioned my finger between us.

"Who would I tell?" He relaxed his arms.

"I'm serious. You tell anyone about what happened and I will run you off the track!" I shoved my socks into my pockets and slipped my trainers back on.

"That's a bit extreme. You shouldn't joke about race safety."

"You're right. I don't joke about race safety. I'm dead serious." I spotted my room key near the door. I scooped it up and faced him once more.

"No goodbye kiss?" A teasing smile pulled at his lips: his soft, very kissable lips.

I scoffed, shook my head, and went for the door handle instead.

Thankfully, I found the corridor empty when I pulled the door back and I made my escape without speaking another word to him.

EIGHTEEN

GREAT BRITAIN

SUNDAY - RACE DAY

He recalled having the best dream of his life. Winter kissing him, her hands all over his body, her breathy moans in his ears. Then he remembered it wasn't a dream at all.

I WOKE from a deep sleep to the sound of a knock at my door. For a glorious second, I rested in a half-delirious state, with no idea where I was or what was going on. Until the events of yesterday came back to me: the terrible Qualifying session and what happened afterwards. I wondered if I'd dreamt up Sterling and me, but the slight ache between my legs said otherwise.

The knocking continued. I clambered to my feet and straightened my PJs. Not bothering with my bed hair, I rushed to the door and pulled it back to find Gem.

"I thought I'd better wake you since I had your phone. Here, I felt bad for taking it," she said, holding my phone out to me. She was already dressed in her Torrin top.

"Did I sleep in? Am I late?" I started to panic, looking at how ready she was.

"You've got plenty of time, but I thought you'd want to get down to the track early."

I sighed, taking my phone back. I glanced at the time on the screen. Only 6.35, and I already had a couple of messages from my mum.

"Yeah, my parents will probably be here early too. I'll get ready. I won't be long."

But Gem didn't leave right away. She stood in my doorway and looked me over.

"Are you okay after yesterday?" she asked.

"Yes. Like you said, it's a new day. A fresh start." Which was true. I was no longer worried about my disastrous Qualifying session. My anger and frustration had gone. But a new set of emotions and worries had replaced them. My biggest concern was someone finding out I slept with Sterling. Two racing drivers hooking up. What would people say? I already knew how the reaction would go. First female driver in F1 in over forty-five years and she slept her way to the top.

"You sure?" Gem asked again.

"Huh?"

"Are you sure you're okay?"

"Yes, I'm good."

"Okay, but if you need to talk, I'm here to listen."

I assured Gem that I was fine and told her I'd meet her in the hotel lobby in thirty minutes. I jumped straight into the shower even though I'd had one last night. I just needed the familiar routine of an ordinary race day. That's what I'd focus on: getting ready and thinking through my plan for the race. Starting in tenth on the grid would bring new challenges. I gave my hair a quick wash and then stepped out. I quickly dried off with a big, fluffy white towel and stood before the sink to brush my hair and moisturise. I looked up at the mirror to find red marks down my neck.

"Shit!" I let go of my towel and leaned closer to the mirror.

The blotchy red marks started on the right side of my neck and trailed down to my chest. What the hell?! How was I going to hide this? Makeup would look too obvious on my neck, and my polo's neckline would be too low, even if I did all the buttons up.

"Ugh!"

I quickly scrambled, brushing and drying my hair. I rushed to get into my underwear and shorts. Pulling my suitcase open, I rummaged through my racing gear. I had some spare inner race shirts and a special fire-resistant top all drivers wore under their race suits. It had a very high neckline. Usually, I wore my team polo and then changed into my race gear at the motorhome, but needs must.

ON THE DRIVE to the track, Gem kept eyeing me in the back of the car.

"What is it?" I asked.

"You're in your race gear already," she said.

"Not all of it. I just want to be ready. Get my head in the zone." I looked out the window at the big, sprawling campsites. Campers were rising, getting breakfast and getting ready for a day of watching high-speed cars. "Hey, can you take my phone again? I don't want any distractions this morning. I want to stay focused."

"Sure." She took my phone from my hand and stashed it away in her bag.

When we got to the track entrance, we signed into the paddock area with our key cards. Fans were already gathered, looking out for an early glimpse of their favourite driver. Gem and I walked down to the Torrin motorhome.

"There you are!" Mum called from outside the motorhome. She pulled me into a tight hug. "Darling, I'm sorry about yesterday."

"But she'll make up for it today," Dad chimed in.

"Thanks." Mum let me go, and Dad pulled me into a hug too. When he released me, I turned to Gem. "You both remember Gem?"

"Of course. Lovely to see you again," Mum said, then turned back to me. "Now, about yesterday."

I groaned.

"It was very unprofessional of Sterling. Not what I'd expect from a three-time World Champion," she said, taking my side. I'd expected a lecture about my role in the whole Qualifying drama. "But..." Here we go.

"But what? It wasn't my fault!"

"I am not saying it's your fault. I have some suggestions, though. You should always try to give yourself space on the track during Qualifying. Really, the team should have done better at timing your pit releases and fast laps so you didn't come close to Sterling."

I sighed. "Mum, let's not. I need to forget about yesterday and focus on today."

"Yes, focus on today's race," Dad agreed, quickly jumping into the discussion.

Mum went quiet for a moment. "You're right. Concentrate on your race day strategy. Why are you in your inner suit already?" she asked, eyeing my clothes. I internally groaned. Instead of replying, I headed inside the Torrin motorhome and the three of them followed me.

Inside, the crew and personnel were busy. Everyone was having breakfast and sitting in the dining area. I saw Michael's back as he headed to his office on the first floor. For breakfast, I had a bowl of porridge with mixed berries, nuts, and a squeeze of honey on top. I also grabbed a fruit salad and a large glass of water.

Gem and I found a free table and I started on my porridge. Dad joined us, sitting opposite me with a steaming mug.

"A lovely lady over there made me a fresh tea. Didn't charge me for it either," he said, taking a small sip.

"Dad, you're a guest of the Torrin team. You can help yourself to tea, coffee, food, and anything in the team motorhome. The chefs will even prepare something for you if you ask nicely."

"I don't know why you guys call it a motorhome. It's more like some high-tech science centre. Nothing like a caravan you hook up to the back of the car."

I shook my head. He'd told this joke at least three times since the start of the season. I finished my porridge and moved on to the fruit, pushing a chunk of melon around the bowl.

"Where's Mum?" I asked him.

Dad shrugged and took another sip of his tea.

I scanned the tables and spotted her sitting with Stefan.

"Oh my God! She's talking to Stefan," I whispered.

Both Gem and my dad turned to look at Mum with Stefan a few tables away. She chatted with animated hand gestures and then the unthinkable happened. Stefan laughed. He actually laughed at what my mum had said.

"Is Stefan laughing?" Gem asked.

Reyna appeared at the edge of our table, also staring at my mum and Stefan.

"Why can't he laugh like that during interviews?" she complained.

"Your mother is a very charming woman," Dad said, turning around.

"Promise me you'll keep her away from the press?" I asked him.

"Don't worry, she's on her best behaviour."

"But she was so good in that interview she did before," Reyna interjected.

"Do you really want her talking to the press after yesterday's Qualifying? You're lucky she didn't march herself off to the stewards and give them a lecture."

"Okay, that's a good point. Don't worry, I'll keep an eye on her during the race," Reyna said before heading over to Stefan and my mum.

"I need some air." I abandoned the rest of my fruit and headed to the stairs. I took them up to the top floor and walked out onto the rooftop garden. The morning light reflected off the shiny wooden floor and I could hear the sound of crowds forming in the distance—fans getting in early to grab their seats.

I went over to the glass barrier that looked over the rest of the paddock. All the team's motorhomes were in a long line ordered by who won the Constructors' Championship last year. Everything was about status in this sport, even down to where the motorhomes were placed.

Someone cleared their throat to my right. I turned to find Sterling standing on the rooftop garden of his team's motorhome. There was about a metre gap between the two structures. He walked over to the very corner of his balcony.

"Why are you here?" I asked.

"Enjoying the view," he said, keeping his eyes on me. His gaze ran over me and his lips quirked into a satisfied smile as if he were replaying last night in his mind.

"Don't look at me like that!" I snapped, going over to the corner closest to the Silvers motorhome. "Why do they put these things so close together?" I looked down at the gap between the two structures.

"How do you want me to look at you, then?" he asked, ignoring my second question.

"Like a normal person would. Like you haven't... You know. We said we wouldn't talk about it!"

"You said we wouldn't talk about it, but I can't help it. You're cute when you get angry."

"Stop it!"

"I thought you'd be more relaxed after last night, less wound up. I slept like a log after you left. I feel ready for the day." He stretched his arms up and his T-shirt rode up, showing a glimpse of the V that went down into his shorts. I couldn't help but look. After he stretched, he leaned forward, resting his forearms on the barrier around his terrace. "Maybe we should've had a second round last night. You might have slept better and feel more relaxed now." I wanted to scream at the arrogant smirk on his lips, but that would only draw people up here.

"I slept fine." Actually, I slept better than fine. I had such a deep sleep that I hadn't even dreamt. I felt pretty ready for the day, apart from the stress of someone finding out what we'd done and the stress of my parents at the track, too. I really hoped they weren't looking for me now.

"How come you're in your inner suit already?" he asked, looking at my top. It seemed everyone was obsessed with my outfit choice today.

"Why? Because you gave me a fucking hickey!" I said in a hushed voice. I pulled the high neck down slightly to show the blotchy red mark on my skin.

"Sorry about that. I get carried away sometimes. I'll be more careful next time."

"Next time? There isn't going to be a next time!"

"Sure there isn't. Anyway, you left scratch marks on my

back, so I don't think you can complain too much about your neck."

"No one will see unless you plan on walking around with your top off!"

"I could if you want?" He went to lift the edge of his shirt.

"Don't you dare!"

Voices came from inside the top floor of the Torrin motorhome.

"I have to go. Do not tell anyone," I whispered.

"Relax. I won't. I promise, and I mean it: I won't," he replied, lowering his voice and sounding serious. "I was only joking with you. I'll see you out there," he added, pointing towards the track. He turned around and headed back inside his motorhome.

NINETEEN

GREAT BRITAIN

SUNDAY - RACE DAY

This was the best race of his life! No one could stop him: from start to finish, he had everything under control.

WHEN THE FIVE red lights went out, I launched my car down the straight and managed to avoid any collisions. It all happened so fast. Cars swarmed around me, the crowd cheered, and I savoured every second of the pursuit down to the first corner. By the end of the first lap, I'd made up three places, but so had Sterling, and he remained in front of me.

By the halfway point, I'd made my way up to third. After my pit stop, I was catching Sterling, who'd succeeded in staying in front of me, but he hadn't pitted yet and his tyres were struggling. My lap times were closing in on his and I caught up to him at the same spot where I'd caught him during Qualifying. Our cars almost touched when we went round the next corner, rear wing to front nose, but he held the position, sticking to the racing line. On the straight, I tailed him, following his slipstream, and I gained on him again. At the next corner, I had more of an advantage. I tried to go down the inside but had to pull back when he turned in early. We both went wide, our cars almost touching again.

On the next straight, he moved over and dived into the pit lane.

"Time to put in your fastest laps!" Ash came on the radio, but he didn't need to tell me. I knew I had to make the most of the next lap while Sterling was in the pits.

Giving it everything I had, I hit every racing line and took the corners perfectly. My car felt so good; everything was coming together and I managed to get in front of Sterling after his pitstop. Now I was in second place and my teammate was still in the lead. Stefan was quite a way out in front, but that wouldn't stop me from chasing him down. I continued to put in my best lap times.

I wasn't the only one pulling exceptional laps. Sterling kept me in his sights. He wasn't gaining on me, but I wasn't losing him either. He was just there, always in the background.

With less than ten laps to go, I started to gain on my team-mate. Stefan came into view, and I got closer and closer to him with every turn of the track.

"Is there something wrong with Stefan's car?" I asked Ash over the radio. Something didn't look right to me and I kept gaining on him. If there was a problem, this could be my chance at another win.

"Possible engine problems," Ash replied and the message encouraged me to continue, but it also encouraged Sterling to move forward.

I was right on Stefan's tail, but he wasn't giving up, even if his engine was. We battled at the next corner, but he remained in front.

"If he has engine problems, he should let me through!" I

said to Ash over the radio. Teams could make those decisions and ask drivers to put the team result before their own ego. I was clearly faster than Stefan and he wasn't just holding me back: he was letting us both slip into Sterling's path. Sterling was right in my mirrors now.

"He's been told to give the place up to you," Ash said, which told me everything I needed to know. Guess Stefan wasn't a team player. That didn't surprise me.

At the next corner, Sterling was at my back while Stefan was in my way. Stefan's car was struggling, but he was still holding on. I went to overtake on the outside. I was almost past him when Sterling came out of nowhere, dived down the inside of Stefan's car and took first place from both of us.

I screamed as I finally passed Stefan and began hunting down Sterling. He made a good exit out of the corner and was already pulling ahead with ease. I kept him in my sights, closing in on him again. As we went down the main straight, the crowd roared. I glanced up at the pit board. Three laps left.

During the next two laps, I closed in on him. On the final lap, I was right behind him. Every corner we took, I tried to get by. I dived, he dodged. I turned in early at the corner, but he kept the momentum out of the turn and reclaimed his position. I could hear the crowd screaming as we continued to battle for first place.

Down the penultimate straight, we were almost side by side, but he kept his nose ahead of mine. I tried to get by him again on the last set of corners, but he had an answer for every move I made. The adrenalin buzzed through my system and I couldn't remember the last time I'd battled with another driver like this.

On the last straight, I pulled up beside him, but he kept his position and went over the finish line in first place. I came second. The crowd erupted into a deafening roar as we both slowed down and made our way back.

"Well done," Ash came on. "I know the end didn't quite work out how we hoped but you went from tenth to finishing second. That was a brilliant recovery."

"Thanks, Ash," I said, not letting my anger at my teammate get the better of me. I'd learnt my lesson from yesterday and I'd keep my rants private from now on.

Race Report
1st – Aiden Sterling
2nd – Winter Jones
3rd – Satoru Hayashi

Championship Driver Standings
Aiden Sterling – 115
Winter Jones – 115
Stefan Brudes – 106

TWENTY

FRANCE

FRIDAY

Everyone thought Stefan Brudes was harmless—the quiet, brooding type—but Aiden knew better.

AFTER THE BRITISH GRAND PRIX, I had a week off. I spent it at home with my parents and tried to focus on my fitness. I followed Gem's exercise and diet plan. She increased my neck-strengthening exercises and core workouts. The negative media coverage of my bad Qualifying session died down after the success of the British Grand Prix. The fans had forgiven Sterling and me for our messy qualifier. Instead, our track battle was all everyone could talk about. There hadn't been such a close finish yet this season. We'd well and truly entertained the fans.

The next race was in France and I travelled there Thursday afternoon, ready for the practice sessions on Friday. There weren't as many media events this week and everything felt quiet compared to the previous race week. I kept my head down and tried to stay focused on the weekend ahead.

We had a drivers' briefing on Friday afternoon and all drivers had to attend. I made my way to one of the rooms used for media interviews. The organisers set up a table at the front for the race director to host the meeting, with chairs in rows before the table.

"Don't worry, I've got my lucky socks on," Benjamin said to Hayashi as I joined them in the second row and sat down in the chair between them.

"Lucky socks?" I asked, looking at Benjamin.

"Yeah, these!" He pulled up his trouser leg and showed me one brightly patterned sock. It had a geometric design in bright yellow, red, and blue. "If I wear them on the Friday before a race weekend, I have a good Qualifying and race day." He dropped his trouser leg and the colourful sock disappeared.

I couldn't help but laugh. "Come on! That's superstitious nonsense. Don't tell me you believe in that stuff?" Benjamin didn't seem like the type: he was always so proper and sensible. I hadn't even heard him swear since the start of the season. He reminded me of an old-fashioned English gentleman, but with bright socks under his very proper clothes.

"Of course I do! I'm telling you, it works!" he replied.

"Don't mess with the socks." Hayashi joined in, nodding along.

"Really? You too?"

"You don't believe in luck?" Benjamin asked me.

"I do, but I don't think it depends on the clothes you wear. Luck is random; it's just luck. There's no system." I shrugged.

"I bet you have a pre-race routine like everyone else," Hayashi said.

"Sure, but that's simply part of getting ready for the race."

"If you did something differently before a race and then had an amazing result, you wouldn't make it part of your routine for the next race? Or if you did something differently and had a bad race? You'd definitely never do that again, right?" Benjamin asked.

"You guys are overthinking it." I shook my head.

"No, we're not. All athletes do it. My friend, the tennis player, has a night-before routine, and he follows it exactly before a big match. Last year, he made it to the semi-finals of Wimbledon. The night before his big match, he got stuck in traffic heading back to the hotel and it threw off his routine. The next day, he lost." Hayashi's eyes were wide.

"Who was your friend playing against for the semi-finals?" I asked, raising an eyebrow.

"Kryvonis," Hayashi replied.

"Didn't he win Wimbledon last year, and isn't he currently ranked number one in the world?" I asked.

Sterling took the seat next to Hayashi at the end of our row, his phone in his hands.

"Aiden, what do you think about routines before a race?" Hayashi asked him, ignoring my questions.

"Has Ben got his lucky socks on today?" He looked at Benjamin, who flashed his ankle at us again.

"You had a brilliant race last time. Ninth to first! Did you switch up your pre-race routine?" Benjamin asked, like it had nothing to do with the Silvers car.

"Hmm... maybe. I didn't go to bed as early as usual the night before." He flipped his phone in his hands and glanced in my direction. I looked away.

"Is this going to be another long meeting?" I asked, quickly changing the subject.

"Let's hope not," Benjamin replied as more drivers took their seats.

Stefan entered the room and took a chair in the back row, closest to the door.

Charles Nielson, the race director, entered the room, took his seat at the head of the table and opened his laptop.

"Are we all here?" he asked.

"Matias is running late. He needed physio," Théo Laurent said. His Cavallo red top was the brightest colour in the room.

Charles looked down at his watch. "He's got exactly five minutes."

Murmurs filled the quiet until Matias finally showed up. He took a seat in the third row and apologised to Charles.

"Okay, let's start with the last race. Does anyone have any concerns from the last GP?" Charles asked the room, and everyone fell into the usual pattern.

The drivers were usually divided into two groups: those who spoke up or had something to complain about, and those who kept quiet in the hope that the meeting wouldn't drag on. I chose to stay quiet. Unless I had a safety concern, I didn't bother speaking. Most of the time, one of the other drivers would point out safety concerns before I had a chance to give my opinion. Normally, it was the more experienced drivers who voiced concerns.

Three drivers spoke about track limits for what felt like forever. I'd hoped for a quick meeting so I could head back to the hotel, go through some strengthening exercises with Gem, and then get an early night ready for Qualifying tomorrow.

Charles typed a few notes on his laptop then finally moved on. "Right. Does anyone have any concerns about this week's race?"

The room remained quiet, and for a moment, I hoped this was the end of the meeting.

"I do."

Everyone turned in their seats to look at Stefan in the back row. He never spoke at these meetings. If he did, it was usually to confirm he'd heard something, with a simple "yes" or "no".

"Stefan?" Charles asked, as surprised as the rest of us.

"The race directors have chosen the soft compound tyre for this track, but I think they made the wrong choice. I think we should ask them to switch to the medium compound tyre." Stefan folded his arms.

Charles clicked on his laptop. "Last year, you raced on softs at this track, Stefan."

"The track has been resurfaced since then. It wears the softs more. Everyone has seen it during practice. It could be unsafe in race conditions."

"You have to look after your tyres in the race then! Don't drive so hard on them!" Théo Laurent interjected. He gestured with his hands. He was one of the most experienced drivers here, and he'd probably sat through many drivers' briefings before.

Stefan glared at him from the back row.

They discussed tyre compounds for almost an hour, but Charles insisted that the soft one was right for the track, so the whole discussion felt pointless.

Finally, Charles ended the meeting and let us go. I filed out with everyone else but watched Stefan heading for the desk, where Charles still sat typing on his laptop. I followed Hayashi and Benjamin out of the room and down the corridor. It opened into a foyer with a reception area and seating.

As I reached the main doors, a hand brushed my arm.

"Hey," Sterling said, tilting his head to the side.

We both stepped out of the walkway and stood near the seating area.

"Stefan is playing a game here," Sterling said in a hushed voice.

"What are you on about?"

"Complaining about the tyre choice and trying to get it changed," he replied.

I frowned at him.

"Stefan loves to play mind games and that was one of them. He's trying to throw you and any other driver off their game, making you second-guess your tyre wear and race strategy."

"It's Stefan: he's not a game player. He doesn't care about that stuff," I replied.

"He blocked you in the last race."

"And I seem to remember someone else blocking me in Qualifying," I added, raising an eyebrow.

"That wasn't intentional and I apologised."

"When did you say sorry?"

"I more than made up for it that evening." He winked.

"Are you being serious right now?" I whispered. His arrogance was on another level.

"I'm trying to be serious, but you always manage to distract me." He placed his hand on my elbow and steered me further away from the door where the others were still leaving the building. "You don't know Stefan like I do. He's a game player and he plays dirty both on and off the track. Do not fall for his quiet, reserved act."

"He's my teammate." And it wasn't an act. Stefan barely spoke to anyone. He was the quietest driver I'd ever met.

"Trust me on this. My dad always used to say it's the quiet ones you need to watch out for the most."

He went still; a faraway look took over his expression. I'd never heard him speak about his dad before and I'd rarely seen him discuss his dad in interviews either, but everyone knew he'd died when Sterling was in his early twenties. When you became an international sporting star, everyone knew your personal business, even the parts you'd rather not share. His posture shifted; he looked uncomfortable, like he hadn't meant to mention his dad and, in doing so, had brought memories to the surface. I knew not to ask questions, not here, not now. Instead, I took the conversation back to a safe territory for us.

"Are you worried about me?" I asked in a teasing voice, placing my hand over my heart to try to distract him.

"I just thought you should be warned." He folded his arms and squared his shoulders.

"Don't worry, I can handle my teammate," I said, smiled at him and turned for the doors.

Sterling caught up to me outside and walked beside me as we both headed back to our team motorhomes.

"I am sorry about ruining your lap time," he said, and then he sped up, strolling over to his motorhome, where someone from his team met him at the door. Before going inside, he looked over his shoulder at me and winked.

He always had to have the last word.

TWENTY-ONE

FRANCE

SATURDAY - QUALIFYING

His Qualifying hadn't gone to plan. It could be worse; second on the grid wasn't bad, but he wondered if maybe his mind had drifted elsewhere.

Qualifying Report
Pole – Heikki Koskinen
2nd – Aiden Sterling
3rd – Winter Jones
4th – Stefan Brudes
5th – Matias da Silveira

DURING QUALIFYING, the car struggled around the Circuit Paul Ricard. The engineers were left scrambling to figure out why and make improvements for Sunday. I got myself up into third. My last lap time squeezed me ahead of my teammate by a fraction of a second. Sterling's teammate had also beaten him, which hadn't happened in a long time.

After a meeting with my engineers and team strategists, Gem and I got ready to leave for the hotel.

"Ready?" Gem called from outside my room. I grabbed my bag and met her in the corridor. As I closed the door, I heard shouting coming from the other side of the motorhome.

"What's that?" I asked Gem.

She shrugged. I walked by her and followed the sound of voices. They were coming from Michael's office at the other end of the corridor.

"Winter, what are you doing?" Gem hissed, following me.

I heard the muffled sound of Michael's voice coming from behind his office door. I hovered outside, curious.

"We should go," Gem whispered, coming up beside me.

"Shh..." I hushed her with a wave of my hand.

"I'm the number one driver!" Stefan shouted.

Gem and I looked at each other with wide eyes.

"Stefan, you know we don't do number ones and number twos in this team," Michael replied, his voice cool and unaffected by Stefan's anger.

"And how did that work out for you last year?" Stefan asked, and I assumed he was referring to the punch-up with his ex-teammate.

"This is a team sport and it's early in the season still. I have everything under control and it's time you started trusting me, Stefan. You want to win this season's Championship, then focus on your driving and let me deal with everything else, okay?"

Michael was the team principal. This was his show and from what I'd seen of him so far, he controlled everything down to the tiniest detail. He was always working and thinking ahead. This wasn't a job for Michael; Torrin was his whole life.

"We shouldn't be listening," Gem whispered.

A phone started ringing, a happy little tune.

"Shit!" Gem fumbled with her bag as she rushed away from the door. I followed, glancing back at the office to check if either Michael or Stefan had heard the noise.

Gem hit "end call" and sent it to voicemail.

"That was your mum," Gem whispered, heading for the stairs.

"What?"

"She's calling me now since you only pick up half her calls."

She was probably calling about tomorrow. Both my parents were coming to watch the race.

"I warned you not to give her your number," I teased as we rushed down the stairs.

The main dining area was quiet. A few crew members were taking a break while one of the strategists worked on a laptop at a table.

"It sounds like Stefan has a problem with me," I said in a hushed voice as we headed out of the motorhome and started down the paddock towards the exit.

"I wouldn't worry. He's probably feeling a bit vulnerable. You're new to the team and you're outperforming him."

"I bet he thought I'd be an easy teammate," I replied.

Gem chuckled. "His biggest mistake."

If Stefan had a problem with me, then it was his issue and not mine. If he couldn't keep up with me, then he'd have to figure that out for himself. At least Michael had handled the situation.

Winter: Hey Sofie! Congrats on your last W win!

Winter: I have a question for you.

Sofie: Ulterior motive I see, but thanks!

Sofie: What's up?

Winter: It's about overbearing parents.

Sofie: I do have experience in that department.

Winter: How do you deal with it?

Sofie: You're asking the wrong person.

Sofie: I've never had much luck dealing with my dad.

Sofie: You know what he's like.

Winter: And you know what my mum's like.

Sofie: Trust me, your mum's not overbearing.

Sofie: She's just overly enthusiastic. She means well.

Winter: I know.

TWENTY-TWO

FRANCE

SUNDAY - AFTER THE RACE

He'd let the win slip through his fingers, but he wasn't about to let Winter slip away so easily.

THE RACE TURNED INTO A DISASTER. I had engine trouble and the team advised me to retire halfway through. My first Did Not Finish of the season. It had to happen at some point. I wanted to be angry but felt more deflated than anything else. I was all geared up, ready to go, and then it all stopped. I felt bad for my team, too. I knew how hard they had worked on my car. Ash took it the hardest.

To top the whole weekend off, Stefan won the race. It could have been worse; Sterling could have won and then I'd have to watch his smug face on all the TV screens. Stefan had the same grumpy face he always had but looked like he enjoyed drinking the champagne. Back at the Torrin garage, half the team celebrated a win, while the other half had to pretend to celebrate while also trying to figure out why my engine had failed.

Once all the drivers finished their media interviews, Reyna gathered the whole team outside our pit garage for team photographs. She managed to get Stefan to put the champagne down for five minutes and assembled everyone around him with the winners' trophies: one for Stefan's first place and one for the Constructors' win.

I had to smile and cheer along while several photographers snapped pictures. Hopefully, I looked happy in the pics and not too sour about my rubbish day.

Stefan continued his celebrations as his manager handed out drinks to his team of engineers, the pit crew, and strategists. Even Michael had a cup. Everyone else headed back inside and started packing away for the next race weekend. I grabbed my phone from my pocket and took a quick picture of my car before the crew packed it up. A message came through from Mum. My parents came to watch me race, only for my car to break. She'd gone back to the Torrin motorhome with Dad and wanted to know how long I'd be. I bet she had a lot of thoughts on my engine troubles, so I lingered in the garage a little longer.

I stepped back outside to make room for a crew member pushing a big trolley of tyres and found Sterling looking out from his pit garage. Members of the Silvers team were busy packing up their cars and kit too. Still clutching my phone, I walked over to the edge of my garage. We stood together, looking out at the pit lane.

"Going to gloat about your brilliant race over my non-existent one?" I asked.

"No, my race was dull, especially compared to the last one."

"You came third. Scored points. Who cares if it was boring?"

He chuckled. "I'd rather race you than him," he said, his voice low and his eyes on Stefan celebrating. I was starting to wonder if there was more to Sterling and Stefan's rivalry. "You're far more entertaining on and off the track."

I shook my head but couldn't help but smile.

"Maybe Benjamin and Hayashi had a point; maybe it's all about luck. Today, we had bad luck because we upset the sporting gods," he said with a smirk.

"You're being ridiculous." I laughed.

"I don't know about that. You and I switched up our pre-game routine at the British GP and we had the best results. Maybe there's something in that. Perhaps we should try it again." He dipped his head and spoke in such a low voice that I had to really strain to hear him.

"We hooked up. That's it. The sporting gods will have to get their entertainment from somewhere else," I whispered back to him.

"Sure you don't want to appease the powers that be?" He arched a brow at me.

"I'd rather borrow Benjamin's lucky socks."

He laughed, that carefree laugh he rarely shared with anyone. I rolled my eyes at him because I wasn't joking. We were not hooking up again. That was a one-off. No matter how much I'd enjoyed myself, it would not happen again.

He reached out and gently took my phone from my fingers. He typed a number in and hit "call". He then pulled his own phone from his pocket. It vibrated in his hand until he hit the "end call" button on my phone.

"In case you change your mind, or the socks don't work," he said, handing my phone back to me.

I took it back, shaking my head, but I didn't delete his number. I saved it.

BACK AT THE MOTORHOME, I found my parents in the dining area. Dad sipped a cup of tea while chatting to a VIP Torrin guest. I grabbed a cold glass of water from the kitchen and joined my parents.

"I'm sorry about your race," Mum said, while Dad gave me a sympathetic smile and then went back to his conversation with his new friend. From what I could hear, they were discussing the different rail networks across Europe.

"Thanks," I replied, taking a sip of water and waiting for Mum to start.

Mum began by offering advice on how I should cope with the disappointing race result. Then she moved on to some criticism, that perhaps I was driving the car too hard, putting too much pressure on the engine, which caused the failure. She briefly offered me some encouragement before moving on to her thoughts on the team's handling of my engine failure.

"They should definitely run tests. Find out exactly what happened," she continued.

"I'm sure they will," I said, pushing my now-empty glass into the middle of the table. I was done with my drink and this conversation.

"But you should ask, make sure you get the results, find out why it happened, and check steps are taken so it doesn't happen again." She paused, and I hoped she'd finished. "You know what..."

"Mum, stop!" I snapped, my voice coming out louder than I meant it to. Dad stopped talking midsentence, and a few heads crooked in our direction. The room went quiet for a moment before people returned to their conversations and heads turned back to their own business.

Heat flushed in my cheeks.

"I'm heading to my room," I said, getting up and rushing towards the stairs.

Mum followed me up to my little room, shutting the door behind her. I pulled my phone out of my pocket, dumped it on the table and then half fell into the little sofa.

"I'm sorry about shouting," I said, breaking the tension. I looked at my fingernails. I'd cut them short the night before, maybe too short; they looked stubby.

"I'm only offering my advice," she said.

"It's too much!" I looked up to face her. "All the messages, the phone calls, making comments about my team's strategy. It's too much!"

Her expression filled with hurt and I felt terrible for snapping.

"Okay," she said, taking in a long breath. "I'll take a step back."

"Mum, I..."

"No, you're right. I need to let you do this your way."

"It's not that I don't want your support. I do. I will always need your support, but I need you to be my mum, not my coach or engineer or strategist."

"I can do that," she replied, giving me a tight smile.

"Thanks," I said, standing up.

She held her arms out and pulled me into a tight hug.

"I'll be here when you need me," she whispered into my ear.

"Thanks Mum, and I'm sorry."

She squeezed me a little tighter and then started to pull back.

"Should we go rescue that poor man from your dad? No one wants to talk about interrailing for that long."

I laughed.

We headed back downstairs, and I felt like a weight had lifted from my shoulders.

Championship Driver Standings

Stefan Brudes – 131

Aiden Sterling – 130

Winter Jones – 115

TWENTY-THREE

GERMANY

SATURDAY - QUALIFYING

During the pre-race press conference, a journalist asked him if everything between Winter Jones and himself was well after the Silverstone battle. He had to work hard to keep the smile off his lips and answer the question as professionally as possible. Luckily, he was well-practised at handling eager reporters. He spent the rest of the interview wondering if he should message her since he had her phone number now, but what should he say? Or maybe he should wait for her to contact him?

WE HAD BACK-TO-BACK RACE WEEKENDS, heading straight from France to Germany. The Nürburgring track was situated in a beautiful region of Germany with mountains, forests, and quaint old towns and villages.

Before Qualifying, I sat on a stool next to Ash in the pit garage as he showed me data from my morning practice session. Ash loved a graph and a spreadsheet. He was going through my times from the last practice session when a noise from the other side of the pit grew louder. I peeked over my shoulder to see three of Stefan's mechanics gathered, talking loudly and each holding a dark blue envelope.

"What's going on?" Mia, one of my mechanics, asked Ash and me.

"I don't know," I replied, watching two of the pit crew walk over to the three mechanics, who were also holding envelopes.

"This is going towards my holiday fund!" one of the pit guys cheered, pulling out a wad of cash from the navy envelope.

"What?" Ash said, frowning.

"Hey, Ruben!" Mia shouted, making both Ash and me wince.

Ruben came over to us.

"What's with the envelopes?" Mia asked him.

"Present from Stefan. His trainer gave us all one. Didn't you get one?" he asked her, and she shook her head.

Ruben went back over to the pit crew.

"That's weird," I said, looking from Mia to Ash.

"No, it's not," Ash replied, clicking the lock screen of his tablet and dumping it down on his workbench with a clatter. "Stefan's being a dick again! I'm going to speak to Michael."

"But..." I started, but Ash was already storming through the garage. I looked at Mia.

"Stefan did this last year. He gave out cash to his side of the garage and pit crew," she explained.

"Okay?" I still felt like I was missing something.

"I think he sees it as an extra incentive for his team. Like if he tips his mechanics, they'll work harder on his car or something. Load of bullshit, and it feels tacky."

"How much money?" I asked, wondering if my side of the garage would expect me to tip them, too.

"Last year, there was three hundred quid in each envelope.

You'll have to ask one of them how much they got this year."
She threw a thumb in the direction of Stefan's mechanics.

"Three hundred!"

"Yeah, that's Stefan."

"Aren't you upset about this? That you didn't get an envelope of cash?" I asked her and wondered if I needed to take a trip to the nearest cash machine. But I wasn't on Stefan's salary, and I couldn't help agreeing with Mia. Handing out envelopes of cash felt tacky. It didn't feel right. It could be against the rules governing how much teams could spend in a year, too. I'd have to check.

"No. I don't need to be bribed to do my job," she said, folding her arms. "You should take it as a compliment."

"What?"

"Stefan only pulls this kind of shit when he feels threatened. Keep beating him on the track and Ruben over there will be able to go on an extended holiday to a private island." She placed a hand lightly on my shoulder and then returned to my car, where the other mechanics were busy working.

It hit me then how I was still the newbie in this team, and everyone knew Stefan's ways much better than I did. Sterling had tried to warn me and I'd brushed him off, thinking I knew better, while no one from my own team had even tried to give me a heads-up about Stefan.

"Hey, where'd Ash go?" Gem came over to me carrying two bottles of water. She handed one to me and put the other down at Ash's workstation. At least Gem was new to the team as well. I wasn't the only outsider here.

"I need to talk to you in private," I said, grabbing her hand and taking her through the garage and back to the team motorhome.

Qualifying Report

Pole – Aiden Sterling

2nd – Winter Jones

3rd – Stefan Brudes

GERMANY

SATURDAY - AFTER QUALIFYING

He knew she'd reach out to him eventually.

THAT EVENING, I paced my hotel room. I'd underestimated my teammate and to make it even worse, no one from my team had thought to warn me of his mind games. I knew it was stupid to get worked up about it. Getting frustrated meant Stefan's plan was working. Qualifying had gone well, but I was letting him get inside my head.

Gem told me to ignore Stefan—to let Michael deal with him—yet here I was, worked up and irritated with myself, too. Not the best state of mind to be in the evening before a race.

I picked my phone up for the third time. I couldn't decide what to do. Opening up my messages for the second time, I finally managed to type out a quick message. This was a bad idea, but I hit send anyway.

Winter: I need to talk to you.
Sterling: Changed your mind? I knew you would.
Winter: No, I just need to talk to you about Stefan.
Sterling: Which hotel are you in?

After giving him the hotel's address, my room number, and strict instructions not to be seen by anyone, twenty minutes later he knocked on my door. I opened it and grabbed his hand, tugging him inside.

"You were right about Stefan," I said as soon as the door shut behind him.

"A 'hello' would be nice, or a 'thank you for sneaking over'. I had to lie to one of my team who saw me leaving my room. I told him I was going to the hotel gym for a late session." He pointed to his trousers. "In jeans. Luckily, he didn't question it." His hair looked a little damp and his skin had that after-shower and moisturiser glow about it. I'd probably interrupted his early night.

"This is important. Tell me what happened between you and Stefan? Clearly, there's history there; otherwise, you wouldn't have warned me about his games."

He sighed and sat down on the edge of my bed. "Stefan and I raced against each other as kids. We're a similar age and our paths crossed as we progressed up through the lower Formulas. It wasn't until Formula 2 that our battles became more serious. We drove for different teams, and every driver was fighting for the win and that shot at an F1 seat. We'd had a few knocks, a few almost-moments, but nothing serious, nothing you wouldn't expect from a bunch of young, over-confident racing drivers."

"What happened?" I asked.

"That season in Formula 2 would end up being my last. I'd

won the previous season, and I was in the lead in points for the current season. Stefan was just behind me in points. There wasn't much between us. Before the last race, I got the call. I'd been offered a seat in an F1 team. The announcement went out before the last Formula 2 race. During the race, Stefan used aggressive moves on me, more so than usual, and we came together on the track. My car spun off, my suspension broke, and I was out. Stefan's car wasn't as badly damaged and he ended up finishing in third. He ended up winning the season."

"But you'd won a bigger prize: a seat in F1."

"Yes. He then came into F1 two years later. He got a seat in Ziegler, but they weren't very competitive, and that's when I moved to Silvers. The Silvers car was more competitive, and so Stefan and I were usually at different ends of the track. When he moved up to Torrin, we had a few close moments, but nothing like that last race in F2. I've kept a close eye on him. I've watched him play games with other drivers and his previous teammates. I'd seen him play mind games with one of his old teammates in F2 and watched what happened to Philippe last year. Stefan got under his skin. I saw him irritate and wind Philippe up until it ended with a punch at the side of the track. Now Philippe is out of F1. His career is dead. He hasn't entered any other race series like ex-F1 drivers usually do."

"At least he got to throw a punch at Stefan, though," I muttered, my fists balled at my sides.

"What has he done?" he asked.

I explained the envelopes of money while I paced back and forth. I also told him about the argument I'd overheard between Stefan and Michael and how frustrated I felt. Sterling made himself at home on my bed. He kicked his shoes off, leaned back against my pillows and folded his arms behind his head as I ranted.

"I'm more bothered by the fact I fell for his quiet guy act, just like you said! I don't care about the money. If he wants to give members of our team money, then he can. It's the way he thinks he can manipulate others that pisses me off." I paused, taking a deep breath. "I can't talk to anyone else about this. I spoke to Gem, my trainer, but she thinks I should ignore him and focus on my own race. She thinks I get too worked up about stuff and it will affect my performance. She's probably right; she usually is. I can't go to Reyna about this. She does the team's PR, there's probably nothing she can do, and I don't want to put her in the middle. Ash, my engineer, is furious. I don't want this to cause a big drama within the team. Inter-team battles lose races. I don't want to go to Michael either. He probably already knows anyway. Ash went to him, but I think Michael will pretend it didn't happen and focus on race strategy. Also, I'm a little afraid of him."

"Wait, you're afraid of your team principal? The fearless Winter Jones? Afraid?"

I rolled my eyes. "I'm not fearless, and he's the one who gave me my seat in F1. He could so easily take it away again."

"Okay, I get that. How long is your contract for?"

"One race season. This is why every race counts. I have to perform, do better every weekend, and prove myself against my teammate. If I don't, then I won't get a contract for next year. It's not like I had a line of teams waiting to sign me up before Torrin came calling."

"I know, I get it. I only had a one-year contract when I first entered F1, too."

"Really?"

"Yes. Everyone starts out as a rookie and we all have to prove ourselves. Some of us have more to prove and more pressure on our shoulders than others. Racers like Stefan Brudes wouldn't understand." He paused and we stared at each other;

a moment of understanding passed between us. "There's only one way to deal with the Stefans of the motorsport world, and that's on the track. Your trainer is right, but you need to take it further. You need to send Stefan a message that he's not going to mess with you, or there will be on-track consequences."

"And how do I do that?"

"If Stefan tries to overtake or pass you, do not let him. Hold your position. Don't give him even a millimetre of space. No matter what."

"You want me to risk damaging my car or crashing into my teammate just to prove a point? That's extreme. I could crash out and lose points. My team would lose points. Michael would be furious."

"Yes, but it's the only way. Stefan will learn that you don't give in to him, and then the next time he tries to pass you, he'll be more cautious. It should stop his silly mind games, too, because he'll know they don't count for shit on the circuit. He can hand out as many envelopes as he likes; they won't stop you on race day. It's about respect. You need to teach him to respect you."

I started pacing again.

"You know I'm right. You've probably done it before," he said.

Had I done it before? I'd had a lot of battles with my teammate Sofie in W. Maybe we both pushed our fights too far, and we'd crashed or damaged our cars a couple of times. That felt different to Stefan and me. Sofie had remained my friend through it all, no matter what happened on the track. We'd been friends for years, best friends, and remained friends no matter what happened on the track. Stefan and I weren't friends.

I sat down on the edge of the bed next to Sterling. My hand brushed against his knee.

"How do I know you're not just giving me this advice to help yourself?"

"My last tip worked out well for you," he replied, unfolding his arms from behind his head and resting them on the bed on either side of him.

"Yes, true, but that advice didn't have a high risk of crashing attached to it. If both Stefan and I crash out, who does that benefit? You. You'll take home all the points and your two biggest rivals will have zero."

"When you put it like that, of course it looks that way, but you know I'm right. It's the only way to deal with Stefan. Think about it. You don't have to do anything. You can take Gem's advice and ignore him. Also, if you keep out-qualifying Stefan, then you might not have to deal with him on the track. If he's a few cars behind you, what can he do?"

"That's true. If I stay ahead of him, there won't be any issues, so that's what I'll do. I'll make sure I'm out in front, in first place," I said, leaning back, placing an arm behind me for support.

"There's a flaw in your plan," he replied, his eyebrow raised.

"Is there?" I smiled sweetly.

"Think you're forgetting about who's in pole position tomorrow." He grinned.

"Don't worry, he won't be any trouble for me," I said, moving, and hooking one leg over him to straddle his lap.

"Did you invite me over here under false pretences?" he asked. His hands moved to my legs, his fingers drawing smooth lines up my thighs.

"No, talking to you helped," I replied and meant it.

"I thought you weren't interested in this? You said you'd rather wear Benjamin's socks," he said.

"I'm doing this because I want to. Maybe I need an outlet

for my frustration, maybe a distraction, or maybe both." I rocked my hips. "Do you have a problem with that? Do you want me to stop?"

"No," he replied. His hands moved up to my hips as I leaned forward and kissed him.

TWENTY-FIVE

GERMANY

SATURDAY - AFTER QUALIFYING

He really didn't think she'd give in and answer his question.

I SUCKED on his bottom lip as I ground my hips against him. His hands gripped my waist and I could feel him harden beneath me. I focused on his lips and tried to ignore that annoying little voice in my head that kept trying to tell me this wasn't a good idea. How could this be bad when it felt so good?

His lips moved from mine, down my jaw to my neck.

"Hey!" I froze and placed my hand on his chest to stop him. "Not my neck again."

"Okay," he replied, looking up at me with a wicked smile. He licked his lips and then lifted the hem of my T-shirt. I raised my arms as he slowly inched it up my body and over my head.

Last time we'd been in a frenzied haze to seek release, but this time Sterling took his time. So did I. My gaze lingered, taking him in, drinking up as much of him as possible. His movements were slow, gentle, and deliberate. His hands moved from my waist up over my shoulder and down my arms like he wanted to touch as much of me as possible. His fingertips drew soft circles up and down my back.

"Taking your time?" I asked, looking down at him.

"I'm not in any rush. Unless you have somewhere else to be?" He quirked a brow and his hands stilled.

"No." I leaned forward and kissed him; his hand slid up my back and his fingers tangled in my hair.

We slowly undressed each other until I was left in only a simple lacy thong, and he was down to his boxers. I felt relaxed around him, like I could be myself and tell him exactly what I wanted. My hands explored every inch of his body while his lips skipped past my neck, going straight to my chest, where he kissed, nipped and sucked. His mouth found one of my nipples and he rolled his tongue over the peak. I moaned and curved into his touch, wanting more.

Suddenly, he flipped me onto my back and the air whooshed out of my lungs. Not giving me a moment to recover, he moved us down the bed so my legs hung off the end, and he stood on the floor between them.

He leaned over me, a hand resting by my head for support, and he kissed his way down my body, down to the band of my thong. I smiled as his fingers moved over the lace, over me, dipping between my legs. He pressed down on my clit and I gasped, bucking my hips.

He chuckled, enjoying my reaction and being in control. He removed my underwear. I lifted my hips to help him, and his fingers followed the lace down my legs to my ankles. My heartbeat quickened with anticipation.

Propping myself on my elbows, I watched him. His dark gaze stayed locked on mine as he knelt between my legs. It was glorious to see him kneeling before me, and my fingers twitched with need. I couldn't decide if I wanted to reach out for him and curl my fingers in his hair, or if I wanted to reach between my legs and lessen the ache that was slowly building there.

He took his time, kissing, teasing me, making me wait. His lips moved up and down both my thighs, getting closer to my core but always stopping.

"Are you playing with me?" I asked, getting impatient. "If you're one of those guys that doesn't like going down on a woman, that's cool, but can you stop teasing me?"

He chuckled. "Don't know what sort of guys you've dated before."

"Then why are you keeping me waiting?"

"I need you to tell me something first," he said, quirking a brow and then going back to sucking on the soft skin of my inner thigh, like a demonstration of what his mouth could do.

"You want me to say 'please'?"

"Hearing you say 'please' would be satisfying, but that's not what I need this time."

"Then what?" I gasped as his lips moved even closer. My whole body seemed to throb with anticipation.

"Tell me who the best F1 driver is, and I'll give you what you want," he said, pulling back and tracing his thumb up my thigh in little circles.

"Are you serious right now?"

"Really serious. I think you know the answer I'm looking for," he said, his hand moving higher and higher until it was almost between my legs.

I groaned, but I was not saying his name.

"I am not..." He planted a kiss on the very edge of my pussy and I gasped. "You're such an arrogant..." He kissed me there again and I let out a frustrated sound.

"Give me a name: you know the one I want. Say it and I'll give you my tongue in return." He licked up my leg in a dramatic sweep.

I let out another frustrated groan and swore under my breath.

"Fine. You!"

"That's not a name," he teased.

"Aiden Sterling! He's the best F1 driver on the grid!" I shouted. "Happy now?"

He didn't answer: his head dipped between my legs and he ran his tongue through the centre of me. I sucked in a sharp breath and let my head fall back against the bed with a moan.

He hooked my left leg over his shoulder and I took a steadying breath. Maybe he was right and I'd been dating the wrong guys.

His tongue circled my clit and I jumped at the contact, but he placed a hand on my stomach to hold me still as he began sucking on my clit. I cried out, a half-moan, half-sob. God, it had been such a long time since anyone had gone down on me.

I fisted the sheets with one hand and reached for him with the other. His tongue, his incredible tongue, continued to play, moving down from my clit and slipping inside me.

"Fuck," I cried out. "Aiden!"

He shifted back, his eyes finding mine, and he watched me as he took his free hand and slipped a finger inside me.

As I moaned his name, his lips returned to my clit. I moved my hips, trying to ride his finger faster, but he held me in place, making sure he controlled everything. He had me exactly where he wanted me, teetering on the edge, and he was the only one who could push me over it. The tension built inside me. I was shaking, moaning, getting closer and closer. When he inserted a second finger, I finally went over the edge.

Panting, slowly coming out of the high, I watched as he stood. With a satisfied smirk, he put both fingers in his mouth and sucked them. I found the action both sexy and annoying, as he looked far too pleased with himself.

"I'll get you back for that," I said, knowing he knew exactly what I meant: making me beg for him and tell him lies.

"Is that a promise or a threat?"

"A promise."

"Looking forward to it." He grinned, and I let that arrogant smile fuel my next move. He'd been in control; now it was my turn.

I slid off the bed and stood before him. His erection tented his boxers. I pulled on the elastic waistband and then let it snap back into place. He shook his head at me and then pulled them off in one fluid motion.

Taking his hand, I guided him to sit on the edge of my bed and then straddled him, my knees on either side of him. His hands moved to my back, holding me against him as we kissed. I could feel him between my legs and I shifted my hips slightly, rubbing his hardness against me. With one move, I could easily have him inside me.

"Do you have a condom?" he asked, breathless, between kisses.

"I'm on birth control and I was tested before the race season started," I said, pulling back slightly to look at him.

"I was tested then too, all clear, but are you sure?"

"Yes. I trust you." We might not be dating or like a real couple—this was just a hook-up—but I trusted him.

"Okay," he replied and pulled me into another kiss.

Breaking away from his lips and gripping onto his shoulders, I rose onto my knees. I could feel him right where I wanted him, needed him. I stared down at him and he looked up at me. Unable to wait any longer, I moved back down, taking his length inside of me. I groaned, taking all of him and rolling my hips.

"Fuck, Winter, you feel so good," he murmured against my neck.

I kissed him, consuming his moans as I shifted my hips again. Ending the kiss, I moved back, placed my hands on his shoulders, and started to move on him: a slow, building pace. I arched my back, relishing every inch of him. His eyes stayed on me, watching me enjoy myself, enjoy him. His hands gripped my hips, tightening as I kept my steady pace.

"You like being in control, don't you?" he asked.

"Not always. Sometimes I like losing control." I leaned in and kissed him, a deep, messy kiss.

His hands moved down from my waist to grip my arse and he stood up, keeping a tight hold of me. My fingers dug into his shoulders as my back hit the wall.

"I want to see you lose control," he whispered into my ear. I shivered and arched into him, the wall hard against my shoulders.

"Then make me," I replied, hooking my legs around his body and wrapping my arms tightly around his shoulders.

With my words, he thrust into me, changing the pace. His hands moved to my hips, positioning me in such a way that I met every one of his thrusts. He increased our speed, and with it, tension began to build as I chased after another release. I let go and got lost in the waves of pleasure taking over my body.

TWENTY-SIX

GERMANY

SUNDAY - RACE DAY

His best friend could keep a secret. She had no reason to worry, and Josh didn't know it was Winter he'd been sneaking around with.

MY ALARM WENT off at six in the morning. My head felt heavy with sleep. When I tried to reach for my phone on the side, my arm wouldn't move. Something was on top of me. No, someone. My eyes flew open as my alarm continued to ring. I was on my side, Sterling tucked up next to me, one of his arms draped over my body.

"Hey! Wake up!" I shoved him off and finally reached for my phone, shutting off the noise.

"Morning," Sterling mumbled as he stretched. Then he sat bolt upright. "Shit. I didn't mean to fall asleep here."

I got out of bed, grabbed my hotel dressing gown, and wrapped it around my naked body.

"What are we going to do? Someone will see you leave!" I began pacing.

Sterling jumped out of bed and started picking up his clothes. He quickly dressed in his boxers and shirt but fumbled with his jeans. He took his phone out of his pocket and chucked the jeans on my bed.

"Hurry, Gem might turn up early!"

"This place has guest parking round the back, right?" he asked, but kept his eyes on his phone, scrolling and typing.

"I don't know!" I threw my hands out to the side.

"It does. Don't worry, I know someone who can help."

"What? You can't tell anyone about this!" I said, getting closer to him.

He put his phone to his ear.

"Sterling, I'm serious, you can't—" He put a finger on my lips, silencing me. I was going to kick his arrogant arse.

"Hey man," he said to whoever answered his call.

"Hey, where are you? I'm at your door," the guy on the other end said.

"Listen, I need a favour." His finger dropped from my lips, but he gave me a pointed look. I rolled my eyes.

"What kind of favour?" the man asked, sounding suspicious already.

"A 'no questions asked' kind of favour."

"Right. What's going on?" He sighed.

"I need picking up from the Liner hotel. The guest parking at the back. Can you sort something out? Keep it between us?"

"I've got my rental. I'll pick you up myself. Leaving now. I'll be about ten or fifteen minutes, and..."

"I know, you can lecture me on the drive back. Thanks, I owe you." He ended the call.

"Who was that?"

"My trainer, Josh. He'll keep this to himself. It might not be the first time he's had to sneak me out of a hotel before." He rubbed the back of his head and then grabbed his jeans off the bed. He started tugging them on.

"And you're sure he won't tell anyone?" I asked. I'd seen his trainer around, but we'd never spoken. Josh looked like a personal trainer; he was so muscular and well-built, even compared to the other drivers and trainers. He looked like he could lift Sterling above his head and not break a sweat.

"He won't. He's one of my oldest and most trusted friends. He doesn't know I was here with you either." He zipped up his jeans, did up the button, and then sat down to put his trainers back on.

"Okay." I let out a long breath. "But you still need to hurry in case my trainer turns up early." I rushed to the door. It had one of those peepholes so you could check to see who was outside. I spied through it to find the corridor empty.

Sterling came up behind me, placing a hand on the small of my back. I moved away from the peephole.

"Is it clear?"

I nodded, reaching for the door handle, but he stopped me. His hand took mine instead. He leaned in and kissed me. It was quick, sweet, and then he was out the door.

Race Report

1st – Winter Jones

2nd – Aiden Sterling

3rd – Stefan Brudes

Championship Driver Standings

Aiden Sterling – 148
Stefan Brudes – 146
Winter Jones – 140

AUSTRIA

THURSDAY

Hiding in a bathroom with Winter on his lap was not how he imagined his evening playing out.

"TELL ME AGAIN?" I asked Reyna in the back of the car. We drove through the Austrian countryside on our way to an event.

"The Torrin team owner, Brenner, throws this yearly event before the Austrian GP," Reyna explained again.

"But he never comes to any of the races?"

"He attends the Austrian race, his home race. He owns a few different sports teams. F1 isn't his only interest. He has a lot on and leaves it all to Michael. Don't ask me to explain the inner workings of a billionaire."

"So, no billionaire jokes tonight?" I teased, fiddling with the Tag watch on my wrist. The company had lent the watch to me for the party. I couldn't keep it. Not that it was my style.

"No, unless you want to risk losing your seat in Torrin. He owns the team: the whole team, Winter," Reyna emphasised.

"Okay, I know, I was only joking," I replied, looking at Reyna's tense posture. "Are you okay?"

She sighed. "After Stefan's last terrible interview, I'm losing the will. But it's okay for Stefan to be a moody bastard; it's not like he'll get fired for it. You know he's friends with Brenner, so he can carry on doing whatever he likes."

"I'm sorry," I said, giving her hand a quick squeeze. "But don't worry. I'll be on my best behaviour. I promise." I grinned at her and she shook her head, but her body relaxed slightly. "Who else will be at this party?" I asked, looking out the window, trying not to seem too interested in her answer. I hadn't seen Sterling since the last race weekend. He hadn't messaged me either, and I refused to message him. Why would I want to hear from him anyway? Not like he gave me two of the best orgasms of my life or anything.

"A lot of people. It's *the* event before the Austrian GP. They'll be international business types, a few local celebrities, and international ones too. I met Dean Scott at last year's party; you know, the movie star."

"Really? That's cool. And from the motorsport world?"

"Brenner invites everyone from the sport—ex-drivers, journalists, team owners and bosses, whole teams—but not everyone turns up."

"Okay." Sterling might be there tonight. "And Stefan, is he going?"

"It's mandatory to attend for Torrin team members. He'll be there since it's his friend's party. At last year's event, they spoke for ages. Longest conversation I ever heard Stefan have."

I rolled my eyes. Of course, Stefan would make sure to keep the team's owner on side even if the guy never came to any races. I'd have to make a good impression if I was going to keep my seat for next season. I smoothed down the fabric on my dress. It was a simple design, a long evening gown that hugged my body in midnight navy, the Torrin team colours. I'd left my hair down and wore a simple silver chain necklace.

The car turned off down a long driveway with trees on either side of the road. Gradually, a grand house came into view. It looked like something out of a period drama or a historical film.

"Wow," I said, staring out the window as the car pulled into a big, looping driveway.

"He had it built around ten years ago. It's not as old as it looks," Reyna explained as I stared up at the many gleaming windows.

The car pulled up to the front of the house and a man dressed in a smart suit stepped forward to open the door for us. Reyna got out and I followed. Another man greeted us, directing us through the doorway into a big, open hallway. My shoes clicked on the marble floors. A staircase went up either side and paintings decorated the walls. I could hear voices and music. A woman dressed in sleek black clothes came up to us with a tray of champagne. We both took a glass and continued to follow our guide further into the house. He spoke about where to find the bar, cloakroom, and bathrooms.

He brought us into a massive room filled with people gathered in groups, talking and laughing. There was a bar at one end, and at the other, a woman played a grand piano. One side of the room had floor-to-ceiling windows, flooding the space with natural light. Two of the glass partitions were pulled back, letting in a light summer breeze.

"There's Michael. Come on," Reyna said, nodding towards the bar where he stood in a small group. Reyna was in business mode, and I wondered if she'd get to enjoy this party or if she'd see it as another day at the office.

"Here they are," I heard Michael say as we approached. He looked at me and tilted his head towards the man who stood next to him. "Sebastian Brenner, our team owner, and this is..."

"Winter Jones!" Sebastian cheered, holding his drink up to me as a greeting. He wore a vibrant magenta suit with a floral shirt underneath. "So glad to finally meet my newest driver. I've heard so much about you."

"All good things, I hope," I replied with a smile, but I glanced at Michael. I couldn't help feeling on edge around him since I'd overheard his argument with Stefan. He'd told Stefan that the team didn't do number one and number two drivers, but he'd also told Stefan that he had everything under control. Did Michael see me as Stefan's equal or as a rookie he could control?

Sebastian laughed. "I like her," he said to Michael, pointing a finger at me.

The four of us chatted for around fifteen minutes. Sebastian asked me general questions about how I was settling into the team, how I was finding F1, and what series I'd raced in. Eventually, he moved on to other guests and I was left at the bar with Michael and Reyna. He kept talking to her about work, marketing plans and some brand sponsorship possibilities. She ended up typing his ideas in her Notes app on her phone. He never stopped working.

My phone buzzed in my small bag. I unhooked it from my shoulder and took out my phone to find a text from Sterling. I tried to suppress my smile as I opened the message.

Sterling: You look like you're really enjoying the party.
Sterling: Does your team principal love the sound of his own voice?

Winter: Haha
Sterling: I've got an idea. A game.
Winter: Really? What sort of game?
Winter: Where are you? I can't see you.

I scanned the crowded room. More people had arrived. I recognised familiar faces from F1—drivers and team members —but couldn't spot Sterling anywhere.

Sterling: Come find me.
Winter: Seriously? I'm not chasing around after you.
Sterling: But you're so good at chasing after me on the track.
Sterling: I'll give you a clue.
Sterling: Near the window.
Sterling: Come on, don't you want to play?
Sterling: Or would you rather listen to your boss for the next hour?
Winter: Arrogant arse.
Winter: And when I catch you?
Sterling: You win a prize.

I focused back on Reyna and Michael's conversation. He was still giving her instructions and her fingers were flying across her phone screen in an effort to keep up.

"Hey, I'll be back in a bit," I said.

Reyna nodded, eyes on her phone, while Michael didn't even register that I'd spoken.

Turning away from them, I pushed my way into the crowd. I sidestepped a giggling couple, drinks in their hands and their bodies pressed close to one another. I squeezed around a group of men in smart suits and passed three fellow drivers.

The trio were from different teams but were known for being close friends. James King, one of the Hunter drivers, always seemed to be at the centre of the group, with Bastiaan Janssen and Rafael Guerra in his orbit. He said something to the other two and they all laughed. Bastiaan sloshed his drink and I narrowly avoided the spill as I passed them.

At the open doorway, I stepped outside into the mild evening air. The sun was still up, but the sky had turned a dusky pink. Guests spilt outside onto an open terrace with potted plants, tables, and chairs scattered around. There was a big outdoor swimming pool and Sterling stood on the far corner. He leaned up against a wall, an open door to his right.

Sterling smiled at me, one of his cocky grins, before turning and disappearing through the open doorway.

I rolled my eyes. This was stupid. I shouldn't have played along, but now that the game had begun, I wanted to win.

Picking up my pace, I walked around the swimming pool and made my way to the door. I stepped into a spacious games room with a couple of pool tables, a big TV, and a darts board. A small group was playing pool, taking turns. I didn't recognise any of them, so they probably weren't from any of the F1 teams.

"Hey, sorry to interrupt, but did someone just pass through here?" I asked.

"Yeah, they went that way," one of the girls replied, pointing towards a door on the other side of the room.

"Thanks."

I followed their directions and came out into a hallway. This wasn't as grand as the entryway to the house—just a simple hall in comparison, with pale blue walls and plush cream carpets.

Sterling: You know, asking for help is cheating.

Winter: No, it's not. You should have specified the rules before we began.

I started along the corridor with no idea where I was going or if I was headed in the right direction. My phone buzzed again.

Sterling: Head for the sound of the party.

Stopping, I listened carefully. I could hear the faint noise of voices and a piano playing. I moved forward and the sound grew. Feeling more confident that I was going in the right direction, I picked up my pace and found myself in the grand hallway again, now empty, with only the chatter and music from the main room filtering into the space.

Sterling: Look up.

I tilted my head to find Sterling above me. He leaned against the banister at the top of the stairs, gazing down at me. Smiling up at him, I headed towards the staircase. My steady footfalls echoed through the space. As I made my way to the top, he started moving, heading down the landing. The carpets upstairs were deep blue and silenced both our footsteps. I followed Sterling, staying a few paces behind him. He turned and took us further into this maze of a building. Then he paused at a door at the end of the corridor, his hand on the handle.

"Found you," I said in a low voice, placing my forefinger on his chest like we'd been playing a game of tag, and now he was it.

He pushed down on the handle and we both stepped into a huge bathroom. A roll-top copper bathtub sat before a large window with views of the open countryside and mountains. A long countertop went down one side with two sinks and two mirrors above. I assumed the tiled partition wall hid a massive walk-in shower. Sterling took my hand and pulled me further inside. We stood facing each other next to the two sinks.

"Did you miss me?" he asked.

"No."

"Liar." He leaned in and kissed me. I wrapped my arms around his neck, pulling him closer to me.

I was a liar. I'd missed this. I'd missed him.

We kissed and kissed, and I lost track of time. My hands wrinkled his shirt while his tangled in my hair. I was so caught up in him that I'd almost forgotten about my plans.

I pulled back.

"What's my prize for finding you?"

"Well..." He looked down.

"There isn't one." I shook my head.

"What about I owe you?" He quirked a brow and gave me one of his signature charming smiles.

"Don't worry, I've got an idea."

I slipped my hand down his chest, slowly inching down to the top button of his trousers. Popping it open, I moved to the zip and yanked it down.

"What are you..." he began, but stopped when I hiked my dress up and dropped down to my knees in front of him.

"What does it look like?" I answered as I began pulling his trousers down to his powerful thighs. "I'm claiming my prize."

"God!" His head tilted back and I rubbed my hand over the hard length straining against his briefs.

Slowly, I began to ease his briefs down. Once he was exposed, I paused and waited. He looked down at me and I stared back, resting a hand on his hip and drawing little circles with my thumb.

"You're going to make me beg, aren't you?"

I licked the head of him in one quick sweep of my tongue. He could play his games, and I could play mine.

"Fuck! This is payback for what I made you say last time?"

I hummed in agreement. "I did make a promise."

"Fine, I can play along, and it's only fair, really. What would you like me to say? Tell you that you're the better driver or that I'm a poor excuse for a World Champion? Something like that?"

I thought about it for a moment.

"No, I don't need that kind of validation of my racing ability. I let my driving do the talking on the track. I'd rather keep it simple. Beg me for it. Tell me what you want."

He stared down at me with wide eyes.

"Go on, or we can rejoin the party if you'd prefer?" I started to move as if to get up from my knees.

"Wait." His hand flew out and tangled in my hair, holding me in place. "Please, Winter, suck me off. I want to fuck your mouth so badly."

I parted my lips and slowly licked them while keeping my eyes locked on his.

"Please, I want those soft lips around my cock." His fingers tightened in my hair.

I stayed still, staring up at him, making him wait.

"Please, Winter. Please," he said, his voice coming out breathy.

I swallowed audibly and reached for his cock, closing my fingers around the base. He groaned and kept his eyes on mine, watching me as I wrapped my lips around him. It was a moment of overwhelming sensation: the feel of his smooth skin, the taste of him, the stretch of my lips. Taking more of him, I slowly slid my mouth down his length.

"Winter," he gasped, and his fingers fisted tighter in my hair.

I let my tongue explore as I moved him in and out of my mouth.

"Fuck! This is too good. You're too good," he said, his voice husky. I was obsessed with the sound of it.

I moaned in agreement. His hand cupped my head and urged my pace on. I took more of him into my mouth as I bobbed up and down. I couldn't stop another moan from escaping from my throat.

I was getting into my own rhythm when he stilled.

"Shit!" he said, and he suddenly jerked away from me. I released him from my mouth and that's when I heard the voices outside the door.

My heart started pounding in my chest. I got to my feet, wiping the back of my hand across my mouth while Sterling tucked himself away. The door handle rattled and I grabbed his arm.

"Quick," I whispered, dragging him into the big walk-in shower. It was huge for a shower, built into its own tiled wall space, and it even had a bench. We went right into the back of the shower. It was like its own little room and from here, I could only see the edge of the counter where the sinks were.

Sterling sat down on the shower bench as the door opened and closed. Two people came in. I could hear the click of high heels along with the lighter clack of flat shoes.

Sterling reached for me and pulled me down onto his lap. My heart thumped in my chest and my skin felt clammy.

"Stay cool," he whispered, his lips pressed to my ear.

"Shall we leave?" the woman asked. She had a slight accent, maybe Scandinavian. "We don't have to stay. We've shown our faces, made a little small talk, and I'd rather go if you're upset." Her voice was familiar.

"I'm not upset," he replied, and I instantly recognised his voice: Matias da Silveira. And the woman with him was his wife, Hannah.

Matias turned the tap on. The water rushed out with a *whoosh*.

"Baby, I know when something is bothering you," she replied in a soft voice. He turned the water off. "Tell me?"

They were both quiet for a moment. I couldn't help leaning forward, trying to sneak a look at them. I glimpsed the edge of Matias's face in the mirror before Sterling pulled me back, holding me firmly against his chest. His lips went to my ear again.

"Do you want to get caught?" he whispered, and a shiver ran down my spine.

"It's my teammate," Matias finally said with a sigh. "He's retiring at the end of the season. Luca told me this afternoon."

"I see," Hannah replied, and I could hear movement, the light rustle of clothes, as if she was wrapping her arms around him in an embrace. "Is that such a bad thing?"

"I knew Théo retiring was a possibility. I like him. We work well together. Who knows who Cavallo will get to replace him? There are rumours that Stefan Brudes is on the lookout for a new team."

I almost choked, holding back my gasp.

"Stefan Brudes? I thought he had a three-year contract with Torrin?"

"Yes, he does, but there's usually a get-out clause. I hope Luca has the sense not to give the seat to him."

"Luca is wise. I'm sure he'll make the best decision for the team and he's got plenty of time to find a new driver."

"True, and the longer they can keep the news quiet, the better. I can't deal with everyone speculating over who it will be."

"I know," she said, her voice soft again. "Shall we go back to the party or back to the hotel? I'd rather not spend the rest of my night in a bathroom," she said in a teasing voice.

They kissed.

"Hotel," he replied, and she laughed.

They left the bathroom, the door clicking closed behind them.

I remained on Sterling's lap, taking in everything we'd heard.

"Théo Laurent is retiring at the end of this season and Stefan has been looking for a new team to join!" I shot to my feet and rushed out of the shower. Sterling followed after me. "Also, you didn't lock the door!" I said, reaching the door handle and sliding the lock closed.

"I was a bit distracted at the time."

"Anyone could have found us!" I covered my hands with my face.

"But nobody saw, and we're okay," he said, reaching for my hands and gently pulling them from my face. He leaned in close to me and kissed me: a soft, gentle kiss. He pulled back to look me in the eyes as if checking to see if I'd calmed down from my mini freak-out.

"Does this mean Stefan is threatened by me if he's looking for another team to join next year?" I asked.

"If he isn't threatened by you, then he should be," he replied, smiling.

"And Théo Laurent is retiring?"

"That's going to cause a stir. Let's hope Cavallo can keep this a secret for as long as possible. If this gets out, silly season will start early."

"Silly season?"

"When news of a possible free seat in a top team gets out, all the drivers' agents and managers start vying for that open spot. If a current driver gets that open seat, then it creates another open spot, like a domino effect."

"Right." And I could be one of those drivers going for that seat if Torrin decided not to renew my contract next year.

Sterling gripped my face in both of his hands. "I know what you're thinking. Torrin would be foolish not to give you a contract for next year. You've currently got more points than your teammate, you're beating him consistently, you've won races in your first season and the season isn't over yet!" His hands slipped from my face.

"But maybe I should look at all my options. I should call my agent. Tell Jean there's an open spot."

"If you do that then word of Laurent's retirement will get out before he's announced it. Agents and managers gossip."

"But this might be my best chance at securing my future!"

"Your best chance is to keep winning. Torrin has to renew your contract. At least wait until after this race weekend. Laurent deserves to announce his retirement plans on his own terms."

I took a deep breath. He was right. "Okay, I'll hold off for now."

He leaned in and brushed his lips against mine, a feather-light touch that made my body buzz. He leaned his forehead against mine, and for a moment, we stayed in that position. I breathed him in and my hands gripped his.

"We should go," I said, finally breaking the tension.

He nodded and we arranged to leave the bathroom one at a time. Sterling went first. While I waited a couple of minutes, I checked my reflection and ran my fingers through my hair to straighten out the tangles Sterling had made. When enough time had passed, I left the bathroom and made my way back to the party.

As I turned the corner for the stairs, I almost bumped into someone. Stefan made a grumbling sound.

"Sorry Stefan, didn't see you there," I said, being as polite as I could to my scheming teammate. He frowned at me and sidestepped to make space. "Enjoying the party?" I asked in an overly cheerful voice, but he walked off in the direction I'd come from. "I'll take that as a no then!" I called after him in a teasing tone.

I hoped he would take Laurent's seat in Cavallo next year.

AUSTRIA

SATURDAY - BEFORE QUALIFYING

All the interviews, promo events, and extras outside of racing were adding up, and he was starting to feel on edge, that anxious feeling creeping up on him again, turning in his stomach and crawling over his skin. He pushed it away as much as he could and carried on like he always did.

EVER SINCE STEFAN'S stunt with the envelopes of cash, tension had built in the team. I sat on a stool in the garage, watching my crew work. The way people moved around the garage and the cars seemed different. The way they spoke to each other was off. There was now a clear division between Stefan's side of the garage and my side. Those working on my car didn't speak to those working on Stefan's.

I felt my stomach tighten into a knot. This was a horrible situation and I wondered if something else had happened after the envelopes to cause a bigger rift. Had Stefan pulled another stunt?

Ash took the stool next to mine, his tablet in his hands, the data from my last practice run on the screen. But I couldn't focus on the numbers. Instead, I asked him about the newly uncomfortable atmosphere.

He sighed and put his tablet down on his workstation.

"Michael made everyone give Stefan the envelopes back, so now that side of the garage is pissed at our side for complaining to Michael." He shook his head.

"Wow. Stefan's really done a number on the team," I said, trying to think of a time when anything like this happened in any other race series I'd taken part in. I drew a blank.

"It will blow over once the race gets going. Ignore it. This has nothing to do with you," he said, picking up his tablet again. He leaned a little closer to me and lowered his voice. "When you win tomorrow and the champagne is flowing, everyone will forget about this nonsense. Everybody loves a win."

I smiled.

A mechanic called for Ash's assistance and he went to help.

I jumped off the stool, grabbed my phone from Ash's workstation, and walked to the pit entrance. Gripping my phone, I stood in the pits watching the other teams get ready for Qualifying. I went back and forth over what to send but kept it simple in the end.

Winter: We have unfinished business.
Sterling: Do we?
Winter: Yes, we were rudely interrupted the other night.

I couldn't help grinning down at my phone.

"Hey," a low voice said, and I looked up to find Sterling's personal trainer, Josh. I quickly hit the lock screen and held my phone behind my back.

"We haven't been introduced yet. I'm Josh." He held his hand out to me. I took it and his fingers wrapped firmly around mine.

"Winter," I replied, and he released my hand.

"You probably already know this, but I'm Aiden's personal trainer. I've known him since we were kids."

"Sure," I replied.

"You seem like a nice enough person, but I think you could be a distraction. Not to mention that you race against each other."

"Err... Not sure what you're on about," I replied with a forced laugh as my heart began to beat faster in my chest. Did Aiden tell him about us after he promised not to?

"I'm very observant and I know my best friend. I know when he's hiding something, and neither of you is very subtle."

"Did he tell you?" I demanded.

"No, but I've seen the looks you give each other."

"I don't give him or anyone looks!"

He chuckled.

"Whatever you think you know, you don't. And you'd better not go spreading rumours," I said in a harsh whisper. I looked up and down the pit lane to check if anyone was watching us.

"I don't gossip. I wouldn't tell anyone. I have my friend's back, which is why I think you should stop whatever is going on between the two of you."

It was my turn to laugh. "Are you warning me off?"

He didn't look impressed by my reaction.

"Aiden's been through a lot and I don't need someone coming along and messing up his progress. I don't want him to get hurt."

"Hurt? Are you messing with me?" I asked because I couldn't believe he was being serious right now. The idea of me hurting Sterling was ridiculous. We were just hooking up occasionally. Having a bit of fun. Sterling knew that. Josh made it sound like I was out to get Sterling.

"I'm serious."

My anger flared, but I managed to keep my voice low so as to not draw attention. "I'm not going to hurt your friend. I know you're looking out for him, but he's a big boy who can make decisions for himself. Also, and most importantly, it's none of your business!" I walked off, back into the Torrin garage, where he couldn't follow.

Qualifying Report
Pole – Winter Jones
2nd – Aiden Sterling
3rd – Stefan Brudes

TWENTY-NINE

AUSTRIA

SATURDAY - AFTER QUALIFYING

*He found himself thinking about her more than he liked to
admit, and he longed for time alone with her.*

ASH WAS RIGHT. After my successful Qualifying session,
the tension in the team dissolved. The team was too busy
enjoying my pole position to worry about Stefan's games.
Stefan secured third place on the grid, behind Sterling. He
stormed off back to the team motorhome, and I hadn't seen him
since. I assumed he was hiding in his room. He didn't even
venture out for dinner.

Gem and I sat down in the motorhome dining area for an
early dinner at six. Qualifying had finished hours ago and I'd
done all my press and media obligations.

I was finishing off my dessert when Reyna came over to our
table.

"Look! It's the interview you did last month!" Reyna waved

the women's fitness magazine and sat down at the table opposite Gem and me.

"Let me see!" Gem said, pushing her empty plate to one side. Reyna opened the magazine to the right page and handed it to Gem.

I leaned closer and read the first few lines. Reyna waited for Gem's reaction to the article.

"They asked you about your dating life?" Gem stated. "*I'm not dating right now. I'm concentrating on my career,*" Gem quoted my words from the interview.

"Luckily, the editor agreed not to include your comment about swearing off men and relationships," Reyna said, glancing at me.

Gem snorted. "Yeah, right!"

"What was wrong with that?" I asked Reyna.

"This version sounds more professional and less like you hate all men," she said, pointing down at the magazine as Gem continued to read.

"I don't think she hates *all* men," Gem commented, a grin tugging at her lips. "I like this bit," she said, quickly changing the subject. She showed Reyna the last paragraph. Reyna nodded in agreement.

"Hopefully, I can arrange more interviews and write-ups like this. Should be easy now you're winning, like, every week," Reyna said.

"Don't jinx it," I replied, closing the magazine.

"I'm only speaking the truth. You're on a roll and the team is working really hard, too." She took her magazine back and headed up the stairs, probably to see Michael in his office.

LATER THAT EVENING, I knocked once on Sterling's hotel room door, as we'd arranged. He opened it and I stepped inside before anyone happened to walk by and see me.

"Hey," I said, unable to keep a smile from my lips at seeing him outside of the racetrack.

"Hey to you too." He wrapped his arms around me and I was engulfed in a fresh citrusy scent that I'd recently learnt was from his favourite moisturiser. He leaned back from the hug to look me up and down, his hands resting on my arms. I'd worn a simple white T-shirt, blue jeans, and a navy bomber jacket. He smiled, an appreciative gleam in his eyes, and I loved how I could wear pretty much anything and he'd still look at me that way.

"Now, where were we before we were interrupted at the party?" He mocked an exaggerated, thoughtful expression. "I think someone was on her knees."

"Really? That's how you want to start this?" I tilted my head to one side.

"It was worth a try." He grinned and leaned in for a kiss, but I stopped him with a hand on his chest.

"Wait. I need to speak to you about something," I said, moving to sit on the edge of his bed.

"Sounds serious." He remained standing, turning to face me and folding his arms.

"It is. Your trainer had words with me today."

"Who? Josh?" Sterling's eyebrows furrowed.

"Yes, he told me to stay away from you and stop whatever is going on between us."

"What?"

"Did you tell him about us?"

"No. Never. I made a promise I wouldn't tell anyone. How did he find out?" His frown deepened.

"Apparently, we've been too obvious about it."

"No, we haven't. I barely speak to you during race weekends."

"He said it's the way we look at each other." I resisted the urge to roll my eyes.

"That's rubbish." He unfolded his arms.

"I know! And he thinks I'm going to hurt you."

Sterling laughed like I had when Josh spoke to me earlier.

"He's very protective of you," I added.

"Yeah, he is." Sterling rubbed the back of his head and sat down beside me on the bed. "I'm sorry he had words with you. I'll talk to him."

"Thanks, but why is he so protective of you?" I couldn't help but ask.

"We've been friends since we were kids. I went through a rough time after my dad died. Josh was there for me. He's seen me at my lowest, helped me back to where I am now."

"He sounds like a good friend. I guess he was looking out for you. I might have told him to keep his nose out of my business and stormed off," I admitted, feeling a bit guilty now.

Sterling laughed so deeply that he jostled the bed. "Don't worry, you were right to do that. It isn't his business. I'll talk to him and he won't tell anyone about us. He knows how to keep a secret."

My stomach did a small flip at his mention of *us*, and I didn't know how to respond or what to think. There shouldn't be an *us*. This was meant to be a casual thing, but maybe it wasn't anymore. The lines had started to blur: or maybe the lines blurred a while ago, and I hadn't noticed.

Us.

"You know, I think you were right," I said, getting to my feet and standing in front of him. He widened the gap between his legs, and I moved in closer to him.

"About what?"

"I was on my knees when we were interrupted," I said, sinking down to the floor.

I GOT an Uber down the road from his hotel. The driver didn't recognise me, or if he did, he didn't say anything and just dropped me off.

Back in my own hotel, I scanned my key card and stepped inside my room.

"Finally, you've returned!"

I froze, finding Gem sitting in one of the chairs by the window, her tablet on her lap. She hit pause on whatever she'd been watching.

"How did you get in here?" I asked, closing the door behind me.

"I knocked on the door earlier: you didn't answer. I rang your phone: you didn't answer. I started to panic that something had happened to you and the hotel receptionist took pity on me and gave me a spare key card to your room."

"Are they allowed to do that?" I asked, putting my phone down on the bedside table and taking my jacket off.

"You went to his room this time," Gem said.

I looked at her.

"Come on, I know about you and Aiden."

I shook my head, went to my suitcase sitting open in the middle of the room and started searching for my PJs. "I don't know what you're talking about."

Gem laughed. "You're a terrible liar. I can read it on your face and you two are very obvious about it."

"No, we're not!" I looked up from my suitcase. Why did people keep saying we were obvious?

"So much for all that talk about not dating and swearing off men." She laughed again.

"We're not dating. How long have you known?"

"I had my suspicions you liked him from the start of the season. You kept going on about beating him on the track, complaining about him, but I knew for certain when I saw those love bites down your neck the morning of Silverstone."

"You've known since Silverstone! Why didn't you say anything?"

"I thought I'd wait for you to tell me," she explained. "But tonight, I got tired of waiting, and I don't like the idea of you sneaking around and no one knowing where you are. What if something happened to you on your way back to the hotel?"

"It's Austria. I'm fine."

"You don't speak the language. You could be recognised and swarmed by fans. You're not an unknown sportsperson anymore. F1 is an international sport with millions of viewers. People know your face. And it's the night before race day!"

I sunk down onto my bed. "Ugh! I know." I covered my face with my hands.

"What's going on with you and Aiden? Is it serious? Do you like him?"

"I don't know. It's not meant to be serious. It was only meant to be a one-off. Then it became a thing, but nothing serious. We just hook up."

"But you like him?" Gem raised a brow.

"No, yes, maybe. I don't know." I shook my head and leaned back on my bed. Gem got up from her chair and came to sit on the other side of the bed, leaning back so we were side by side, both staring up at the ceiling. "The sex is great. Amazing. But I like talking to him too. He gave me good advice on dealing with Stefan more than once. I feel like he's shared stuff with me that he wouldn't share with a one-night stand. He makes me laugh and I can be myself with him. He gets the racing stuff, too," I added, thinking about my ex and how he really didn't understand my love of racing. "I don't have to explain things to him: he just gets it. He gets me."

My phone buzzed against the nightstand. I picked it up to find a message from Sterling asking if I made it back okay. "And he checks to see if I'm okay." It felt good to talk to Gem about Sterling and voice what I'd barely admitted to myself.

"I think you more than like him. You're falling for him," Gem said.

"What! No, I'm not. I can't!" I sat up and turned towards her. "He's my competitor, my track rival. We can't be together like a normal couple. What would everyone say? We race against each other. You know exactly how that would play out, especially with the press, and I would come out worse for it."

"You don't know how people would react," Gem said, sitting up so we were face to face again.

"You know it would be made out to be a big thing. I can imagine people accusing me of sleeping my way to the top of the podium. You saw the reaction when Sterling and I messed up our Qualifying in Silverstone."

"Maybe it would be bad at first, but people would get over it. The press would move on to other news or some other gossip."

"I still don't have a contract for next season. It could affect my chances of securing another contract."

"Then what do you do—tell Sterling you can't see him anymore?" Gem asked, and I frowned at the idea. My stomach twisted at the thought. "Or carry on sneaking around?"

"I don't know what to do."

"You like him and he clearly likes you. I've seen the way he looks at you. So do nothing. You don't have to figure it out right away. Just don't get caught while you're exploring your options," she said, giving me a reassuring smile.

"What is it with the way we look at each other? I'm not giving him looks and he isn't giving me looks back." I shook my head.

"Sure, you keep telling yourself that." She laughed. "At least things will be easier from now on."

"Easier?" I asked.

"I can help cover for you, make sure you get back to your hotel safely," she explained.

"You don't have to cover for me."

"I'll just add it to my bill alongside my fee for motivational pep talks. Reyna still owes me for hers."

I leaned forward and pulled her into a tight hug. Gem really was the best trainer I'd ever had, a best friend like the sister I never had. I finally released her and leaned back on my pillows again. Gem copied me, leaning back next to me.

"So, I'm curious, is the sex really that good?" She laughed.

"Yes."

AUSTRIA

SUNDAY - RACE DAY

Rain was Formula One's version of a wild card. All bets were off, but if he had to place a stake on a racer other than himself, he'd place his bet on Winter.

THE RAIN HIT AROUND MIDDAY. We hadn't had a wet race yet, and it looked like this would be the first one of the season. Heavy grey clouds blanketed the sky, and the rain poured. A haze hung around the circuit.

I stood trackside next to Gem. She held a big blue umbrella to shelter us both. I'd already got a bit wet driving the car from the pits out onto the grid. The rain had washed out the usual fanfare before the start. There were fewer VIPs walking the grid, and the fans in the stands weren't as noisy. They huddled in coats, in plastic ponchos and under umbrellas. Camera crews still walked up and down trying to get interviews with drivers, but they had to keep wiping the water from the camera lens.

They also had to watch out for the gazebos raised over the cars so the teams could carry on working without getting rained on.

My gaze drifted across the track to Sterling. He stood near his car, in deep conversation with a team member, probably chatting about strategy and how the weather would impact their plans. Or perhaps they were discussing the best strategy to get in front of me. Josh stood beside them, holding up an umbrella that was too small for the three of them. The rain bounced off the umbrella's canopy and fell onto Sterling's back, trickling down his race suit.

I watched Sterling talking with energetic hand gestures and a concentrated expression. He took racing so seriously, every aspect of it, you could see the passion for it as he spoke.

"See, you're giving him a look," Gem whispered in my ear.

"I'm observing and exploring my options like you said last night," I whispered back.

"Try to look less dreamy while doing it." She chuckled.

"Shut up! I never look dreamily at anyone or anything."

She continued to laugh.

"His trainer is giving us the evils," Gem said, and my gaze moved from Sterling to Josh, who was glaring in our direction.

"Josh doesn't approve," I explained.

"He knows?"

"He figured it out like you did, but unlike you, he's not a fan."

"Why not? You're a catch! He should be happy for Aiden," she whispered the last part.

"Apparently, I'm a distraction. I might hurt him, too."

"Rubbish. I should have a chat with him later."

"Don't. Sterling said he'd talk to him anyway."

The rain continued to pelt against the umbrella.

"Are you going to be okay in this rain?" Gem asked.

"Sure. I'm British. This is my weather."

"Just checking, you don't need a motivational chat."

"Nah, I'm good. You better not charge me for one." I joked, giving her a wry smile.

Ash ran over to us, ducking under the umbrella.

"News from race control. We're starting under the safety car. Rain is too heavy, but satellite data suggests it will ease about ten minutes after the start."

"Thanks, anything else I should know?"

After discussing race strategy, I got back in the car. The teams began to pack away all the equipment. The gazebos were folded away, and the rain pelted against my car and helmet. This was going to be a challenging race. Visibility would be poor even at low speeds.

Under a safety car start, there would be no warm-up lap. I didn't need a formation lap to know I wouldn't be able to see much in this weather. The flashing lights of the safety car would have to guide me, along with my memory of the track layout. At least we were at a circuit I'd raced at a few times before. Would hate to think what it would be like to race at a brand-new circuit in these conditions.

Lined up in pole position, I waited for the safety car to go. I glanced across to see Sterling in second. His helmet bobbed as if he was nodding at me; I nodded back and stared straight ahead at the safety car. Its lights changed, and it began to pull away. I followed along with all the other cars, a procession until the rain eased and the race could begin in full.

THE CROWD CHEERED as Sterling sprayed champagne at me. I got him back with my own. The rain had eventually eased off, and I'd come home with the winner's trophy. Another one to add to the growing collection, more points to add, and hopefully another step closer to securing my future in this sport. If I kept this up, I would win the Championship, and then every team would want to offer me a seat in their car for next year. I could do this; I could secure my future in F1.

Race Report
1st – Winter Jones
2nd – Aiden Sterling
3rd – Benjamin Knight

Championship Driver Standings
Aiden Sterling – 166
Winter Jones – 165
Stefan Brudes – 154

GREAT BRITAIN

FRIDAY - A WEEKEND OFF

For a moment, he let himself get carried away talking on the phone to her, chatting like they were more than racing rivals, more than a hook-up, and much more than just friends.

I SHOULD HAVE PLANNED MORE interesting Friday night activities than hiding in my bedroom. I'd come home for the weekend off and Mum had gotten on my nerves today. After our talk in France, she'd backed off. She'd stopped offering me so much advice, especially when it came to my team and strategy. However, she did try to give me fitness guidance. It wasn't like I had my own personal trainer or anything. What did she think Gem's job was?

She also brought up my contract for next year, and perhaps she was right to worry about my F1 future. I knew I should call Jean, my agent. It was her job to secure me a seat, after all. After my last win, it should be easy for her to start negotiations with Torrin or put some calls in to other top teams.

I propped myself up against my pillows, watching some reality TV rubbish on my laptop while eating a chocolate bar that wasn't on Gem's nutritional plan. My phone started ringing as the show got interesting. Two of the girls had finally figured out they'd been dating the same guy. I hit pause, not wanting to miss the action, and reached for my phone.

Video call: Aiden Sterling

"Shit." I chucked the chocolate bar wrapper on the floor, wiped my mouth with the back of my hand, and pulled my hair loose from the very messy ponytail it was in. Why would he video call me? Especially when I was in my PJs, looking like a mess, and eating chocolate in bed.

I could ignore it, but I hit the "answer" button.

His face filled the screen and he looked as gorgeous and perfect as always. I could see a dark shirt collar, meaning he wasn't already in bed like I was.

"Hey," he said, holding his phone back further. I could make out the back of a couch and the edge of a picture frame on the wall behind him.

"Hey, what's up?" I asked, trying to sound cool and not like I was freaking out about his unexpected call.

"I'm good, you?"

"Yeah, just having a quiet night in."

He squinted at the camera. "Where are you?" he asked.

"In my bedroom," I replied, wondering why he was still squinting at me.

"What wallpaper is that?"

"Oh shit," I muttered, glancing behind me to my childhood wallpaper. It was a horrible pink with a ditsy floral pattern. Didn't everyone go through a pink phase growing up? I moved so I was leaning further back into the pillows and he couldn't see the terrible decorating choices I'd made as a young teen. "I'm at my parents. This is my childhood bedroom," I admitted.

"Cute." He grinned at me, that infuriating grin of his, the one he used whenever he teased me.

"Whatever you're about to say, don't."

"I wasn't going to say anything." He feigned innocence, placing a hand over his heart. "So you're visiting your parents?"

"Not exactly. I live here. I moved back in last year. I broke up with my ex halfway through the W season. With all the travelling, I didn't have time to look for a new place, and it wasn't like I'd be home much either. When the season finished, I just couldn't be bothered to find somewhere new. Then everything happened with F1, and I was back travelling again. I never unpacked properly," I confessed and flipped the camera so he could see the pile of cardboard boxes by my wardrobe.

"That is a lot of boxes," he commented, and I flipped the camera back around. "Wait, you mean to tell me the current F1 Championship leader is living at home with her parents?" His teasing grin was back.

"Hey! Don't judge; moving is stressful!"

"I'm not judging. I find it interesting."

"I think someone is jealous of someone else's Championship points."

"Nah, I'm cool. Next race is one of my all-time favourites. I'll take the lead back with ease."

"Will you now?" I asked, unable to keep the smile from my lips. I tried to hide it and would deny it if asked, but I loved these back-and-forth arguments with him about racing.

"Sure!"

"Why did you call? Apart from informing me of your strategy for the next race?" I asked.

"I thought you might miss me."

I laughed. "You actually interrupted my show as it was getting interesting."

"I can be far more interesting than a TV show."

"Really? How?"

"I'm more interactive." He winked.

"Did you interrupt my evening for phone sex? Because sadly my vibrator is packed away in one of those boxes. Not risking my mum snooping and finding it in one of my drawers."

"You really need to move out."

"Aw, you sound concerned for me."

"I am! You should be able to have personal time in your own home without worrying about getting interrupted."

I laughed again. "I did think about moving. I thought about where I wanted to live, where I should live—around here or closer to the Torrin factory base? Or should I move abroad like all the other drivers so I'm more central for travelling to races? But where? Which country? Then what sort of property: apartment or house? Do I rent or try to buy? Can I afford it on my current pay? Do I risk taking out a big mortgage when I don't have a contract for next season? And then I got a headache and stopped thinking about moving out."

He stared at me and blinked twice. "When you put it like that..."

"Sorry, did I ruin your plan to try and seduce me over the phone with a rant about my living situation?"

"Sort of, but maybe I can help. You're an F1 driver: move to Monaco. Rent an apartment for a year, see if you like living in the city, and then buy a place a year later when you've secured a long-term contract or a few big sponsorship deals. There, sorted."

"You make it sound so easy."

"Because it is."

"And you live in Monaco?"

"Sure."

"And if I lived there too, you wouldn't have to make do with phone sex. Your booty call would be a drive away."

He laughed. "I hadn't thought of that, but seriously, you should look into it. Almost all the drivers have places in Monaco. You have to live here for at least a year or two. It's like a rite of passage."

"I'll consider it."

In the end, we talked for almost an hour. He told me about his family and how his mum was currently on a world cruise seeing the sights. I chatted about my family too, mostly about my F1-obsessed Mum, who also named both her children after seasons because my dad wouldn't let her name us after F1 teams. By the time I hung up, I'd forgotten all about my cheesy reality show, and instead, I fell into an effortless sleep.

THIRTY-TWO

RACE REPORTS

Hungary

First – Winter Jones
Second – Aiden Sterling
Third – Heikki Koskinen

Tenth – Stefan Brudes

Turkey

First – Matias da Silveira
Second – Winter Jones
Third – Aiden Sterling

DNF – Stefan Brudes

Championship Driver Standings

Winter Jones – 208

Aiden Sterling – 199

Stefan Brudes – 155

THIRTY-THREE

GREAT BRITAIN

THE SUMMER BREAK

He couldn't be expected to go four weeks without seeing her!

FIVE DAYS. Only five days had passed since the last race ended and the summer break began. Five days, and I was already feeling agitated at my parents' house. On the third day, I started sneaking down to the small gym in the converted garage because if Mum knew I was working out, she'd watch and offer me pointers, or worse, she'd want to join in. I now ran on the treadmill in a heightened state, aware of every sound my footsteps made and constantly looking over my shoulder to check that the door was still closed. I knew Mum meant well, but I still needed my own space and right now, I didn't have it.

The summer break was meant to be relaxing, a chance to recharge, ready for the last part of the Championship season. I felt more stressed now than I did before my first race.

I finished my workout and managed to sneak back up to my room without anyone noticing me. I took a quick shower, dressed in some comfortable clothes, and grabbed my phone off the charger.

Winter: You were right
Sterling: Thanks, I usually am, but what was I right about this time?

I rolled my eyes, imagining his grinning face as he wrote the message.

Winter: About how I need my own space. I need to move out. I might not survive the whole summer break.
Sterling: Book a flight. Come to Monaco. Sorted.
Winter: I can't just drop everything and fly out to Monaco!
Sterling: Why not? Do you have important plans? If you do, cancel them.
Winter: And what am I going to do in Monaco? Are you going to show me around? How will that work? We can't be seen in public together outside of a race weekend.
Sterling: Minor details. I can figure something out.
Sterling: Book a flight and let me know when you're here.
Winter: Stop bossing me around!

I shouldn't book a flight and jet off to Monaco. Or should I? It's not like I had loads of plans for the rest of the week. I'd promised to meet up with some old friends at the end of next week and Mum had begun organising a family lunch for Sunday with my brother. I hadn't seen him since the start of the season and couldn't remember the last message I'd sent him, but that was normal for us. We didn't have one of those close, supportive sibling relationships. We'd grown further apart in recent years, and family gatherings always felt forced or awkward. He hated motorsport or had no interest in it at all. While I knew very little about his art career, he always made me feel ignorant and poorly educated whenever I tried to take an interest.

That made the decision for me. Guess they'd have to have Sunday lunch without me.

THIRTY-FOUR

MONACO

THE SUMMER BREAK

He told her he loved her hair because it was too soon to say more than that.

I GOT to the hotel after three. The receptionist beamed at me as she checked me in and told me about how she really got into F1 this year. She'd watched races on and off with her dad, but she'd followed every race this season. She started telling me about the hotel's gym facilities, pool, and spa.

"You can book treatments too!" She handed me a small brochure for the spa.

"Thanks."

"Here's your key. You're on the third floor, room twenty-five. The lift will take you straight up, and then turn right. Do you need help with your bag?" she asked, still smiling.

"No, I'm good, thanks!" I said, wheeling my suitcase away and heading for the lift.

The hotel was modern, with new carpets, white walls and

subtle styling. My room was simple but had a great view of the coast. I took a minute to take it all in. It felt odd staying at a hotel without gearing up for a race weekend, without Gem in a room nearby, or the whole team down the corridor. This time it was only me. No race to worry about, no tight schedule or publicity events to attend. I was on holiday. I decided to try to relax and do whatever people did while on holiday.

I ran a bath in the big, free-standing tub. I held off messaging Sterling and instead sank into the hot, steamy water. He could wait a little longer. I let myself soak until my finger-tips went wrinkly. After my bath, I unpacked my suitcase and picked out a cute summer dress. I hadn't worn a dress of my own choosing in so long. The last dress I'd worn, Reyna had final approval on. I zipped up the cute white cotton sundress and found my phone.

Winter: Checked into my hotel!

The three dots popped onto the screen as soon as the message was sent, like he'd been impatiently staring at his phone, waiting for my message.

Sterling: Do you want to come over to mine?
Winter: Nah, I just flew all the way out here to stare at the pretty view.
Sterling: Wouldn't put it past you. You do like pretty views.
Sterling: I'll send a car over to pick you up in ten minutes.

THE CAR SERVICE picked me up outside the front of the hotel. The driver asked for my name and that was it; he didn't speak to me for the rest of the journey. We headed further and further out of the city, driving along coastal roads, and even though I wasn't super familiar with the local area, I was pretty sure we'd left the tiny city-state of Monaco and crossed into France. The views were stunning, with the sparkling blue seas to the right and green rocky hills to the left. We drove up into the hills until the driver pulled off the main road and down into a narrow driveway. The car stopped outside a garage door. The door began to rise and the driver pulled into an underground garage.

When we finally stopped, I remained in the car, unsure what to do. The driver looked at me in his mirrors and a frown furrowed his bushy brows. I quickly opened the door and hopped out to find Aiden leaning against a doorway, a grin on his lips. The car pulled out of the garage and drove off.

I went straight up to him.

"You lied: you don't live in Monaco. Also, who the hell was that guy?" I asked, looking at his garage door as it closed automatically.

He laughed, reached for my hand, and pulled me through the doorway and into his home.

"I used to live in Monaco but moved out here a couple of years ago. There's more space and privacy if you live just outside the city. And that was Marco. He runs a local car service. He's a quiet, serious man with no interest in gossip, who his customers are or where he drops them off."

He took me through a small storeroom into a bright, open-plan living space. Big windows looked down the valley to the sea.

"Wow," I stepped further into his home, my eyes moving from the view to roam around the room.

He hung back, watching me take in the space. It was all white walls and modern furniture—nothing too dark or bright, nothing to distract the eye too much. The views were the main focal point. His kitchen was to my right, with white cupboards and black marble countertops. The whole place was spotless, with no clutter or mess. Only his kettle sat on the worktop.

He reached for my hand and spun me to face him. His eyes went up and down my body.

"You look different," he said.

"Good-different?"

He reached up to a lock of my hair and tucked it behind my ear. I'd left my hair to dry naturally and let it hang loose for a change.

"Good, definitely good," he said, his voice a little husky, and he leaned in, gently pressing his lips to mine. I wrapped my arms around his neck and leaned into the kiss, into him, pressing my body against his. A quiet moan broke through his lips as he ended the kiss and moved back to look me over again.

We hadn't seen each other in what felt like forever. We hadn't been alone together in ages either, and we'd never been alone like this before, without a time limit or worrying about getting caught.

"Is it just us?" I asked, my voice quiet.

"Yes. Just us."

We kissed again, hard and fast. My arms tightened around his shoulders and he pushed me backwards until I hit the edge of his kitchen island, the cool marble top biting into me. I pulled back, breaking the kiss.

"Did you miss me? Or did you miss this?" I asked.

"You. I missed you." He gripped my waist and lifted me up. My legs instantly wrapped around him as he sat me down on his kitchen counter. We kissed, heated and rushed. I put a hand on his chest and he moved back; his eyes looked me over, intense and full of lust.

"Okay, maybe I missed this too. Kissing you, touching you, being close to you."

My hands moved over his defined muscles and then up to his face. I traced my thumb over his lips: his soft, very kissable lips. My eyes stayed fixed on him, taking him all in.

"I missed you too," I said as I brushed over his jaw. A part of me wanted to say more, to admit feelings I hadn't yet admitted to myself. Looking at him, I felt like he wanted to say more too. He was holding back as much as I was. It was like we were both standing on the edge of a cliff and if one of us said too much, we would find ourselves toppling over. I wasn't sure I was ready for the fall or to find out what awaited us at the bottom of that cliff. It was safer to stay here on the edge, stay in the moment.

"What are you doing?" he asked.

"Looking at you and enjoying the view," I replied, one hand moving up over his cheek to brush his hairline. "Are you growing your hair out?" I asked, noting the tiny difference in its length since I'd last seen him.

"Not really. I usually keep it short for racing—makes life easier getting in and out of the gear—but I don't bother during the summer and winter breaks." My hands slipped down from his face and back to his chest.

"My mum's always telling me I should cut my hair short for the same reason."

He reached up and slid his hand into my hair, tangling his fingers in it. "I love your hair." He leaned in closer to me, our lips almost brushing. He tightened his grip, lifting my chin.

"You should make the most of it then," I whispered.

"Really?" he whispered back, tracing his thumb over my lips.

"Yes," I said, shifting forward off the countertop and gliding down his body, feeling every part of him against me as I fell onto my feet.

His hand dropped from my hair and he stepped back to give me enough space to move. Slowly, I reached under the hem of my dress and pulled my lacy thong down until it dropped around my feet. I stepped out of the lace, picked it up in a quick sweep and chucked it into his living space.

A wicked grin took over his face as he guided me so I faced the counter. He placed my hands flat on the marble top and pressed his body against mine. This was our safe territory. Less chat about feelings and all the unsaid words between us, more action.

A thrill shot through me and I wished I'd taken more than my underwear off.

"Was this what you had in mind?" He used one hand to gather my hair into a loose ponytail and wrapped it around his fingers. His other hand snaked around my body, pulling me tightly against him. I could feel how hard he was already and I couldn't help pressing my thighs together.

"Yes. Better."

His hand slipped from my waist down to my bare legs. His fingers brushed up my thigh, under my dress, going higher and higher until they reached between my legs. He cupped me roughly and I gasped.

He tugged my hair and I arched my neck towards his shoulder. His lips found my neck; his kisses moved up until his mouth was at my ear.

"You don't have to be quiet here. We're not in a hotel. You can scream my name if you like."

"That depends," I said, my voice breathy.

"On what?"

"On whether you can make me scream," I teased, knowing

how he loved a challenge, even if it was a pointless one—I already knew he could make me cry out. At least this time, I wouldn't have to worry about getting caught with him.

He didn't reply. Instead, his fingers moved roughly between my legs, pressing down on my clit, and then making agonisingly slow circles. The friction wasn't enough. I wanted more. I started to move my hips, grinding against him.

"Patience."

"You know I have none. I like going fast."

He laughed and his chest vibrated against my back. "Ask me then. Beg me."

"Please?"

He instantly increased his pace, rubbing two of his fingers against my clit. The tension began to build and I moaned loudly. I closed my eyes as he pressed his fingers against me even harder, a throbbing sensation forming.

When one of his fingers sunk inside me, I cried out.

"Aiden!"

"So tight, so perfect, just for me," he said into my ear.

"Yes!"

Normally, I'd never let anyone speak to me like that, in such a possessive way, but Aiden could. He could have me, and have me, and have me.

I was so close that the pressure built to almost painful levels, and I started rocking my hips again, frantic to find release. But he stopped; his finger slipped out and his hand unravelled from my hair. I was about to protest when I heard the sound of his zipper.

His fingers played with the hem of my dress.

"Please?" I begged again.

"Do you always get what you want?" he asked, and I could hear the teasing grin in his voice, although it was huskier than usual, like he was only just holding on.

"Yes!" I gripped the edge of the counter even tighter, my knuckles turning white.

He pushed my dress up, and suddenly, he was there, at my entrance, pressing himself against me.

"Fuck," he swore as he pushed into me in one hard thrust. Both his hands gripped my hips, his fingers digging in.

"Oh my God!"

He pulled out only to slam back in again. I could feel myself stretching around him, adjusting to his size. In this position, everything felt deeper. He pulled out, thrust back in, again and again, at a relentless pace. Fast, like I'd asked for.

"You feel fucking amazing!" he gasped.

I could only moan in response.

He moved me even harder, hitting the right spot. I cried out; the tension began building again. My whole body felt like it was throbbing with anticipation, my release so close. His hands tightened on my hips and I couldn't work out if I was holding him or he was holding me.

"Aiden, I'm so close!"

His movements became even more rough, demanding, and relentless in chasing down our pleasure.

"Winter." His voice was rough, raw, and my name on his lips was what pushed me over.

"Aiden!" I screamed.

My orgasm ripped through me as he continued. Both his hands dug into my hips as his own orgasm took over.

We both slumped forward, my hands still gripping the counter, and we were both breathing heavily. Seconds, minutes, went by until he finally slipped out of me and gently pulled me around to face him. He kissed me, deep and slow. My body felt boneless but buzzed.

"What now?" I asked, still a little breathless as I tried to straighten my dress out.

"I should show you around properly. Let's start with my bedroom." He winked.

I laughed but let him take my hand and lead me into his home.

HOURS LATER, we both lounged on the floor. I had his bedsheet wrapped around me while he wore only his boxers. We leaned against his sofa with an open takeaway pizza box between us and a movie I was only half watching on the TV.

"Mhmm... this pizza is amazing! I haven't had pizza in so long," I said between mouthfuls of warm bread and greasy cheese. "Don't tell my trainer."

"As long as you don't tell mine."

"They'll know, though. They always do. I bet Gem is putting together my post-holiday training plan as we speak."

He laughed and reached for another slice.

"I would have liked to take you out somewhere," he said before taking another bite.

A lump formed in my throat. We were standing at that metaphorical cliff edge again with a big question looming over our heads: what were we to each other? At some point, we'd have to get off this brink, have the talk, and figure out what the hell this was between us. I knew one thing for sure—it wasn't casual anymore. I'd flown to another country to spend time with him outside of a race weekend.

I swallowed the lump in my throat. That conversation could wait a little longer. I wasn't going to risk spoiling the evening, and I didn't even know how to start or what I wanted to say.

"But this has been amazing, especially the pizza."

"Just the pizza?" he asked, turning to me and raising an eyebrow.

"Hmm..." I mocked a thoughtful expression.

"I'll make you forget about that pizza later," he said, placing his hand on my exposed knee, and his eyes glanced towards the hall that led to his bedroom.

"You know I paid for my own hotel room."

"Ah, what a waste." He leaned in and kissed me.

THIRTY-FIVE

MONACO

THE SUMMER BREAK

He had to take her out. They couldn't hide away in his place all the time, even if he knew they had plenty of ways to keep themselves entertained. There had to be somewhere they could go where no one would recognise them or interrupt their time together. A place came to mind, and he wondered if he could pull it off or if it would be too risky.

I DIDN'T GET BACK to my hotel until late morning. There was no Gem waiting for me this time, but she did send me a message to check that I was getting enough training. I still had the rest of the season to go and couldn't let anything slip. *There's no such thing as a summer break for serious athletes,* she'd written in her message. With her words in my head, I got changed, headed down to the hotel gym, and then showered after my workout session.

Putting on another cute summer dress, one with a blue and yellow floral print, I decided to head out into the city and explore. I should try to see what the city was like when it wasn't decked out for a race weekend or packed with F1 fans.

I walked from the hotel in the warm summer sunshine, pausing at a few shop windows to peek inside. I found a cute coffee shop with little round tables and umbrellas outside and headed in to grab a drink and something to eat. It wasn't too busy and they had a display full of pastries. I ordered a coffee and a cream-filled pastry.

"Two racing drivers in one day," the young woman at the counter said after taking my order.

"Really?" I asked, raising an eyebrow.

"It happens occasionally," she said, tipping her head towards a collection of photographs on the wall. Some were typical scenic photographs, but others had photos of F1 cars on the Monaco track going back decades and photos of past F1 drivers, too. I wanted to ask her which driver had been in before me but held off, not wanting to seem too nosy. "You'll get used to it," she added.

"I'm just visiting, but thinking about moving," I said.

"Please come back if you do make the move. We can add another World Champion to our wall," she said.

"I'm not Champion yet," I said, but couldn't help returning her smile.

"We'll see," she replied.

I sat, drank my coffee, and enjoyed the buzz of the little shop. Customers came and went with their orders, the coffee machine hissed, and cars drove past outside.

While finishing my pastry, I got a message from Aiden.

Sterling: I have a plan.
Winter: What sort of plan?
Sterling: Do you trust me?
Winter: Yes.

MARCO, the silent and serious taxi driver, picked me up once
again, but he didn't take me to Aiden's house this time. He
dropped me off outside a cliffside restaurant. I stood staring at
the sleek modern building, wondering what on earth Aiden had
planned. Why would he want me dropped off here and why
would I need a bikini at a restaurant? We couldn't dine out like
a normal couple in a normal restaurant. A family walked past
me on their way inside and I kept my head down, looking at my
phone, hoping they weren't F1 fans. A message buzzed on my
phone.

Following a narrow footpath, I headed past the restaurant
and down to the car park. Only a handful of cars were there,
including a sleek silver sports car. As I got closer, I could make
out the car's details. It was the newest Silvers sportscar, the one
they featured in the promotional video at the start of the season
in Australia, when I'd first met Aiden.

His window slid down as I approached. He flipped his
aviator sunglasses up to get a better look at me. He wore a
simple, crisp white T-shirt and looked effortlessly cool, as
always.

Neither of us spoke. He tapped a finger on the screen on
the dash and the passenger door opened like a silent command.
I walked over and slid inside. He pressed his finger on the
screen again and the door shut by itself.

"Fancy," I said, and he grinned at me like a kid with a new toy. "Are you going to explain this plan of yours?"

"Not yet."

"And no one's going to spot us together in your car?"

"Tinted windows." He pushed his sunglasses back down to cover his eyes.

I glanced at the car's dash, the smooth steering wheel, and the way his hands gripped it.

"Impressive."

"Just you wait."

He put the car into reverse, pulled out of the parking spot, and effortlessly sped off down the coastal road.

We drove along a scenic route, less busy but with lots of winding corners and flashes of coastal views. His car hugged the curves of the road and Aiden kept an even, smooth speed.

"Are you trying to impress me with your driving skills? Because I already know you can drive. We race each other and I beat you often, remember?"

He laughed. "How could I forget? No, I thought you'd appreciate this smooth ride."

"I'd appreciate it more if you let me drive."

"Nice try. This is my car and only I get behind the wheel."

"We'll see about that."

We drove for well over an hour into the French country-side. Aiden turned down a very narrow road that became rougher as we continued along it, more like a track than a road.

"Are you sure you know where you're going?" I asked as a stone flicked up from the ground and bounced along the shiny bonnet.

"Yes, and it's worth it."

The tiny lane opened into a small clearing surrounded by trees on one side and an old, half-fallen wall on the other. A gateway was in the wall. Beyond the gate was another tiny track road.

"I see: you can't beat me on the racetrack, so you're going to abandon me in the middle of nowhere."

He laughed, turning the engine off. "If that was true, why would I ask you to bring swimwear?"

He opened both our doors with the touch of a button. We both got out, and he opened the tiny boot and took out a couple of towels. I frowned at him.

"Listen," he said, and I paused.

I could hear the crash of waves.

"It's this way." He shut the boot and headed for a gap in the wall, the towels under his arm. He didn't even bother locking his £300,000 sports car. I glanced at the shiny silver car, then back to his figure disappearing down a tiny footpath. Shaking my head, I rushed to catch up to him, squeezing through the gap in the wall. The trail winded through trees and undergrowth. As we continued, the footpath turned to sand, the trees thinned out, and rocks took their place. The ground became even more rocky and sandy; we had to squeeze through a gap between two boulders, but once we were through, the view opened onto a small beach.

Cliffs and rocks protected the cove on either side and in the middle, golden sand warmed under the summer sun. The sea lapped in a gentle rhythm and a few gulls called from above.

"Wow," I said.

"Told you it would be worth it." Aiden gave me a smug grin and started walking further onto the sand.

He paused suddenly and my eyes followed his gaze. We weren't the only ones on the secret beach. A dog bounded into the water, its owner walking along the shore. The lady didn't pay us any attention; she continued to walk, her dog's lead in one hand.

I stood beside Aiden and we both looked out to sea.

"I didn't think beaches like this still existed. It's so beautiful and quiet. How do people not know about this place?"

"The locals do. It's not the easiest place to access. There's another way in further down, but it's very rocky. It's probably where she's headed," he said, looking at the dog walker, now much further along the beach than us. Her Labrador continued to jump in and out of the sea, having the time of its life.

"And you're sure we're okay here? Maybe this isn't a good idea. Someone might spot us together."

"It's deserted. It will be fine. We won't stay too long, just long enough for a swim." He chucked the towels down and pulled off his shirt. I watched the fabric slip over every single one of his muscles. He discarded the shirt on the sand and turned to me with a crooked grin. He knew I couldn't help but admire him. He slipped his trainers off and pulled his socks off. He was already wearing his swimming shorts, a dark navy pair.

"Coming?" Aiden asked, but he didn't wait for a reply. He started for the sea.

I watched him for a moment: his easy, relaxed strides—not a care rested on his shoulders. Here, away from the track, the pressure, and the people, he was at ease; a deeper ease I hadn't seen before. I wanted that—to forget it all for a moment and simply exist. I took in the deserted beach. The dog walker had gone. If there was ever a time to relax freely, it was now.

I unzipped my dress and pulled it over my head. I'd worn my bikini underneath, a simple black bikini with secure straps —sexy but still practical for swimming. I slipped my shoes off and left my stuff in a pile next to Aiden's clothes and towels. My toes sunk into the soft sand and the grains were warm between my toes. I started to run, chasing him down and quickly catching him.

"Keep up!" I shouted as I ran straight for the sea.

He shouted in surprise. I looked over my shoulder to see him speeding after me. My footsteps struck damp sand, where the sea had recently lapped, and then my feet hit the shallow waves. Water splashed and hands grabbed me from behind.

"Gotcha!"

"I still beat you to the sea!" I said, slowing my pace as the water reached my knees. It was cool against my warm skin, but I kept going, getting used to the temperature.

We both waded in until we could kick our feet off the bottom and swim. The waves rolled in gently against the shore, and my arms and legs cut through the clear blue.

We swam for a few minutes, going further out, but kept the beach in sight. Together, we came to a spot and treaded water, our bodies bobbing up and down with the movement of the waves.

"This was a good plan," I said, pushing my wet hair back out of my face.

"Told you."

"Try not to be too smug about it." I splashed him and he splashed me back. I went to splash him again, but he reached for my hand and pulled my body against his in the water. My legs entwined with his, and he brushed a finger down my cheek, leaving a trail of water droplets behind. I wrapped my arms around his neck and pulled his lips to mine. We kissed with no one but the sea to witness, the sun high above us and a gentle breeze brushing against us.

THIRTY-SIX

MONACO

THE SUMMER BREAK

He'd love to tell everyone Winter Jones was his girlfriend, but for now, they'd keep the labels to themselves. One day, he'd get to shout about it, he hoped.

WE RACED back to the shore, and this time, he won our mini swimming competition. His smug smile was on full display, but he was a more gracious winner than I would have been. It was one of his many qualities that I loved. He enjoyed a good competition as much as I did, but he never seemed intimidated by me, never worried about losing to a girl, and was not threatened by my racing achievements or attitude. He was challenged by me but in a good way. Everything I threw at him on- and off-track, he met head-on, on equal ground. Maybe we weren't rivals after all but were partners playing a game together and enjoying every second of it.

Aiden wrapped one big towel around both of us, my body pressed against his as he rubbed us both down. He laid out the other towel, and we stretched out on it, letting the sun dry us off.

We looked out at the bay at the cloudless blue sky.

"Thank you," I said, looking over at him.

"For what?"

"For bringing me here. For inviting me over. For suggesting I come to Monaco."

"I was being selfish. I didn't want to go four weeks without seeing you."

I smiled and then leaned in for a quick kiss.

"I'm going to get sand in your clean, shiny sportscar," I whispered, pulling back from his lips.

He laughed.

WE RETURNED to Aiden's place, showered together in his massive walk-in shower, and he gave me a pair of boxers and a T-shirt to wear. He made us dinner and I watched him carefully prepare our meal in his kitchen. He kept looking up and catching me watching. He'd smile every time and then go back to chopping vegetables. I felt so comfortable in his home, sitting on his couch with a glass in my hand. I could get used to this.

I got up from his couch and started to roam his living space, taking in the details of his home. He watched me from the kitchen as I picked up a book from his coffee table. The title read *River Kings* and I looked up at him.

"Viking history?" I asked, raising an eyebrow.

"It's really interesting," he replied and went back to his cooking.

I smiled, put the book back on the table, and continued my exploration. I traced a light finger on the edge of the big picture frame on the wall. The painting was an abstract piece with bold blocks of different colours: blue, grey, and black. As I came to the end of the painting, I paused at a small side table. He had a collection of photo frames arranged on the table. In the middle of them was a family photograph, with a young Aiden in the middle, both his parents on either side of him, all smiling at the camera. I could tell from his dad's posture that he was hunching slightly; he must have been very tall. His pale skin was crinkled around his eyes and his brown hair had a grey streak. His mum's smile was beautiful, her face framed by thick black curls.

Aiden came over to me and placed a gentle hand on my back. "Dinner is almost ready."

"Will your mum be at any of the races after the break?" I asked. I hadn't seen her at any of the tracks, but Aiden had said she'd gone travelling this year with a friend.

"She's still on a cruise but might make the season's last race." He smiled down at the photo. "She's been to all the races before, though, and I'm happy she's travelling and getting to do something that's just for her."

"That's an idea! I wonder if I can convince my mum to go on a yearlong cruise."

He laughed.

After dinner, we watched a movie but turned it off halfway through when neither of us could keep our hands off each other. Over an hour later, I was curled up in Aiden's bed, his arms wrapped around me, feeling tired but content. We cuddled in the darkness, knowing we should sleep but not yet ready to say goodnight. I realised I could get used to this, used to spending my whole day with him, laughing, talking, being near each other.

His arms tightened around me; my back pressed against his chest. His nose trailed up and down my neck. I shivered at the sensation. We should have slept. My body was exhausted, but at the same time, I couldn't get enough of him.

"I know it's probably too soon, but I have to say it, get it out," he whispered in my ear. "I think I'm falling in love with you."

I froze. For a moment, I couldn't reply; I couldn't admit my feelings out loud, even though I knew them to be true. I'd known it for some time and wanted to pretend otherwise, but Aiden had found a way into my heart. I let out a long breath. I could do this. I could step off the cliff of uncertainty.

"I feel the same," I whispered into the dark. They were the only words I could get out, could allow myself to voice.

His arms lightly squeezed me again and I knew he understood. Eventually, I'd be ready to use the word "love", but I wasn't there yet.

"And I want more, even though I'm nervous to ask. I don't know what you want. You're not always the easiest to read," he said against my neck. It was like here, in the dark, we could admit our feelings and fears.

I let out a nervous breath. "I want more too, but I didn't expect to want more. This wasn't part of the plan. I wasn't looking for a relationship and wasn't meant to want one."

He let go of my middle and shifted in the bed. His hand reached for mine and I turned to face him. Only a little sliver of light slipped through his blinds. I could just make out the features of his face.

"What do you mean by that?"

"I went through a bad breakup last year and was just done. So done. I wanted to focus on my career and forget anything else. My plan was to race and win, and that was it."

"What happened?"

"We drifted apart long before we actually broke up, but I

think it happened so slowly I didn't realise. There were signs but I ignored them and made excuses. I don't think he ever understood my love of racing. When we first started dating, he loved it. I was his cool girlfriend, the one who raced cars, and he loved telling his friends that. As the years went on, he got tired of all my constant travelling, tired of everything that came with a life of motorsport: the early morning gym sessions, the training, the sponsor events. I missed birthdays and important events."

"You can't help where the race calendar falls. It's not like you could miss a race weekend for a party."

"You say that because you get it. You're from this world. Athletes understand the dedication it takes to compete. He wasn't a sportsperson and he didn't get it."

"And I'm guessing motorsport being historically a very masculine-dominated sport and industry didn't help either?"

"No, it didn't. As the years went by, I stopped being the 'cool girl' with an interesting job. He didn't understand my passion. It wasn't a job to me: it was my life, my dream. I wanted to race in F1 and I wasn't going to stop trying to reach the top level of motorsport. Not ever. Not for him."

"What? He asked you to stop racing?" His voice became a whisper.

"Not exactly, but I knew that's what he wanted. He kept telling me F1 was never going to happen. *Not every driver makes it to F1.* Too many drivers competing for too few race seats, which is true: it's unbelievably competitive. In the end, it all came to a head when I had to miss his parents' big anniversary party because I had a race. I think he wanted me to make a choice and I chose racing."

"Good. Now you're winning races and leading the Championship. I really hope someone is shoving that in his face."

I laughed. "My mum sometimes bumps into his mum at the supermarket and I'm pretty sure she drops it into every conversation. Then again, she drops my career into every conversation with anyone she meets."

He chuckled. "But I get it, though. Why you weren't looking for anything serious."

"I wasted years on him. I didn't want to get into another relationship, and maybe I was scared of putting myself out there again. Or scared of finding someone only for them not to understand me, but..." I trailed off, still trying to figure everything out in my head.

"But?"

"I like you and I know it would be different with us. You get me. I know that. Except there are other concerns."

"How us being together would affect our racing careers."

"Exactly. Who knows how our teams would react? How the wider racing world would respond? The media? The fans? And I still don't have a contract for next season."

He took hold of my hand and squeezed. "It might be time to call your agent and put some pressure on them to secure you a contract."

"Has Théo Laurent announced his retirement plans yet?"

"No, not unless he has in the last few hours. It's probably still too early in the season to announce it."

"I thought Torrin would have extended my contract by now, at the very least." I sighed.

"Same. I wonder what they're playing at? You're leading in Championship points. You'd think they'd be keen to get you signed for next season before another team snaps you up."

"I don't know what's going on."

"Call your agent tomorrow. Put some pressure on them to secure you a race seat for next year. If they can't, you'll find someone else who can."

I nodded. "And us?"

He wrapped his arms around my middle and put his forehead to mine. "For now, we keep this between us: whatever this is, we don't have to put a label on it if you don't want to or if you're not ready to. We keep us private for as long as possible, or at least until you secure a seat for next year. I get your concerns about how people will react. We don't need that kind of outside pressure. We don't have to rush. We can take our time, learn more about each other while also fighting on the track for wins."

"I like the sound of that, but I don't mind putting a label on us. If you want?" I smiled.

"Really?"

"I guess I could call you my boyfriend. Obviously, not in front of anyone if we're keeping this private, but I don't mind the way it sounds," I said in a teasing tone.

"And I can call you my girlfriend? Just between you and me."

"Sure." We both grinned at each other like a couple of lovesick teenagers.

It felt silly—boyfriend and girlfriend—because what was between us felt so much more than those simple titles.

His arms pulled me tighter against his body. I snuggled against him, getting comfortable again.

He leaned closer, his lips brushing against my ear.

"Goodnight, girlfriend."

THIRTY-SEVEN

BELGIUM

SUNDAY - RACE DAY

Some days, he'd wake up and feel off. He knew this was a common experience for many, especially for superstitious racing drivers. There was never a particular reason why he felt off. He'd wake up, and something felt wrong, and as the morning progressed, small things wouldn't go to plan, tiny insignificant moments, like dropping his toothbrush, putting his T-shirt on back to front, or forgetting to charge his phone, but they all added up. This would throw him off even more, and that's when he'd find himself spiralling.

Qualifying Report
Pole – Winter Jones
2nd – Aiden Sterling
3rd – Satoru Hayashi

ON RACE DAY, I woke up next to Aiden. My six o'clock alarm vibrated my phone on the bedside table. Reaching out an arm, I hit "end", and then Aiden pulled me back against his chest into a tight hug.

"I have to go," I said.

"Five more minutes."

"Better not push our luck."

Gem had helped arrange for me to spend my nights in Aiden's hotel room, but I needed to get back before anyone noticed. Gem was proving to have some top-level sneaky skills. She could switch careers and work in the Secret Service if she ever got sick of personal training.

"You're probably right. I need to get down to the paddock early anyway," he said, and his arms relaxed from around me.

"Why?"

"The team's PR manager arranged an interview with a Belgian reporter."

"On race day? Before the race?"

"I know." He shook his head and sat up, grabbing his phone from the side. "Damn. Forgot to charge it last night." He sighed.

"You okay?" I asked as I got up and reached for my clothes on the floor. "You could refuse the interview or try to rearrange it," I said as I quickly changed, tugging my jeans on in a hurry.

"I don't want to cause a fuss. I also agreed to do an interview with Astrid Carlson, but we haven't settled on a date yet. I keep pushing it back."

"Wait! An interview with Astrid Carlson?"

"Yes."

"Why would you push that back? She's only the best and most well-respected sports journalist around and so knowledgeable on F1. I'd love to do an interview with her," I said, thinking about what it would be like to sit down with her. She'd interviewed all the greats. She was the last journalist to interview

Hartman before he tragically crashed in 1982. It was still early in her career back then, and she was one of only a few women breaking into motorsport journalism.

He shrugged and got out of bed. "I don't know. I'm over all the interviews. Not in the head space for them."

He headed for the bathroom, his posture stiff. I was about to call him back and ask if something was wrong when my phone started ringing. The screen flashed with my agent's name.

"Hey Jean, any news?"

"Torrin won't budge yet," she replied.

"Why? What's holding them back? You said you'd get my contract sorted before the end of summer break! It's been weeks! Is it the money that's stopping them?"

"No. They want to wait until the last quarter of the season. That's all they'll tell me. I'm sorry, Winter."

"That's bullshit!" I snapped. "What about other teams? Maybe if I get an offer from another team, Torrin will hurry to sign me for next year."

"I had an offer from Ziegler."

"Ziegler! Really? They're at the back of the field. Their car has been shit this season and I don't see that changing for next year!"

"I'm sorry, Winter. All the top teams have drivers with a minimum of two- or three-year contracts," she explained, and I had to fight the urge to tell her that wasn't true, that soon Cavallo would have an open spot when Théo Laurent announced his retirement. "Waiting for Torrin is our best option. They will offer you a contract for next year, I'm sure of it; we just need to be patient."

"Maybe I should speak to Michael and just ask him face to face what's holding it up," I suggested.

"No, that's not how it's done. I will sort this out."

I sighed. "Okay, okay."

"And when Torrin comes to me, I'll make sure to negotiate a Championship fee for your new contract. Trust me. I've got this."

"I haven't won yet. There's still the rest of the season to go."

She made a dismissive sound down the phone. "You've got this. I'll talk to you later." She hung up.

"Ugh." I threw my phone down on the bed.

"Not good news then." I turned to find Aiden leaning against the doorframe. He'd obviously heard most of my conversation.

"No." I sighed, reaching for my phone and sliding it into my back pocket. "Maybe that will change after today's race. There are only six races left. Why won't Torrin hurry up and re-sign me?"

"Maybe you should consider telling your agent about Théo Laurent's retirement."

"But you said I should wait for his announcement."

"Yeah, I did, but you need the security of knowing you've got a seat. Ask your agent if she can keep a secret."

I laughed and shook my head. "I already know she can't. I'll wait until after this race. Maybe if I win this one, Torrin will finally ready the paperwork."

"What is it like to be that confident? So sure you're going to beat me and win?" he asked, quirking a brow.

"Hah! Says you! You're just as confident and self-assured."

"Not the way you are," he replied, the humour gone from his expression. "You just have it all under control." He walked over and pulled me into his arms in a tight hug. He only released me so he could kiss me, hard and deep, like he wasn't sure when he'd next get to kiss me.

When we broke the kiss, I grabbed his hand and gave it a squeeze. "Sure you're alright?" I asked again.

"Sure." He squeezed my hand in return.

"Okay, if you're sure. I should go. I'll see you on the track. In my mirrors!" I teased.

THIRTY-EIGHT

BELGIUM

SUNDAY - RACE DAY

The imposter syndrome never went away, no matter how hard he worked, how many races he won or how many Championship titles he had. Three world titles and it still wasn't enough for the niggling doubt. The imposter was always there in the background ready to strike him when he found himself low, ready to eat away at him and tell him how worthless and useless he was.

AS USUAL, fans packed the stands and the grid was a frenzy of activity. I stood beside Gem, not too far from my car, my team surrounding it.

Benjamin walked by and paused to say hello.

"Winter." He gave me a polite nod.

"Hey Benjamin, how's it going?"

"Good, good," he said as someone in his team colours beckoned him over to a camera crew. "Sorry, gotta go, catch up later?"

"Sure!" I shouted as he headed over to a reporter and started answering questions.

"Hey, Winter! Guess what?" Hayashi appeared almost out of nowhere, taking the spot where Benjamin had been standing moments ago.

"What's up?"

He looked around, his eyes flicking over the crowded paddock, and then he leaned in closer to me.

"I stole Benjamin's lucky socks," he whispered to me.

"What?"

"Shhh... I don't want him to find out." He hushed me, and I leaned in closer. "I switched his lucky socks with an almost identical pair before summer break. It was an experiment to test your theory on how it was all superstition. Benjamin qualified well yesterday, so I guess you were right all along."

"Hmm..." I suddenly felt bad for taking away their belief in good luck charms. "Unless the new socks are also lucky."

He laughed and headed for the top of the grid where the drivers would gather for the national anthem.

"You will need to explain what the hell that was about. Lucky socks?" Gem asked.

"I'll tell you later," I replied, glancing up and down the track. It was still packed with teams, camera crews, reporters, and VIP guests, but we didn't have long until the start. "Have you seen Aiden?" I asked.

She frowned and looked around the busy grid, searching the faces of Aiden's team. They crowded around his car, working on it, checking everything over.

"No, but we've not got long now." She looked down at her watch. "We've got about ten minutes until the national anthem."

"Where is he?" I kept looking up and down, checking to see if any of the TV crews were interviewing him.

"I saw him get out of his car on the grid, but after that, I don't know. I haven't seen him since. Was there something wrong this morning?" Gem asked, looking concerned.

"I don't know." I thought about this morning. Maybe he seemed more on edge than usual; there was a tension in him, but he didn't say anything to me.

Gem elbowed me.

"What?"

"Someone is trying to get our attention," she whispered in my ear, and I followed her eyeline to where Josh, Aiden's trainer, stood not too far from the walkway to the paddock.

He subtly tilted his head towards the paddock.

"I think he wants to talk to us," Gem said. I looked back at her with a frown. Josh had made it clear he didn't like me very much. "Come on, let's see what he wants. Head for the paddock; I'll tell Ash we're going for a quick bathroom break."

She elbowed me again before dashing over to where Ash stood with Michael next to the car. I went towards the walkway. Josh turned before I could reach him and started walking ahead. Gem caught up to me and we both followed Josh. He paused briefly.

"What's going on?" I asked him.

"Follow me to the team motorhomes."

"We've not got long until the race starts!"

"I'm well aware, thanks." He turned and continued into the paddock area at a fast pace.

"So charming," Gem said, but I hurried forward, heading towards the shiny glass-fronted Torrin Motorhome. This close to the race, there were still plenty of people around. I paced towards where Josh stood beside the Silvers's motorhome. Gem shadowed me.

"What's going on? I'm getting worried now," I asked in a hushed voice.

"He's down there. He won't listen to me. You're my last resort." He tilted his head to the gap between the Torrin motorhome and the Silvers's.

"Okay," I replied, feeling uneasy.

He reached for my arm. "I'm sorry about the way I acted towards you before. I was just looking out for him."

"I get that. You were trying to be a good friend, but you should know I'm not a distraction and I care about him too."

"I know that now and I'm sorry."

I went down the gap. There were a few emergency exit doors and I avoided a couple of cables sticking out of the side of Torrin. At the end, I turned the corner to Silvers's side and found Aiden sitting on the ground, his back leaning against the motorhome.

"Hey," I said, and he looked up at me. I could see the stress lining his face and how he held his shoulders, tense and rigid. The easy, relaxed expression he wore at every race had gone.

"Josh shouldn't have gotten you."

"What's going on?" I asked as I sat down beside him.

"You're going to miss the race," he said, not answering my question.

"So are you, but we still have a little time. They haven't done the anthem yet. I wouldn't mind missing that, though."

He sighed but still wouldn't answer me.

"What would they do if two of the drivers didn't show up, especially the two on the front row?" I asked.

He shrugged. "Probably get fined."

"I don't know what's going on. You don't have to tell me, but I'm here."

"You shouldn't stay. You'll miss the race," he repeated, both his hands gripping his knees, his knuckles sharp.

"So will you!"

He lifted both hands from his knees and they shook ever-so-slightly. He flexed his fingers once, twice, before balling them into fists at his side.

"I want to explain," he said.

"You can later, after the race."

"Leave me here." He shook his head.

"Really? I thought you had plans to beat me this weekend?"

He clenched his jaw, not replying.

"There is no race without you. There's no race for me if you're not there pushing me to my limits. I need you on the front row lined up beside me." I got to my feet and held my hand out to him. "Please?"

A moment passed and it felt like the seconds slowed down, a painful beat of time. Finally, he placed his hand in mine and stood up.

"Sure?" I asked.

"Yes."

I nodded and we both walked back down the gap. His hand slipped from mine as we emerged into the paddock. Gem and Josh greeted us there. The four of us split up and made our way back to the grid just in time.

* * *

THE RACE DIDN'T GO AS PLANNED: not for me and Torrin, or Aiden and the Silvers team.

Satoru Hayashi won his first race with the Stewart team. The Stewart car had been in the midfield most of the season, but in recent races, they'd upgraded the car, and Hayashi had been finishing closer to the top of the grid. Or perhaps Benjamin's socks really were lucky.

Some weekends didn't go your way and there was nothing anyone could do about it. The team made a bad call with my pitstops, then a car went off-track and the safety car came out. A bit of bad luck. I went from first down to fourth, but I managed to fight my way back up to second and kept my tyres in good condition. I wasn't the only driver with bad luck. When I fell back, so did Aiden, but he disappeared, slipping further back down the order. Instead of silver, my mirrors were full of my teammate's blue and red car. Stefan hounded me until the very last second of the race. Even when the chequered flag fell, he came up beside me, still on my back.

I tried to ignore Stefan and instead focused on celebrating Hayashi's first win. I kept to myself in the cool-down room and didn't speak a word to Stefan. The cameras were still on us and there were microphones too. I didn't trust myself to speak in case I said something I didn't want to be recorded and sent out live to the entire world.

On the podium, I couldn't avoid Stefan. After receiving our trophies, he sprayed me with champagne, looking happy about our team's successful comeback during the race. I played along, spraying him back, smiling and cheering with the team below the podium, but my mind was elsewhere. I wanted to know where Aiden had finished and if he'd been okay during the race. I wanted to get this performance over with.

We all posed for photographs—the top three—with Hayashi in the middle, Stefan on his left and me on his right. Hayashi had no idea about the tension between Stefan and me: he was too busy enjoying his win, holding his trophy up for everyone to see.

After the photographs, Stefan caught me before I could escape.

"You were a bit late to the track earlier. Not very professional of you," Stefan said.

"You're the last person I'd take advice from on how to be a

professional racing driver," I replied, pushing past him and heading straight for the exit.

———

Championship Driver Standings

Winter Jones – 226

Aiden Sterling – 201

Stefan Brudes – 170

THIRTY-NINE

BELGIUM

SUNDAY - AFTER THE RACE

Sometimes, he felt like who he was on the inside didn't match up with how he appeared on the outside. Maybe it was his own fault. He'd spent years carefully curating himself so he could be the perfect racing driver on-track and off-track, too. There weren't many who knew his real self: only the select few he let in.

THE DAY FELT ENDLESS; the interviews after the race seemed to drag and the team debrief took forever. I swore Stefan had more to say about this race than all the previous races put together. Usually, he didn't speak at all, maybe a handful of yeses and nos, but not this time. It's as if he knew I had somewhere else I wanted to be. Our strategist's words went over my head, a muddled jumble of track times and pit stops. I knew I should concentrate, stay focused, but I couldn't stop my mind going elsewhere.

When I was finally able to leave the circuit, I headed

straight back to my hotel, changed quickly, and sent a message to Aiden. He was already back in his hotel room. As soon as I'd changed, I went over to his.

"Hey," he said, answering the door and letting me inside.

As soon as the door closed, I pulled him into a hug. "I'm sorry about your race," I said into his neck.

"The team made a bad call with my pitstops," he replied, his arms wrapped around me. "I should probably explain about earlier," he added and I could feel him tense.

I let my arms slip from around him and took a step back. "You don't have to explain if you don't want to or if you're not ready to share."

"No, I want to. You're a part of my life. You should know." He rubbed the back of his head.

I moved to his bed and sat down.

"I suffer from anxiety. This year was meant to be different. I thought I'd finally got a handle on it, but it crept up on me today after that stupid interview." He sat down next to me. "I've always suffered from it; that, and imposter syndrome. I've always felt this pressure on my shoulders, even as a kid messing around in a go-kart. Pressure to perform, be better than my peers and show everyone what I could achieve."

He shifted slightly but I stayed quiet, giving him time to speak.

"I didn't think much of it as a kid. Everyone gets nervous before a race. It was just part of the sport, but the anxiety got worse after my dad passed away. I was getting through it, grieving but doing okay, dealing with it all, going about life, and then all of a sudden, it felt like I couldn't breathe, like everything was bearing down on me. I felt like I'd let my dad down. I'd reached F1, but I got there too late. Dad passed away months before I signed for a seat in F1. It wasn't just my dream to be an F1 driver: it was his dream, too, to see me in F1. If only I'd gotten there faster."

"But..." I started.

"I know. I know it's stupid, and I know he was proud of me, but I can't help putting pressure on myself to do more, get further, and achieve more and faster. Be a role model. Be inspiring to kids who look like me. I needed to be perfect, the best version of myself. I thought things would get better after I won my first Championship. Like I'd done it, I could relax now. I no longer had to prove myself or justify my place in F1. The next race season, the anxiety got worse, not better, and the imposter syndrome hit harder; winning my second Championship came at a cost to my mental health. But after winning my third World Championship title, I thought I'd turned a corner. It hadn't been as bad that year. I spent the last winter break in therapy and just trying to disconnect from everything and get the pressure off. I wanted to finally be free of it. That's why I didn't recognise you at the start of this season. I stayed away from all media. Josh ran my socials and I ignored the news; I ignored everything. Josh only told me what I needed to know while I worked on myself, both mentally and physically. I focused on prepping for the new season because when I'm focused on racing, on the driving and only the driving, I'm fine. When I'm in the car, I'm good. It's all the other stuff—interviews, media, the race build-up—it adds onto the pressure I already put on myself."

"Is that why you missed the media session in Silverstone?"

"Yes."

"But you're so good at interviews. You're so good with journalists and reporters, so professional but natural and charming. That first drivers' briefing at the start of the season, I thought you were perfect and I was jealous of you, at how good at it you were."

"On the outside, it looks that way." He sighed. "It's not been as bad this season, partly thanks to therapy and reducing media interactions. I'm still trying to figure out my boundaries and then stick to them, but it's easier in theory than in practice."

"I get that, and it probably doesn't help that everyone wants to talk to the three-time World Champion. It's hard to say no, too."

"Exactly, and I don't like letting people down. This year has been better on the whole. I haven't been so caught up in my own head. Add that to my regular therapy sessions, less media shit and Josh handling my training: I've felt so good this season. I felt like I'd finally overcome it. Then this morning hit, and it felt ten times worse because I'd fooled myself into thinking it wouldn't happen again."

"I'm sorry," I said, not knowing what else to say.

"Don't be."

"Thank you for trusting me with this."

"Only my manager, my therapist, Josh, and my mum know about my anxiety. I know people are far more open with their mental health these days, but I think the sporting world still has a long way to go. I'd rather people didn't know. Look at how that tennis player was treated when she refused to do interviews after a match because of her mental health. In the end, her sport fined her for not showing up," he said.

My heart broke for him, for the fined tennis star, for every sportsperson who ever had to hide their health problems in fear of being treated differently or in fear of losing their career in the sport they'd dedicated their life to.

"I get it. You know I won't tell anyone. If there's anything I can do, then let me know?"

"Carry on being you. I don't want this to change us. I still want to see that face you make whenever I tease you," he replied, a smile tugging at his lips.

"What face? I don't make a face!"

He laughed. "That one."

"I'm not—"

He cut me off by pressing his lips to mine. I got lost in the kiss for a moment but slowly pulled back. One of my hands reached for his and I squeezed it. "I need to ask this—will us sneaking around, trying to keep this private, add to the pressure?"

"No. No way. This, us..." He gestured at us with his free hand. "We are separate from all of that. We might race together, or rather against each other, but us being together is something different, something that's ours. You, us, is not a problem here. Okay?"

I felt like he had to say that last part to make sure I understood.

I nodded.

"You're not going to go easy on me on the track now, are you?" he asked. The very edges of his lips quirked as he fought a teasing grin.

I scoffed. "You wish! The Championship is mine!"

"Don't get ahead of yourself. I'm not that far behind you in points."

"The important word in your statement is 'behind', and that is where you will stay." I teased.

He leaned in and kissed me hard. When he pulled back, he left me gasping for air.

"We'll see. Rookie drivers always slip up at some point."

I got up and moved to straddle him. "Like you said, we'll see about that."

FORTY

THE NETHERLANDS
SATURDAY - QUALIFYING

There was a special place in racing driver hell for arseholes like Stefan Brudes.

MY PHONE STARTED RINGING as I put my shoes on. I'd stayed in Aiden's hotel room again and was getting ready to leave.

"News?" I asked, using my new way of answering Jean's calls, which she was used to by this point.

"Yes, I have news," she replied, and I held my breath, waiting for her next words. "I'm very close to securing a deal with Torrin for next year. A two-year contract."

I exhaled. "How much longer before it's a done deal?"

"Not long, I promise. All we need to work out is pay. This is the final stage."

"Thank you." I wanted to say more, the relief wanting to burst out of me.

222

"Since you're still leading the Championship, you should be paid a Championship fee," Jean said.

"I agree, but I also want to make sure I have a drive for next year. Don't push them too far, Jean," I warned her, my relief vanishing. It wasn't done until the contracts were signed.

"I know what I'm doing. Everything is under control."

"Call me when it's agreed?"

"For sure!" She hung up.

As I put my phone into my bag, Aiden came out of the bathroom.

"Was it Jean?"

"Yes," I replied and told him everything she had told me.

He pulled me into a hug. "Maybe we should go public after you've signed your new contract."

I pulled back from the hug and looked up at him.

"I think we should wait until the end of this season. It could take Torrin that long to settle on my new contract. I think it's better to wait until the winter break when there's less of a spotlight on us. I can already imagine what the press will say." That I slept my way to the top. Or that Aiden and I helped each other out on the track.

"People will talk no matter what, but we can wait until after the end of the season. It's getting harder to keep this a secret, though. I want to hold your hand and kiss you in public."

"Hold my hand?"

"Yeah." He smiled and pulled my hand into his, entwining our fingers.

"You're such a softy. The three-time Formula One World Champion wants to hold hands?" I teased.

"Just to be clear, only your hand. And a person can have many different interests." He grinned, leaned in, and kissed me.

THE DUTCH CIRCUIT was packed with fans, every stand at full capacity, and a heavy dance beat played on speakers around the track. The atmosphere pulsed with energy. The Dutch fans really knew how to start a party.

I'd gotten into the last round of Qualifying. The car felt good on this track and my team put a fresh set of soft tyres on before the last Qualifying session started. My car waited in the garage, my team working around me. Stefan's car sat in the bay next to mine. He'd also made it into the last part of Qualifying. As soon as the final session started, the team released his car first and he headed straight out onto the track. I followed him down the pit lane and onto the circuit.

I managed to put in a couple of fast laps. Aiden, Stefan, and I battled it out for pole position, all of us trying to get around the track in the fastest time. One of us would post the quickest lap, only for the next one to steal it from them.

With less than a minute left of the session, I was halfway around the track on a hot lap, trying to beat everyone else to pole position. I started to catch the car in front of me and as I got closer, I recognised the familiar team colours. It was Stefan, but he didn't look like he was on a quick lap like I was. I kept my pace. If he was heading back to the pits, he should let me by so I could finish my final Qualifying time.

But of course, he didn't let me pass. He sped up, trying to keep in front of me, but I wasn't going to let him ruin my best lap. I kept pushing, and down the straight, I moved to get past him, and then he swerved in the breaking zone. My reflexes reacted on impulse, and I veered off to avoid him. My car went wide at the next corner, sliding over the white lines. I swore as I re-joined the track. Stefan pulled ahead of me. We both continued our laps, but I knew the near-miss had ruined my lap time.

"Did you see that?" I said over the radio to Ash as I crossed the finish line. The last Qualifying session had ended, and there was no time left for me to do another fast run.

"Yes."

"What the hell was he doing? He cost me my lap! Who's on pole?"

"Stefan," Ash replied, his voice clipped.

"Fuck! He did that on purpose!" I shouted, not caring that the live TV coverage had access to all the drivers' radio transmissions. "Where am I on the grid for tomorrow?"

"Box the car."

I wanted to scream down the radio. Instead, I carried on to the pits.

Back in the garage, I got out of the car in a state of rage. All I could think about was Stefan's dirty driving on the track. The rush of racing still pulsed through my body and I had no outlet for it. I glanced at one of the screens showing the TV coverage. All the drivers' final Qualifying lap times went down the left side of the screen in a list. I spotted my name with the fourth fastest time. I'd start fourth on the grid for tomorrow's race. Matias da Silveira had secured third place, Aiden had second, and my cheating teammate had pole position. The camera cut to Stefan looking pleased with his result, smirking and running his fingers through his messy hair.

Yanking my gloves off, I chucked them back into my car as the team worked on it. No one spoke to me and I couldn't see Ash anywhere. I tugged my helmet off and gripped it under my arm. Maybe I could throw it at Stefan. My feet started moving without any thought, heading towards the pit lane, knowing exactly where Stefan would be. I'd tell him what I thought of him and his dangerous driving. It wasn't just about how he ruined my lap time; I could have crashed, we both could have crashed, and in this high-speed sport, any accident could be your last. There was no room for errors in Formula One and there was no place for reckless drivers like Stefan. He'd risked both of us.

I got to the garage doorway, about to step out into the pit lane, when someone grabbed my hand and I turned to find Gem. Her fingers tightened around mine in a vice-like grip.

"Don't," she said, her voice low.

"I'm—" I began, but she cut me off.

"I know that look, but don't. Do not act in anger. Not when you're straight out of the car. Walk away. A scene is what Stefan wants. Don't give him the satisfaction."

"I could have crashed, Gem!" I shouted, pulling on her hand, but she kept me in place.

"I know, but this isn't the way." Her hand tightened even more and she held my gaze, her face calm but determined. A moment passed between us. The world continued as we stood there, the team working in the garage, the fans cheering in the stands, and music playing from a speaker outside the pits. I could feel the fast beat of my heart in my chest and the firm, steady hold of Gem's hand.

"Okay," I breathed.

Gem nodded, but she didn't release me. "Carry on as normal. It's another Qualifying result. Not the result you were aiming for, but you can come back stronger in the race."

I nodded along to her words and Gem loosened her grip on me.

"Ash is with Michael. Let him fight this one for you, away from the cameras. The team or the stewards will deal with Stefan. Okay?"

"Okay," I repeated, and she finally let go of my hand. I took in a deep breath. "Thank you."

"Anytime," she replied, and we both went back into the garage.

HOURS LATER, I felt more grounded: still angry, but not so on edge, not so clouded by adrenalin and rage that I'd do something stupid. Almost every part of the race weekend was captured by live cameras, not to mention the journalists and fans everywhere. Nothing went unnoticed at race weekends. No one could avoid the gossip and politics. I was so lucky to have Gem. She knew me so well, and she knew if I sounded off at Stefan, even if I was in the right, there would be negative backlash and questions asked of me. It would fan the flames instead of dampening them.

Ash wanted to make a formal complaint to the race stewards about Stefan's dangerous driving, but Michael insisted the incident would be handled internally by the team and he would speak to Stefan himself. I wanted to go to the stewards, too, but I also didn't want to go against Michael's decision. Not when I still hadn't secured my race seat for next season. Jean was so close to getting me that contract, so I couldn't risk messing that up.

Right now, it looked like Stefan would get away with it. I doubt he'd take much notice of Michael's talk. Stefan did whatever he wanted and got away with it, over and over again. I didn't understand why. Sure, he was an adequate racing driver and experienced, but he'd never won a Championship and he was still behind me in points. Why did everyone let his poor behaviour slide? Then I remembered his friendship with the Torrin team owner. Perhaps that was why.

After all the interviews and a long chat with Ash, Gem and I returned to the team motorhome for dinner. She kept a close eye on me even though I reassured her that I'd calmed down. I wouldn't do anything reckless. There was nothing I could do now anyway. Michael had spoken: end of discussion. I hadn't seen Stefan since Qualifying. Perhaps he had some awareness of what he'd done. The atmosphere in the motorhome felt subdued—not the response you'd expect from a team with a car in pole position for tomorrow's race.

Team members ate their dinner in a near-silent state. Two of our strategists worked on their laptops while they ate, muttering a few words to each other between mouthfuls. I continued to chase a piece of melon around my bowl. Gem had finished her meal five minutes ago, her plate and bowl discarded to one side, as she looked down at her phone instead. Probably messaging her girlfriend and explaining what happened today. Emily watched F1 but she wasn't a hardcore fan. Gem often had to explain the politics of the sport to her.

Reyna came down the stairs from the offices and headed straight to our table. She took the empty seat beside me, placing her trusty tablet down on the table before her.

"I'm sorry about today," she said in a hushed voice.

I was about to tell her not to apologise for Stefan when shouting came from outside. Every head in the room looked up at the same time. The shouting continued, getting louder.

"What's going on?" Reyna asked.

One of the strategists abandoned his laptop and walked to the main doors. They slid open and I heard Aiden's voice. I dropped my fork into my bowl with a clatter, and suddenly, everyone in the motorhome was rushing to see what was going on outside.

Qualifying Report

Pole – Stefan Brudes

2nd – Aiden Sterling

3rd – Matias da Silveira

4th – Winter Jones

FORTY-ONE

THE NETHERLANDS

SATURDAY - AFTER QUALIFYING

He really wanted to punch his smug face. Consequences be damned.

I PUSHED through the small crowd that had formed at the motorhome doorway with Gem right behind me. Squeezing past one of Stefan's engineers, I stepped outside to find Aiden and Stefan facing off. Benjamin held Stefan back; he was shorter than Stefan, but he gripped his left shoulder. Josh put an arm out to hold Aiden back. Some of Aiden's team gathered behind him, like backup, all in their Silvers team colours. Stefan's trainer stood beside him, a smirk on his lips, making no attempt to intervene.

"You bastard!" Aiden shouted.

"I don't know what you're on about," Stefan said, his voice cool.

"You swerved in the breaking zone. It's a cheap, desperate move, and you know it!"

"I was nowhere near you on-track during Quali." Stefan shrugged; the very edges of his lips twitched like he was trying not to smile.

"I'm not talking about me, you fucking idiot!" Aiden pushed against Josh's arm, trying to get closer to Stefan.

My heart started beating double at his words and my palms became clammy. Gem pushed her way to me.

"This isn't good," Gem whispered in my ear. I shook my head.

Reyna squeezed through to stand at my other shoulder. "What's going on?" she asked again, looking at Stefan and Aiden.

"Then who are you talking about?" Stefan asked, and his gaze darted to me. He smirked.

"She could have crashed because of you!"

Stefan shrugged again and Aiden lunged for him. His hand reached out for Stefan, his fingers skimming the front of Stefan's race suit before Josh pushed him back. Josh didn't give Aiden a chance to fight back. Josh gripped his shoulder and pulled him away from Stefan and the crowd. Together, they disappeared into the Silvers motorhome.

"Shit," Gem muttered.

"He knows," I whispered. My heart pounded in my chest. I didn't know how, but Stefan knew about Aidan and me. He had to. It's why he kept looking at me and smirking. Why else would he provoke Aiden in this way?

"Who knows? And what?" Reyna asked, looking at me and then Gem.

The crowd began to disperse, but Stefan remained in the middle of the paddock. Our gazes locked for a second and he threw me a crooked smile.

"Come on. Let's get out of here," Gem said.

We headed back inside the Torrin motorhome, the dining

area now full of loud chatter as everyone started to discuss what had gone on between Stefan and Aiden. A few pairs of eyes landed on me.

"Upstairs, both of you. I want to know what just happened," Reyna said to me and Gem in a hushed voice. "I know something is going on."

Gem looked at me, waiting for my decision. It wasn't her secret to tell.

"Fine, let's go." The three of us headed for my private room upstairs.

"OKAY," Reyna said, her voice breathy, after I'd told her about Aiden and me. She paced my tiny room in the motorhome while Gem and I perched on the edge of the little sofa. "Okay, okay..."

"I'm not sure she's okay," Gem whispered in my ear.

"This is fine. I can handle this." Reyna continued to pace the tiny space and she spoke like she was giving herself a pep talk. She turned around to face us suddenly. "I need to start damage control."

"What?" I asked, looking up at her.

"It's my job to handle any PR for the team and you. I'll need to figure out who witnessed the almost-fight and check to see if anyone is linking you and Aiden online, too." She grabbed her tablet from my desk, opening it and scrolling. She muttered something about setting up Google alerts and I wondered if she'd forgotten that Gem and I were still here.

She stopped again and looked up from her screen.

"Why didn't you tell me sooner?" she asked.

"I'm sorry. It just sort of happened, and I wanted to keep it as quiet as possible. So did Aiden."

Reyna shook her head. "Secrets never stay secret for long."

"And now Stefan knows," I replied, proving Reyna's point.

"What? No, he doesn't. What makes you say that?" Gem asked.

"The way he antagonised Aiden. He knows!"

"Stefan antagonises everyone at every opportunity," Gem argued.

I opened my mouth to try and explain how I had a gut feeling Stefan knew, but Reyna jumped in.

"I will handle everything from now on. I'll make sure no one from the media or press witnessed the fight. Let's hope no one caught it on camera, and if they did, let's also hope the sound quality is poor. Hopefully, all the music playing around the circuit interfered. If someone did catch it on camera, then I can play it off as them fighting over the Championship and not even mention you."

"And Stefan?" I asked her.

"If he does know, then I'll kindly remind him that I handle both your PR and his. He wouldn't dare push me, not now. I've had enough of his sullen interviews and difficult behaviour this season. If I can push positive publicity out there, I can also put negative publicity out there, too."

"You're kinda scary," Gem said, leaning back into the sofa.

"Don't mess with the woman who controls your public image." She looked back down at her screen again.

"You're not going to tell Michael, are you?" I doubt Michael would be keen to sign me for another two years if he knew I was involved with a driver from our team's main rival.

"I won't tell him," Reyna replied, still looking down at her screen.

"And if he asks about the fight?" I pushed, needing to know where her loyalties lay. Michael was her boss.

"I'll lie. He doesn't need to know."

"You don't have to lie for me."

"No, I don't have to, but I will." She looked up from her screen and I smiled at her. Gem and Reyna had my back, and with them by my side, helping to keep my secret, I could relax a little—or try to. If only Reyna had a say on my contract for next season. There was no way I could fully relax until I knew I had a drive for next year.

FORTY-TWO

THE NETHERLANDS

SATURDAY - AFTER QUALIFYING

Shit. He'd messed up.

I KNOCKED on the hotel room door, feeling uneasy. A mix of emotions filled my head. I wanted to see Aiden, but I felt annoyed with him, too. Low wall lights cast the deserted corridor in shadows. The door swung back a couple of seconds later and I walked inside.

"Hey," Aiden said, leaning in to kiss me, but I placed a hand on his chest to stop him.

"We need to talk," I said, folding my arms.

"About what I did earlier?"

"Yes."

"I was angry," he started.

"I know, so was I!"

"Someone had to tell him how dangerous his driving was," Aiden continued, folding his arms, too.

"And you had to be the one to tell him?"

"Someone needed to since no one reported him to the race stewards."

"My team decided to deal with it internally. Do you really think Stefan was going to listen to you? He doesn't listen to anyone, not even the stewards. All you did was cause a scene, and you were the one who warned me of Stefan's game-playing in the first place! You're meant to know what he's like!"

"I know." He sighed. His hands fell to his sides and he walked over to the window. "But there's a difference between game-playing and dangerous driving that risks others' lives. I couldn't let it slide, not when it concerned you."

I took in a breath and closed my eyes for a second, feeling conflicted. He cared about me, wanted me to be safe, and wanted the best for me, but he'd interfered in my race. It wasn't his place to get involved in my battle with Stefan. He wouldn't want me shouting at another driver who'd pulled a reckless move on him. I'd wanted to rage at Stefan when I first got out of the car, but Gem stopped me, and that was the right decision. I thought I'd avoided an awkward confrontation, only for Aiden to cause one later on. Now, everyone would be wondering why Aiden had defended me. Reyna might be able to keep it quiet publicly, but those inside the world of F1 would be talking. Benjamin had held Stefan back from Aiden, and he must have questions about what really caused their almost-fight.

I moved to stand closer to Aiden. He remained in front of the window with his back to me, looking at the darkening evening sky.

"I don't need you to fight my battles for me," I said.

"That's not what I was doing."

"It's how it looked, and you risked letting everyone know about us!"

"I was careful."

"No, you weren't. You were angry," I argued, and he turned around to face me.

"I was, and I had every right to be. Stefan deserved it!"

"You got involved in my team's business; you crossed a line."

"I did and I'd do it again! I know you want us to keep our relationship separate from racing, but it doesn't work like that." He took a step closer to me. "What we have started because we're both in this sport together and I can't switch my feelings off when it suits you."

"When it suits me?"

"I want you, want us, want it all, but I'm holding back to keep everything a secret for you."

"And you know why I can't go public. I still haven't got my contract for next year."

"But is that the only reason or just an excuse to keep me at a distance because you're scared of what this is—what we could be?" He took hold of my hand.

"My contract is the reason and you know that! And you don't get to decide how fast or slow I take this relationship. You still don't have the right to get involved in my team's business!" I pulled my hand free from his. "I'm leaving."

"Winter, don't."

I moved to the door. "I need calm before the race tomorrow and I'm not going to get that here." I yanked the door open, strode back out into the hallway, and let the door slam behind me.

I returned to my hotel room feeling empty. As I entered, my phone buzzed in my pocket. I took it out to find a message from Aiden.

Aiden: I'm sorry.

FORTY-THREE

THE NETHERLANDS
SUNDAY - RACE REPORT

He planned on apologising for confronting her teammate, but then everything happened and he found himself in the middle of a media storm.

NOTHING FELT right in the morning. I woke up at six after the worst night's sleep I'd had all year. I tossed and turned for hours before finally drifting off in the early hours. When my alarm woke me up, I felt disoriented for a split second. My arm reached out to find the other side of the bed empty. Then I remembered last night. This wasn't the bed I'd intended on waking in.

I reached for my phone and stopped the alarm. There was another message from Aiden.

Aiden: I shouldn't have reacted how I did yesterday. If another driver had pulled that move on me, I would have been angry, but I wouldn't have responded. But it wasn't me: it was you, and you are my weakness. I'll try to do better next time. I'm sorry.

Winter: I'm sorry, too. I shouldn't have taken my anger out on you. I am serious about us being together, but maybe I am scared because we're moving so fast, and maybe I haven't felt this way about someone in a long time. Let's talk after the race.

THE MORNING WENT by like it always did. I discussed my strategy with the team and Ash went through my Qualifying data. I ignored Stefan, and he ignored me. The same routine. Another race weekend. Reyna told me she'd seen nothing linking me to Aiden and Stefan's confrontation yesterday.

The grid was busy with the usual pre-race build-up, along with the added excitement of the Dutch fans. Loud music played across the track again and the fans cheered in the stands. I tried to use the upbeat atmosphere to get myself ready for the race. Fourth wasn't the worst position to be in. I could fight my way up, especially if I got a good start.

I stood with Gem at the side of the track; my car lined up in fourth before me. My team worked around the car, Ash at the front talking with one of the strategists and mechanics. Michael stood beside Stefan's car at the front of the grid. Reyna hovered near Stefan as a TV pundit tried to interview him. I could tell from Reyna's expression that Stefan wasn't making an effort to answer the questions.

A normal race weekend.

Suddenly, the atmosphere changed. The chatter and noise quietened down. The music still beat heavily in the air, but there was less general sound around the circuit. Guests on the grid, VIPs, and the media started looking down at their phones, and whispers moved through the crowd in a wave. Heads looked up and a few pairs of eyes turned in my direction.

"What's going on?" I whispered to Gem.

"I don't know."

A camera crew turned to face me, moving away from interviewing Matias da Silveira mid-question. A puzzled expression took over his face as the interviewer wrapped up and started towards me. The noise in the crowd increased again and chatter filled the air, fighting against the pulse of the music.

"What?" Gem started to ask but Reyna dived towards us. She gripped my hand and started pulling me towards the edge of the track. Gem followed closely behind me.

My stomach flipped. I knew something was wrong. I glanced over my shoulder as reporters and camera crews fought each other to reach us.

"Reyna?" I asked, panicking.

She held her phone out to me. It buzzed constantly, with alerts and messages coming in. Little notifications kept popping up at the top of the screen. She clicked on a news app, opened an article, and handed me the phone. I took it with numb fingers, already knowing what it had to be.

I read the headline with my heart in my throat.

Racing Rivals or Secret Lovers?

Under the headline were photos of Aiden and me kissing on that French beach during the summer break. A couple of the images were grainy like they'd been taken from a distance, and the photographer had zoomed in to capture our faces. They might not have been the clearest images, but it was unmistakably Aiden and me together. One image showed us leaning towards each other, both of us sitting on a towel laid out on the sand. The next photo showed us kissing, lips locked, hands on each other. The last photo showed us breaking apart.

"I'm sorry," Reyna said under her breath as my thumb flew over the screen, scrolling through the article, not really reading it but taking in the odd word here and there. I closed the app and instead opened the web browser, typing in my own name and hitting "go". A list of articles referring to Aiden and me came up instantly. My heart thudded in my chest as I scrolled down the page, seeing more posts about us.

Reporters, TV pundits, and journalists started to crowd around where we stood and began to shout questions at me. Usually, they'd ask about my race strategy, or tyre choices, or how I felt about my chances of a win. Now they asked about Aiden.

"No more interviews!" Reyna shouted, and she pulled me closer to the barrier at the edge of the track. Gem stood in front of me like a bodyguard and Ash and a couple of the mechanics came over to tell the scrum of people to disperse. Racing drivers didn't have to give interviews before the race and journalists were meant to respect that choice.

Everything blurred around me: the noise and frenzied crowd. I zoned out the questions and Reyna's shouts; instead, my eyes searched further up the grid to where another crowd gathered around Aiden. I found his face in the chaos, but his gaze didn't meet mine, too distracted. Josh stepped in front of him and shouted something to a reporter. It looked like he was telling him to fuck off. The Silvers team quickly took control of the situation and the media moved back. Team members formed a block between Aiden and the cameras and reporters.

"Should we go back to the motorhome?" Gem asked Reyna.

"No, it's too close to the start now. Better to wait it out. Everyone except the teams will be called off the grid soon."

"What now?" I asked no one in particular, not expecting an answer.

"Nothing. We wait for the start. It's business as usual. You race like you always do," Gem replied, her voice hard.

I looked at her and I nodded in reply. Yes, I could do this.

The minutes stretched on. It felt like the longest build-up to a race I'd ever experienced. Eventually, all the VIPs and the media left the grid. The teams continued working on the cars until the very last moment. As the clock ticked down, I got ready, putting on my helmet and gloves. Standing beside my car, I looked over at Aiden's car. He looked back at me as he got in. I had no idea what was going through his head, or whether his mind was spinning like mine. One emotion stood out in my whirling thoughts: anger. I was angry at the fuss. So what if Aiden and I were together? Why did people care so much about other people's dating lives? I was angry at myself, too. The deserted beach hadn't been deserted after all. I knew we shouldn't have gone there. I'd told Aiden it was a bad idea, but he'd insisted we'd be fine.

Getting into my car, I took in a steadying breath and told myself to focus on the race. I started to play out the start in my head. I saw the red lights go out and imagined how I would make it down to the first corner. Then I visualised the next corner and the next, but my thoughts went back to the kiss on the beach.

Everyone got ready for the warm-up lap. I followed the car in front, going along the track, warming my tyres, and trying to get my head focused. I needed a good start if I was going to make up for my poor Qualifying. I had to get up to third or second within the first few laps.

After finishing the warm-up, all the cars pulled up onto the grid in formation. I stopped my car in the fourth slot and looked up, waiting for the five red lights to come on and then go out.

I GOT BOGGED down during my start. Three cars got by me before the first corner, including a Hunter, and their team were having one of their worst years in F1. Their cars had shocking performance and one had gotten past me. I tried to make up for it. I had a fast car and I knew I could get past James King in the Hunter in front, but he knew it too and drove defensively. King seemed to predict my every move and the frustration began to build. I got desperate and went down the inside on a corner not known for overtaking. King didn't expect the move, but I didn't get by. My tyres locked up and our cars touched, my front left hitting the side of his car with a heavy jolt. He spun off in front and I went off the track. My car hit the barrier with another thud. It jolted me, my body straining against the seatbelt.

My race was over in a matter of seconds.

"Are you okay?" Ash asked over the radio.

"Yes," I replied, but I wanted to say no.

No, I wasn't okay.

Championship Driver Standings

Winter Jones – 226

Aiden Sterling – 216

Stefan Brudes - 195

FORTY-FOUR

THE NETHERLANDS
SUNDAY - AFTER THE RACE

The wrong words kept spilling from his mouth and it all felt out of control. He could tell she was spiralling and he wanted to fix it for her, for them, but he couldn't seem to make everything okay again.

I HAD to watch the rest of the race from the garage in the pit lane. A painful experience. Nothing like watching your team-mate win a race after you've crashed out of it.

As soon as the race ended, I headed back to the team's motorhome. It was like going against the direction of traffic. While everyone else headed to the pits to celebrate Stefan's win, I returned to my room to hide away from the world. My phone wouldn't stop ringing and vibrating. It buzzed on the desk in my room, but I ignored it while I changed out of my race suit and into a clean polo and a pair of shorts.

Gem joined me at some point. She sat beside me and leaned back on the tiny sofa. We didn't talk; she knew when I needed space or quiet, but it was good to have her here. She kept eyeing my phone on the table as it continued to blow up with messages and calls.

"I think your mum is calling," she said, leaning over the table to look at the name flashing up on the screen.

"I can't talk to her right now." I shook my head.

"Maybe you should turn it off." She picked up my humming phone and held it out to me.

I took it, sent my mum's call to voicemail, and held down the power button. Silence filled the space once the device was off.

A small knock sounded on the door.

"Come in!" I answered.

The door opened enough for Reyna to pop her head through.

"Michael wants to speak to you. He's in his office," she said.

"Tell him she's unavailable," Gem answered.

"No, it's fine. I can't avoid this." I stood up, stretched, and followed Reyna out and down the corridor to Michael's office.

She knocked on his door, opened it for me, and I walked inside. Michael had the blinds pulled down low and only one small desk light switched on, leaving most of the room in shadow. He sat at his desk in the centre of the office, working on his laptop. He didn't look up from his screen as I entered.

"Take a seat," he said in a flat voice. I'd always found him difficult to read, to pick up on his mood, and he rarely showed emotion. But right now, there was a small crease in his forehead.

I took the seat opposite his.

"Do you have anything to say first?" he asked, finally looking up from his laptop.

"I made a mistake out on the track today. It won't happen again," I replied.

"I'm not talking about the on-track mess."

"What I do in my private life has nothing to do with my racing."

"Really?" He turned his laptop around so I could see the photos of Sterling and me kissing on the beach. I ignored the screen, refusing to look at the images. "This comes out moments before the race and then you crash. What if you've accidentally given Sterling an advantage? Given him Torrin information?"

I scoffed. "That's ridiculous."

Michael leaned back in his chair, that same quiet fury on his face. He folded his arms, waiting.

"It is possible for two people to keep their personal lives separate from their work lives." I folded my arms and held my ground. This wasn't the first case of two racing drivers dating. Maybe not in F1, but still, it wasn't unthinkable. Plenty of people had relationships with work colleagues and they managed to keep their work lives professional.

Michael unfolded his arms and pulled his laptop back around to face him. He started typing like we'd already finished our conversation.

"I'm afraid it's not possible for me to sign your new contract right now. Our team owner isn't happy about the negative press coverage." He spoke without looking at me, keeping his eyes on his screen instead.

"How is it negative or bad for Torrin?" I asked. From what I'd see of the headlines, they were all focused on Aiden and me, not really mentioning either of our teams. Not yet.

"It's a scandal and Brenner doesn't like it. I won't consider signing you for next season until after this race season is over."

"A few headlines and you won't sign me? I'm leading in Championship points! You should have signed my new contract weeks ago."

"You might be leading in points, but you crashed today. You're still a rookie driver in your first season, and I don't see a line of other teams looking to sign you up. We will wait until the end of this season and then the team will make a decision."

He had me there. No one else was interested in signing me.

"This is about Stefan. You don't want to sign me because you don't want to upset him. Stefan can't stand the fact that I beat him most weekends. That I'm a better driver."

"My decision has nothing to do with your teammate squabbles."

"Teammate squabbles? You're the one who's constantly babying Stefan. You've prioritised him over me even when I was winning and he wasn't."

Michael finally looked up from his computer. "Stefan had a difficult start to the year, but he's caught up to you in points, especially after today's performance." He slammed his laptop shut. "I'm sick of dealing with these petty driver arguments."

"Then you're a bad team manager. You let the spoilt driver do whatever he likes. Same as last year when Stefan got into a fight at the side of the racetrack. You let that happen and I'm not the problem here. Neither is what I choose to do in my free time."

Michael leaned forward, placing both elbows on the desk.

"Here's the truth. I brought you to this team. I didn't expect you to win races: you were here to fill the second seat, maybe get Torrin some extra publicity and some extra coverage for having the only woman on the grid. I thought you'd be an easy driver to handle and be okay playing second to Stefan. You winning a few races was a bonus. You kept us in the points when Stefan wasn't doing so well. I brought you to my team and gave you one of my cars so Torrin could have a drama-free season and the team could finally win a Championship. That's it."

My heart thumped in my chest. I could almost hear the blood pumping in my ears.

"You might have won races, but you won because I let you win. Torrin is my team, my car, and from now on, you will keep your head down and get on with finishing the season. I will make a final decision on your new contract after the season is over. Tell your agent to back off, too."

"Fuck you and your contract! I only drive for teams who actually want me to race and win! I'm not here to fill a spare seat!"

I shot to my feet and rushed out the door. I couldn't spend another second in the same room as him. The door slammed behind me, and I stormed back to my own room, trying to hold back the tears threatening to spill from my eyes.

Back in my room, I closed the door and leaned against it, letting my head fall back and closing my eyes.

"Hey, are you okay?" Aiden asked. I opened my eyes to find him standing up from the sofa. Both Gem and Reyna had gone.

"What are you doing in here?" He couldn't be here, not in Torrin's motorhome wearing his Silvers T-shirt.

"Gem snuck me in," he explained, reaching me and taking my hand. "Hey, you're upset. I know this was the situation we were trying to avoid, but we can figure it out and deal with the fallout together." He reached up to my face and brushed away one of the traitorous tears that had escaped my eyes.

"It's not that," I said, pushing his hand from my face. "You need to leave. Michael is fuming. He won't want you here in his motorhome."

"What happened?"

"I don't have a contract for next year." The words felt heavy and final as I spoke them. All the weeks of hoping and wishing to get my contract signed, and now it was over. A few harsh words and I had no race seat for next year, no plan, and no idea what to do next. How could I finish racing the rest of the season knowing I was racing for a team principal who saw me at best as a seat filler and, at worst, as a publicity stunt?

"What? Because of us? Torrin won't sign you for next year because of me?"

I shook my head. "Not exactly. Yes, Michael wasn't happy about us sneaking around and said he would decide on my contract after this season. But I refused his offer."

"I don't understand." Aiden's eyebrows drew together and his hand squeezed mine.

"Michael told me he only gave me the seat in Torrin to be an easy, pliable teammate for Stefan. I was never meant to win or lead the Championship. I was filling a space. So I told him he could forget my contract for next year. I told him to fuck off."

Aiden froze at my words.

"He... he said that?"

I nodded.

"I can't believe it," he said, his voice almost a whisper, like he was still trying to process what had happened. "I'm sorry, Winter." He pulled me into a tight hug and I got lost in him for a moment, feeling nothing but his arms around me and forgetting the world outside these four walls. Eventually, he pulled back. "Have you spoken to your agent yet? Jean will find you another drive for next year."

"No, not yet." I moved around him and sat down on the sofa. "I switched my phone off. Too many messages and phone calls. Too many people wanting to know what's going on with those photos of us on the beach together."

"Shit, right, the photos." He rubbed the back of his head, moved my desk chair out and sat down to face me. We both stared at each other.

"So, you're not sorry about the photos then?" I asked, my voice hollowed out.

"I'm sorry about the situation, but it wasn't me who took the photos, Winter."

"I know that," I snapped, looking away from him. "But you took us to that beach in the first place. I told you it wasn't a good idea, that someone might see us together, and they did!"

He let out a long breath. "I've been to that beach hundreds of times and no one has ever spotted me. The paparazzi have never photographed me there before and it's never been busy with tourists either. As far as I knew, it was deserted the day we went there."

"Except it wasn't! But you insisted it was okay and I stupidly went along with it! I should have said no!" I stood up, not enjoying his piercing gaze on me.

He stood up too, his eyes back on mine. "Seriously, is this the argument you want to have right now? I can't take back what is done. It's out there now."

"If we hadn't gotten caught on that beach, our relationship would still be private. Michael wouldn't know about us and he would have signed my contract this weekend."

"Really? You'd want to pretend that the news coming out is what stopped him from signing you for next year? You'd want to race for him, knowing why he signed you in the first place? After he spoke to you the way he did?"

"No, I don't want to race for his team now, but I never would have found out. Ignorance is bliss, as they say."

"You're directing your anger at the wrong person. You're trying to push me away again."

"I'm not!" I shut my eyes, unable to look at him.

"You have every right to be upset, but this isn't my fault." He rested a hand on my arm; his fingers trailed down my skin, along my forearm, until he reached my fingers. He took hold of my hand.

"I think I need some space. Some time to figure everything out," I said.

His hand dropped from mine. "If that's what you really want?"

"It is."

I opened my eyes and finally faced him. I watched him step back and walk out the door, leaving me in the silent, empty room.

***

Mum: 12 missed calls
Mum: 5 voicemails

FORTY-FIVE

GREAT BRITAIN

A WEEKEND OFF

*He really wanted to call her, but she'd asked for space and he
would respect her wishes.*

TURNS out the best place to hide from all your problems was
at your personal trainer's house. Gem and Emily were excellent
hosts, and with a break between the last and the next race, I
didn't have anywhere else to go. I was stuck and needed somewhere I could lay low and avoid any press, too.

I couldn't go home and face my parents. The thought of
seeing Mum's disappointed face was too much. Or worse,
seeing her "I told you so" face. At least she'd given up trying to
call me. I was too cowardly to even listen to her voicemail
messages. She'd always been the biggest supporter of my racing
career. She'd given up so much of her time taking me karting as
a kid; she'd helped me move up through the Formulas and
financed so much of my career in its early stages. And I'd

repaid her by sleeping with my F1 rival and losing my drive for next year.

I couldn't crash at Aiden's because I'd asked him for space and we hadn't spoken since then. He hadn't messaged or called, but I couldn't blame him, since I'd asked him for time. Why would he want to speak to me when I tried to blame him for everything?

Gem's house was on the outskirts of London, down a quiet street. When Emily got home from work, we ate dinner around their kitchen table with the TV on in the background.

I offered to make them dinner, but Gem took over, muttering something about my terrible cooking skills.

"I know things haven't been great, but having you here has its benefits," Gem said between mouthfuls of pasta.

"Really?" I looked up from my bowl of pasta. I thought they might have had enough of playing host to me by now.

"I can make sure you're sticking to my exercise plan."

Emily shook her head at Gem and took her empty bowl to the sink.

"What? It's true. Singapore is next and physical fitness will be key."

"I'm sure it is key, but perhaps you could try to be a bit more supportive," Emily said, leaving her dish in the sink and returning to the table to kiss Gem on the top of the head. "I said I'd call my dad this evening, so I'll be upstairs." She left the room.

"I'm sorry. Am I being a bad friend? I thought that was supportive," Gem said.

"It was, and you're letting me stay here. That's more than enough."

"You're always welcome here, but are you sure you're okay?"

I finished my last mouthful of pasta and placed my fork down gently in my bowl.

"I'm okay. Jean said she's working on getting me a seat for next year and she advised me to ignore all the media attention. She thinks it's best to refuse any interviews unless they're about my racing and racing alone. I agree with her. I'm not interested in answering questions about my personal life, especially when I don't even have the answers."

"Still nothing from Aiden?"

I shook my head and looked down at my hands.

"He'll call and the rest will blow over. There'll be some other news to gossip about next week," Gem replied, pushing her empty bowl forward.

"It's been over a week now. Yesterday, I had to log out of all my social accounts because it still hasn't blown over. Complete strangers are messaging me on a couple of my socials and I can't keep up with the 'delete' and 'block' buttons."

"Is it still that bad? I haven't really seen much chat about you."

"Probably because most of your feed is either cute cats or workout videos." Gem didn't follow many F1 accounts on her socials. "And yes, it is still bad. I've had my integrity as a competitive sportswoman questioned by some so-called 'sports commentators'. The gossip columnists just want the details of my relationship and rumours are flying all over the place. The F1 fanboys are questioning my driving ability and whether Aiden let me pass him at certain races this year. And the sexist internet trolls are saying this is exactly why women shouldn't be in F1."

"You really need to stop looking."

"I have now. I've deleted most of my apps."

"I'm sure there are still plenty of people out there who support you. The negative voices are always the loudest and outshout the quiet majority. Most people don't even watch F1. They don't even know who you are. They watch players kick a football round a field at weekends, not cars."

"Thanks." I couldn't help but smile at her words. Gem was probably right. I needed to shut out the negative stuff and get on with my life. "It's just that I don't know what I'm supposed to do now."

"That's easy. You race. You turn up at the next track and you race. Simple."

"Is it, though? What about everything else?"

"Forget about everything else. You have one job: to drive. If Aiden doesn't call, then leave him to sulk. Let Jean handle your contract. That's her job, not yours. Ignore Michael; as long as you stick to your current contractual obligations, then you don't have to speak to him outside of that. Let Reyna deal with any media stuff because that's her job. You race. That's it."

"Maybe you should start charging me for your motivational speeches. They're very good."

"I know." She stood, grabbed both our bowls and headed to the sink.

FORTY-SIX

RACE REPORTS

Singapore

1 st – Stefan Brudes

2 nd – Benjamin Knight

3 rd – Aiden Sterling

6 th – Winter Jones

Japan

1 st – Benjamin Knight

2 nd – Matias da Silveira

3 rd – Satoru Hayashi

DNF – Winter Jones

United States
1st – Matias da Silveira
2nd – Stefan Brudes
3rd – Aiden Sterling

9th – Winter Jones

Championship Driver Standings
Aiden Sterling – 256
Stefan Brudes – 250
Winter Jones – 236

THE LAST THREE races were a disaster. I felt helpless as I watched my Championship lead shrink. Aiden and Stefan caught up to me with wins and podium finishes. Their point scores rose above mine and I'd lost my Championship lead.

I kept trying, pushing myself to do better, race faster, but it all felt out of control. The overthinking seeped into my driving. I made moves I wouldn't normally make, turned into corners too soon, and made stupid rookie mistakes. The more I tried to improve, the more I fell behind. Luck was against me in Japan when someone else crashed into me at the first corner. I didn't see them. They came out of nowhere. I had no warning and no chance to get out of the way.

The Championship was slowly slipping away, no matter how hard I tried to hold onto it.

My luck and driving had become so bad that Ash convinced himself someone in the team on Stefan's side of the garage was sabotaging my car. I wouldn't put it past Michael to sink to that level, but he never worked on either of the Torrin cars. He stayed in his office or on the pit wall. I trusted my engineers and mechanics. I knew they'd never do anything to my car or let anyone untrustworthy near it, either. It didn't stop Ash from working extra to double- and triple-check every tiny detail. He was first in the garage at dawn and the last to leave at night. The man needed to sleep. Nothing was wrong with my car. It was me. I was the problem.

My poor racing results weren't the most depressing part of the last four weeks. I hadn't spoken to Aiden and he didn't reach out to me either. Race weekends became a painful game of hide-and-seek. I didn't want to see him knowing he was actively ignoring me. In Singapore, I tried to catch his eye during the drivers' safety briefing. I thought after two weeks, he'd want to speak to me. We could talk and try to work something out. He blanked me. So I decided to blank him back and I spent the next two races trying to avoid him, which was difficult since there were so many moments the drivers had to be near each other during the weekend. I managed to get out of a media briefing with him. Reyna convinced the organisers to take Stefan in my place instead. I'm not sure how she managed to swap us, since Stefan was every journalist's worst nightmare.

After the race in Austin, I caved. Before leaving my hotel room, I sent him a blunt message.

Winter: Are you going to ignore me at every race now? It's been five weeks and you've said nothing to me.
Aiden: You told me you needed space and time. I'm giving you space and time. I know what I want. I've told you, but do you know what you want yet?

I typed out several replies. My fingers sped over the letters, only for my thumb to hit the "delete" button. In the end, I couldn't reply. I wanted Aiden but didn't want everything else that came with him. I didn't want the attention, the rumours and speculation, or the questioning of my racing ability. I wished I could go back to when it was only us and nobody else knew. Even though the trip to the secluded beach had become our downfall, I wanted to go back to that moment—a quiet but perfect moment with him when nothing else mattered.

FORTY-SEVEN

MEXICO

SATURDAY - QUALIFYING

THE BAD LUCK CONTINUED. I found myself qualifying in tenth place for the Mexican Grand Prix. I couldn't get heat into my tyres and no matter what I did, I couldn't increase my lap times. The whole Qualifying session became painful and I was glad when it came to an end.

I didn't think it could get much worse, but when Gem and I tried to get dinner in the city that evening, we were ambushed by reporters as we tried to enter a restaurant. Gem thought a change of scenery would be good for me, but we didn't even make it inside. Instead, we rushed back to the car with reporters bombarding me with questions about Aiden, my poor Qualifying, and whether my Championship dreams were over like my relationship clearly was.

"Fuck them!" Gem said as our driver sped off down the road, leaving the flashing cameras behind on the pavement. "I really wanted to eat at that place, too. The reviews were really good."

"Do they deliver?" I asked, my head spinning from all the shouting and flashing lights.

"I'll check." Gem took her phone out.

They did deliver. Gem and I ate in my room, and when we were done, I convinced her I wanted an early night, so she left me alone. I put some quiet music on and busied my hands with pointless tasks. Halfway through repacking my suitcase, a knock sounded on the door, making me jump. For a split second, I thought it might be Aiden and I rushed to open it. But how would he know which room I was in? He hadn't messaged to ask.

I pulled back the door to find my mum standing before me.

"Winter."

"Mum," I replied, my voice cracking.

She pulled me into a tight hug and tears started to form in the corners of my eyes.

She pulled back and looked me up and down. "Let's go inside and talk."

I nodded and she came into my room, closing the door behind her.

"You've been avoiding me," she stated, sitting at the small table in the corner of my room.

"I know; I'm sorry," I replied, waiting for her to tell me off for messing everything up. I stood by the bed, folding my arms.

"Don't apologise; you needed space, and I understand that," she said and I blinked at her.

"What?"

"I was trying to respect your boundaries like you asked me to, but after the last race, I thought it was about time we talked. Do you want to tell me what's going on?" she asked.

"Don't you already know? It's been reported everywhere."

"I'd rather hear your version." She pulled the other chair out at the table and gestured to it. I took a deep breath and joined her.

I TOLD HER EVERYTHING, or almost everything, skipping over some details about Aiden and me. When I told her about what Michael had said and my response, I expected her to tell me I'd made a mistake.

"Good. You don't want to drive for a team that doesn't value you and only wanted you for publicity. Sounds like whoever they put in that car will always play second to Stefan. You're better off out of that situation. You did the right thing."

"You think? I've kinda been thinking I reacted too quickly. Maybe I should have kept my mouth shut. He could have kicked me out of the team then and there. Then I'd definitely be out of the Championship."

"No, you made the right choice. Michael wouldn't dare kick you out mid-season. You're too popular with the fans. It would cause even more scandal."

"You sure about my popularity?" I asked, raising an eyebrow and thinking about all the gossip.

"Ignore the sports commentators and online trolls. You've always been popular with the real fans, even before you entered F1."

"But you would say that: you're my mum."

"I am, and I think we should get out of this room for a bit. Let's go to the hotel bar. Have a drink." She stood.

"I can't. I have a race tomorrow. I have to be up early, remember?"

"It's not late and it's one drink. Come on?" She brushed a hand over my shoulder as she made her way across my room to the door.

I followed her, grabbing my room key as I went.

"How did you even know which hotel I was in?" I asked as we walked to the lift.

"Reyna gave me the details. She booked me into a room down the hall from yours," she said, pressing the button.

I shook my head, smiling. "Of course she did."

"She was worried about you and messaged me to see if I'd spoken to you." The lift doors opened and we stepped inside. "When I told her we hadn't spoken, she suggested I come out and visit you."

"Clever," I replied, pressing the button for the ground floor.

"She's good at her job. Shame she works for Torrin, though."

"I know," I sighed. If I managed to find another F1 team to take me on, I'd get a new public relations manager, and it was hard to imagine working with someone who wasn't Reyna.

"Is Dad with you?" I asked. We started moving down the floors.

"Yes. I left him in our room watching some old movie on the TV."

The lift opened on the ground floor and we made our way through the lobby to the bar. The low lights and quiet background music had a calming effect. It wasn't busy either; a few guests lounged on the sofas by the windows. Mum made a beeline for the bar, taking a seat at one of the stools. I grabbed the stool next to hers as a barman came over to take our order.

"Two small glasses of wine: this one looks good," she said, pointing to the drink menu.

"Mum, I can't drink before a race, especially wine!" I said in a hushed voice as the barman walked away to get our order.

"A couple of sips won't hurt." She waved me off.

"You know I don't drink during the season—not unless it's champagne, winner's champagne."

"If there was ever a time for a drink, now is it," she replied as the barman placed our glasses down before us. Mum told him to charge it to her room.

She held her glass up and nodded for me to do the same. I picked mine up, the glass cold. "Gem won't be happy. Do you know how high the sugar content in wine is?" I muttered.

Mum ignored me. "Let's cheers to your success." She moved her glass to mine, clinked them together, and then took a deep sip.

"Success?" I put my glass down without taking a drink.

"Yes, your success. Darling, I know you've had a bit of a hard time recently, but you need to look at the bigger picture. Think about where you were last year, and now here you are, in Formula One, living your dream, and you even led the Championship."

"Not anymore, though."

"Stop that. Almost a year ago, you were chatting about giving up, retiring from racing, and now you're here. Look how far you've come and it's not over yet."

"I know, I know," I replied.

"But do you? Remember when you crashed at the penultimate race in the British Juniors series?"

"That's not the same as this." I shook my head.

"Isn't it? You were down, on the back foot, but you went to the following race, and you fought back and won. What about that race in Spain when you were sixteen? You went from the back of the grid to the front. And your first year in the W series. That wasn't an easy one, but you never gave up. This is no different. If anything, you're in a better position now. There are only a few points between you and your competitors."

She was right. She was always right. I needed to stop focusing on the negatives or the things I couldn't change. "Okay, I see what you're saying."

"Let's make another toast, and you have to take a sip this time." She exaggerated a glare at me.

I laughed and held my glass out to hers.

"To winning the Championship," she said and we touched glasses. I took the smallest sip and placed my drink down again.

FORTY-EIGHT

MEXICO

SUNDAY - RACE DAY

MY ALARM WOKE me at six and I got straight up, taking a quick shower and changing into my Torrin top and shorts. I felt more energetic after Mum's pep talk, like I could do this—I could recover from my poor Qualifying and fight for the top spot. I had to believe it was possible and as Mum said, we'd been here before—bad races, poor results—and we'd come back fighting.

Unfortunately, I couldn't help but look at the Torrin logo on my polo differently now. Before my argument with Michael, I'd worn the Torrin colours with pride. Now, I couldn't wait to take them off after the race.

My phone buzzed on the bedside table as I came out of the bathroom.

Mum: Come to my room as soon as you're ready.

I frowned at her text. I'd told her not to worry about getting up early and escorting me to the circuit. She should enjoy the weekend with Dad and head down to the track in their own time. I grabbed my room key with my phone and went to her room down the corridor.

At the door, I knocked once before it flung back. I walked inside to find the room a hive of activity. She'd transformed the whole space, pushing the queen-sized bed to one side and bringing in two tables. Ash, my mechanic, and one of the team's strategists worked on the table closest to the window. They worked on laptops and had papers scattered over the table. Ash had his headset on and was talking to someone. The other table was set closer to the door, with Gem and Reyna sitting on one side, and an empty seat between them. Reyna worked on her tablet as usual while Gem had her phone in one hand, looking a bit lost. My mum stood in the middle of the room, switching from one table to the next, like a queen holding court.

I slowly stepped inside.

"What's going on?" I asked. Mum ushered me further into the room and shut the door behind me.

"I've put together a group of key people to help you win the Championship."

"Mum, these people already help me. You didn't need to drag them into your hotel room."

"And have this meeting in the Torrin motorhome or garage where someone from Stefan's crew could listen in and gain an advantage? I don't think so."

"What advantage is there to gain? Have you forgotten that my last three races were a disaster? Stefan has the advantage now."

She picked up a pen from the table and headed to a big roll of white paper she'd taped to the wall. She started noting down a list of numbers and I realised she was writing down the points I'd won at each race of the season so far. She then started listing Stefan's points and Aiden's, too.

"It's not over until it's mathematically impossible. You can still win the Championship. We're not done yet." My chance of winning was so slim, but Mum was right: it wasn't impossible.

"I'm not sure if the hotel will be pleased you've taped paper to the walls," I said.

"Take a seat," Mum said.

I took the empty chair between Reyna and Gem. Mum stood on the other side of the table before the three of us, like a teacher about to instruct a lesson.

I glanced around the room again.

"Where's Dad?" I asked. Maybe she'd locked him in the bathroom or perhaps he'd gone in there willingly to hide from this chaos.

"He's at the Torrin motorhome having breakfast and keeping a close eye on your teammate and his strategist." She picked up her phone from the table and glanced down at it. "Right now, Stefan is having breakfast with his engineer and two of the strategists. Dad said one of the ladies who does the catering for the team is helping him listen in on their conversation. Stefan was rude to her about a meal she prepared at the last race, so she's a willing accomplice." She walked over to my strategist and handed her phone to him. "If my husband calls, answer it, and hopefully, he'll have something good on Stefan's race plans."

Gem leaned into me. "Remind me never to get on the wrong side of your mum," she whispered.

"Right! In order for you to race at your best, you need a clear head," Mum began, taking command of the room again.

"My head is clear and I'm good." That was true. After last night's chat with Mum, I was feeling better about myself and my racing. It wasn't all doom and gloom.

Mum shook her head. "You still have unanswered questions and I know you—you won't be able to fully focus with those questions floating around."

I instantly thought of Aiden. I wasn't the one who needed a question answered: it was him.

"Mum, I'm good."

Mum looked at Reyna. Reyna opened her tablet and showed the article that broke the story about Aiden and me.

"Who leaked the story? Who took these photos?" Mum asked, pointing to the images of Aiden and me kissing on the beach. Mum turned around to face her paper on the wall.

I gestured to Reyna to swipe away from the photos of me kissing Aiden. My mum didn't need to see them. Embarrassment heated my cheeks even though I bet thousands, maybe even millions, of people had seen them by now; I still didn't want my mum looking at them.

"Reyna?" Mum turned back around.

"I'm sure the photos were taken with a phone camera. Not a camera the paparazzi use. This isn't a professional job. The quality is poor and the images are blurry, like whoever took them was rushed or moving while taking them. I've contacted someone I know who works at the paper and I'm working to see if I can get them to admit who gave them the photos," Reyna explained.

"It could have been anyone. A random member of the public who happened to be walking along that beach," I said.

"If that was true, why didn't the news come out sooner? The paper would have released the photos during the summer break, close to when they were taken, not over a month later. The timing is odd. Like someone waited to release them, waited for the moment when it would throw you off your game the most."

"Are you suggesting someone in F1 leaked them to the press?" I asked.

"Yes, sadly, I think so." Reyna sighed.

"Your friend at the newspaper will never give up their source," I told her.

"They will, but only for something in return. An exclusive interview with you."

I shook my head.

"Tell them Winter will give them an exclusive interview once she's won the Championship, but only after she's won."

"Mum! I'm not doing interviews where they'll only want to ask about my dating life."

"If you don't win the Championship, then you won't have to do the interview. If you do win, then you've got at least a few weeks until you'd have to give them the interview, and you'll be World Champion. They'd be fools to sit there and just ask you questions about your love life. They wouldn't do that to a man who'd just won the Championship, would they?" Mum asked.

"It's clever and it could work. I'll contact my friend and make the offer," Reyna said. "But it's up to you, Winter. Do you want to know who leaked the photographs?"

Did I want to know? Knowing who was behind it wouldn't change anything. It wouldn't take us back in time and stop the photos from getting published, but maybe Mum was right. If I knew who'd done it, I'd have some sort of peace of mind. I'd know who I couldn't trust in this sport. If I knew who, then I'd know who to be mad at, or who to get revenge on.

"Yes, I want to know."

"Okay. I'll see what I can do." Reyna picked up her tablet and left the room.

"There's just one last question to ask," my mum said. "Winter, what do you want?"

I stared at her. It was the same question Aiden had asked me, but I hadn't been able to give him an answer. Or maybe I knew I couldn't give him the answer he wanted to hear.

"What do you want?" she asked again.

"To be the Formula One World Champion."

"Then let's make it happen."

Winter: I'm sorry for pushing you away. You were right. I took my anger out on you and used it as an excuse to push you away. I'm sorry I did that to you, and I'm sorry I kept you waiting for a reply. I know what I want now. I want to be the World Champion. It's what I've wanted all my life. I have to give it everything I've got, and I need to do this by myself.

Aiden: I understand, but I still believe we could fight for the Championship on-track and be together off-track. We could have it all if we wanted to: if you wanted to?

Race Report

1st – Stefan Brudes

2nd – Aiden Sterling

3rd – Winter Jones

Championship Driver Standings

Stefan Brudes – 275

Aiden Sterling – 274

Winter Jones – 251

FORTY-NINE

BRAZIL

FRIDAY

THE CAR FELT good during Friday practice. I felt good, too. This was the last race of the season and my last chance to win, but I was confident after Mexico, where I fought back up to third. I proved to myself I could do it, that I could recover from a bad day; now I had to prove it to everyone else and win the Championship.

I pulled my car into the Torrin garage. My mechanics swarmed as it idled in its bay. I got out and started to pull my helmet off. Reyna lingered at the back of the garage, watching me. She tilted her head towards the exit out back. Gathering my helmet, gloves, and balaclava, I put them down next to Ash's workstation and told him I'd be back in a few minutes to go through my practice data.

Reyna and I made our way to the back of the garage and we huddled together in a tight corridor.

"I know who leaked the photos," she said in a hushed voice.

"Who was it?" I asked.

"Are you sure you want to know? You could put this behind you. Focus on the weekend instead. I can tell you after the race?" she asked, her eyes darting towards one of Stefan's strategists as they walked past us.

"Just tell me." At this point, the worst had already happened and I wasn't going to let anything else throw me off.

"It was Stefan, or someone from his team, his manager or trainer. That's what my friend told me. They received the photos of you and Aiden at the end of that week and decided to run the story at the weekend."

I stared at her for a moment, taking in her serious expression as she waited for me to respond. I burst into hysterical laughter.

"Hah! Of course it was Stefan! Who else would it be?" I continued to laugh. I should have known it was him. Last year, he punched his teammate. This year, he went to the papers.

"Are you okay?" She raised an eyebrow as I recovered from my laughter.

"I'm fine." I waved her off, catching my breath. "Actually, I'm better than fine. Thank you for finding out for me." I pulled her into a tight hug, catching her off guard. She felt stiff in my arms but relaxed as I released her. "Thanks again," I said, moving past her and heading towards the exit into the paddock.

"Wait, where are you going?" she called after me.

I waved a hand but kept going. There was something I had to do.

I FOUND Stefan in the middle of the paddock, not far from the Torrin motorhome. He stood with his manager and personal trainer, the three of them talking. The paddock was busy, with teams having finished the practice session. A few fans were walking up and down with their passes on show around their necks and a few reporters were lingering looking for interviews.

I walked straight up to the three of them and stared right at Stefan.

"So, it was you who sent the photos of me and Aiden to the press?" I said, my voice loud but calm. A few heads turned in our direction.

"I don't think this is an appropriate time to have this—" Stefan's manager began, his German accent thick, but I cut him off.

"I wasn't speaking to you." I kept my gaze on Stefan.

"It was me," he finally replied, with a casual "so what" shrug. "I'd noticed you and Sterling during the race season, having private conversations and eyeing each other whenever you thought no one was looking. At first, I thought he was giving you tips on racing against me, but then I spotted you in Monaco during the summer break, at one of my favourite restaurants, too. I was curious, because why would you be in Monaco when you didn't live there? I had a hunch and so I followed you. I saw an opportunity and took it." He shrugged again, like none of this was a big deal, as if he hadn't acted like a crazy stalker tailing us down to the beach that day. He must have put in a lot of effort to get those photos: followed us in a car into France and stayed hidden on the beach. What a creep.

"And then you kept the photos for a few weeks?"

"I wanted to wait for the right moment to really put you and Aiden off your game, and the plan worked well."

I couldn't stop another laugh from escaping me. "But they didn't work! They didn't stop Aiden from staying with you in the points and I've caught back up to you now. Your actions have proven something really important to me," I said.

He frowned. "Proven what?"

I took a small step towards him and leaned towards his ear.

"I'm in your head and that means I've already won," I whispered to him and moved back. "You're a pathetic, desperate little man. You had to sink to such low levels to beat me. You've got nothing on me now," I spoke louder so everyone could hear.

I started to walk away, leaving the three men stunned.

"You don't even have a drive for next year!" Stefan shouted after me and I could hear his manager telling him to calm down.

"For now!" I shouted back, not even turning to face him.

"I'm still in the Championship lead!"

"For now!" I repeated, heading for the Torrin motorhome. "See you on the track!"

I smiled to myself. Stefan wouldn't be a problem for me anymore. As I reached the Torrin motorhome, I spotted Sterling outside the Silvers motorhome. His gaze seemed to burn and stayed on me until I stepped inside and out of view.

Inside, I took in a deep breath.

"Hey, you okay?" Gem said, getting up from the table she'd been sitting at with my parents. Mum looked up at my sudden arrival.

"Better than ever," I said, meaning it.

"We weren't expecting you back yet. Was practice okay?" Mum asked, concern creasing her forehead.

"All good, car felt great, and I'm ready for tomorrow."

"Excellent!" Mum grinned.

"Do you have my phone?" I asked her. She took my phone out of her bag and handed it to me. "Thanks, I'll be right back."

Leaving my family, I went upstairs and out onto the rooftop deck, hitting Jean's contact as I went. The sun beat down on me and I unzipped the top half of my race suit as I waited for Jean to pick up.

"Hello Winter, I don't have any updates to share yet," she

said by way of greeting, but I'd gotten used to our blunt method of communicating with each other. No small talk, just business.

"I know for certain that there's going to be a seat available at Cavallo Rosso next season," I said. I'd kept Théo Laurent's retirement a secret for long enough and I had to put myself first now. It was the last race of the year. If the gossip got out now, then he wouldn't have to deal with it for long.

"At Cavallo Rosso? I've already tried them. They said both their drivers have contracts."

"Try again. Forget other teams and focus all your persuasive powers on them. One of their drivers is retiring this year. They will have a free spot. Tell them I'm going to win the Championship and the number One would look good on their red car," I said.

"Who's retiring, Laurent or da Silveira? How do you know this?"

"It doesn't matter who or how. Get me into that team," I said and she went quiet for a moment.

"Okay, I'll make some calls."

"Thanks, Jean."

"You focus on Qualifying. Getting onto pole will make my job a whole lot easier."

"Don't worry. I've got this."

BRAZIL

SATURDAY - AFTER QUALIFYING

Qualifying Report
Pole – Winter Jones
2nd – Aiden Sterling
3rd – Stefan Brudes

AFTER QUALIFYING and all my media commitments, I walked into the Torrin motorhome with Reyna. No matter what happened tomorrow, this would be one of the final times I'd hang out in the Torrin motorhome with these people and this team. I tried not to get too caught up in those thoughts; I had to stay focused. I had pole position, so now all I had to do was keep that lead, win the race, and hope both my Championship rivals had terrible race results.

A buzz of chatter hummed in the air. Both Reyna and I approached the table where my parents and Gem sat. My mum and dad were looking over at one of the big screens in the corner. Gem had her head down, staring at her phone. The TV screen showed the live coverage of the Qualifying weekend. Two of the British TV pundits stood in the pits talking. No sound came out of the speakers, but delayed subtitles ran across the screen in black, blocky letters.

"What's going on?" I asked.

Mum turned away from the screen. "Théo Laurent just announced his retirement from F1."

"Oh, I see," I replied, trying to sound surprised. Gem looked up from her phone and frowned at me.

"This is going to shake things up," Mum continued, turning back to the screen to try to keep up with whatever the pundits were saying. "A lot of drivers will be after that seat. Cavallo is a top team. I know they haven't had the best season this year, but it's Cavallo." Mum loved the F1 gossip. She couldn't help getting sucked in.

Gem got up suddenly. "Upstairs," she said, looking at me and then Reyna. I nodded, reached for my mum's bag and grabbed my phone out of it. Reyna and I followed Gem up to the rooftop garden.

A few team members loitered around the terrace. The three of us gathered at the railing overlooking the paddock.

"You didn't seem surprised about Théo Laurent," Gem said.

"I'm surprised it took him this long to announce it!"

"You knew?" Reyna asked.

"Good thing I called Jean yesterday. At least she's had a little head start over the other drivers' managers and agents," I muttered, wishing I'd told her weeks ago.

"I still want to know how you knew before all of us." Reyna crossed her arms.

"I accidentally found out. It was back when Aiden and I

were sneaking around. Might have snuck into one of the bathrooms at Brenner's party. Then Matias da Silveira and his wife came into the bathroom. Aiden and I hid, but we overheard their conversation, which happened to be about his teammate's retirement plans."

"That was months ago, and you didn't say anything? You could have gone after his seat before anyone else," Reyna said.

"I know, but Aiden convinced me not to say anything. It wasn't fair to let slip Laurent's retirement plans before he announced it on his own terms. You know how managers and agents like to talk. It would have been all over the F1 news in a matter of days."

"Really, a bathroom?" Gem asked, with a smirk on her lips.

"I know, I'm super classy. I was caught up in the moment."

"Caught up and falling in love," she teased.

"I... Don't say that," I hushed, glancing around, hoping no one else had overheard.

"What? Like it's not true?" Gem stared at me.

"I... I..."

"Exactly," Gem said, looking smug. "After the race, you should really try to sort your head out and then maybe go speak to Aiden. The gossip has settled down now. Everyone has other news to obsess over."

"I need to stay focused. No distractions."

"That's why I said after the race," Gem repeated.

"Reyna," a voice called from the doorway. Michael stood there, an impatient frown creasing his forehead. I couldn't wait to be free from him after tomorrow.

"I have to go," Reyna sighed. "Shame the Cavallo's PR guy isn't retiring too," she muttered, making her way across the terrace to Michael.

"I need to make a quick call," I told Gem.

"Calling Loverboy?"

I glared at her.

"Okay, okay, I was only teasing." She laughed and wandered back inside.

I hit Jean's contact and started walking along beside the rail as the phone rang.

"If you can predict the future, you could have at least told me the lottery numbers," Jean said, answering my call.

"Haha, did you call Cavallo?" I asked.

"I did."

"And?" I asked, taking in a deep breath.

"Cavallo are unsure, or they're just keeping their cards close to their chest right now."

"Did you tell them this Championship is mine?"

"You haven't won it yet, Winter," she reminded me.

I let out a huff. "I'm on pole and it's the last race of the season. It's mine."

Jean went quiet for a moment. "I'll contact them again."

"Good, but wait, I have a favour to ask."

She sighed. "Go on then. What do you want?"

FIFTY-ONE

BRAZIL

SUNDAY - RACE DAY

He was either about to make a grand gesture or make a stupid mistake, but he had to at least try.

I GOT out of the shower and started drying off, slowly wrapping my hair up in a towel and trying to focus on the small actions of my morning routine. I kept my hands busy and my mind on the task of getting ready. I could not let my thoughts wander to the impending race; better to stay in the moment, focus on the feel of my moisturiser, the stretch of my socks as I pulled them on, and the hum of the hairdryer as it blasted me with hot air. My phone kept buzzing on the side table, but I ignored it. Mum said she'd meet me at eight and we planned on going down to the track together a bit later than my usual time. That way, I was less likely to bump into Stefan, Michael, or any other distractions.

I switched my phone to silent and carried on getting ready.

Half an hour later, someone started banging on my door.

I wrenched it back to find Gem.

"Why aren't you answering your phone?"

"It's on silent. I didn't want to be disturbed," I said like it was obvious. "What's going on? Has something happened? Are my parents okay?" I asked, starting to panic. Gem knew the plan for the morning.

"Your parents are fine, don't worry, but you should really check your messages."

"Or you could tell me what's going on?" I replied, frowning at her and the way her lips curved slightly, like she was trying not to smile.

"Follow the link I sent you. That's all," she said, turning around and starting back down the hallway.

I leaned out my door to watch her go.

"Gem!"

"Check your messages!" she shouted back before disappearing around the corner.

"What the hell?" I muttered, closing the door and grabbing my phone.

I perched on the edge of my bed as my home screen came to life and a bunch of notifications filled the screen. I went straight to Gem's messages, and as she'd said, there was a link to a sports news article with Aiden's name on it.

My stomach flipped as I clicked the link. The article opened and a video started automatically. Intro music played before Aiden and Astrid Carlson came on the screen. They were sitting in two armchairs, angled, sort of facing each other. This wasn't some tabloid interview. Astrid Carlson's sports journalism was highly respected throughout the sporting world.

"Let's start with the year you've had," she began. "You're on the eve of what could be your fourth World Championship title! Did you expect to be here when you started the season?"

Aiden leaned back, looking thoughtful, taking his time to

answer. Normally, he breezed through interviews and always appeared to know exactly what to say with a smile here and a look at the camera there. This felt different.

"If I'm honest, no."

"No? You had doubts about the car at the start of the season?"

"No, the car was great. I had complete faith in my team and they'd worked hard over the winter before the start of the season."

"Then what was it?"

"Me. My third title had really taken its toll on me; that whole year had been a tough one, and I doubted whether I could do it all over again. I wondered if I even wanted to do it all over again. Part of me questioned if I'd fallen out of love with racing, whether my passion and determination had faded. You need passion to be in this sport, to keep bringing your best every day, to stay focused and push through those tougher moments. If I didn't love it anymore, then I questioned why I should stay in F1."

"But you didn't quit. You came back for another season," she added.

He sighed. "I did. I had a contract, I'd made a commitment to my team, to the fans, and I wasn't going to let them down, but I didn't believe I'd be fighting for another Championship win."

"Then what changed? Because here you are, one of three drivers about to battle it out at the last race of the season for the title."

"That's easy. I fell back in love with racing again," he replied, finally smiling.

"And how did that happen?"

"Someone showed me how," he replied, and suddenly my heart started beating faster.

"I see," she replied with a knowing smile.

"At first, when Winter joined F1, I had a new competitor. She challenged me and I wanted to be better, race better and faster than her. Then there was her passion for this sport, her determination and drive to beat me and everyone else. It was infectious. Racing her on the track was thrilling, and then I got to know her off-track: she's funny, witty, and she knew how to put me in my place out of the car too. And to all the doubters and haters saying I went easy on her: they're wrong. I've never had to up my game like I have this season. To those sports commentators questioning her integrity and her actions— shouldn't you be questioning mine too, or at least to the same level? The only time she pursued me was on the track. I'm the one who pursued her, wanted more with her than a racing rivalry."

"And for clarification, for anyone who's been living under a rock the past few weeks, you're talking about Winter Jones, who you're currently fighting against for the Championship title?" she asked.

"Yes," he confirmed. My heart continued to race.

"I know you don't like discussing your personal life," she began, then paused, as if trying to think of the right question to ask next.

"No, it's okay. I wanted a chance to put the record straight, to hopefully put an end to some of the rumours and specula-tion, and to challenge some of the negativity thrown at Winter instead of me. If you're going to criticise her, then you should criticise me too."

"Anything in particular you want to set straight?"

"We dated for a few months, but we kept it to ourselves to avoid the negative attention and scrutiny," he said, sounding so unsure of himself that it almost hurt me to watch him like this.

"For a few months? So, you're not together anymore?"

"The media attention has been hard on her, on us both."

"And that's why you agreed to this interview with me? To set the record straight?"

"Perhaps." He smiled. "It's not the first time racing drivers have dated. Perhaps not in F1, but we're certainly not the first opponents or athletes to get together outside of their sport. Hopefully, with a bit of time, people can see it's not such a big deal."

"I guess you'll find out when this interview goes live." She chuckled.

He laughed with her, one of his media-friendly laughs.

"But you're back to racing at your best now?"

"Yes, better than ever, but we'll see if I decide to continue."

"Continue?"

"If Winter doesn't race next year, then I might call it quits because, for me, there's no F1 without her now."

"Really?" She leaned forward in her seat, her eyes a little wider.

"Yes."

Astrid Carlson wound up the interview and I stared at my phone screen as an advert played, his words repeating in my head.

There's no F1 without her.

FIFTY-TWO

BRAZIL

SUNDAY - RACE DAY

He kissed her and didn't care that the world was watching.

AFTER WATCHING AIDEN'S INTERVIEW, I called Reyna and asked her if she could work her magic and sneak me into Aiden's hotel. It was still early in the morning, ten past seven, and he had to be in his hotel room. I hoped he was. Reyna promised to do her best, and while I waited for her to call back with good news, I messaged Gem and asked her to keep my parents busy for an hour or so.

Gem: What do you mean, keep them busy?
Winter: Tell them I've already gone down to the track and I'll meet them at the motorhome.
Gem: And if they ask why you've changed the plan?
Winter: I don't know. Make an excuse. I'm in a strategy meeting or something.

Gem: You're going to see him, aren't you? Don't worry, you can owe me for covering for you.

After another call with Reyna and a carefully arranged car service, I was escorted into a side entrance of Aiden's hotel by a security guard. Reyna really did work her magic and then some.

At Aiden's door, I knocked once. The loud noise echoed down the corridor. Muffled sounds came from behind the door and then it swung back.

For a moment, we stared at each other, his face surprised. This was the first time we'd been alone together since the argument after everyone found out.

"Are you going to invite me in?" I asked.

"Yes," he replied. He held the door open wide and I walked inside.

His room was about twice the size of mine and had a separate little sitting area with two sofas facing each other and a coffee table in the middle. A big arched doorway led into his bedroom. The bed was made and everything was neat and tidy, exactly the way he liked it.

"I saw your interview." We stood facing each other.

"I'm sorry; I know you didn't want interviews or for us to talk openly about what happened with us, but I needed to say something." He rubbed the back of his head. "I was sick of all the rumours and seeing criticism thrown your way. I probably should have asked you before agreeing to it, but I didn't know where we stood. You were pissed at me and—"

I reached for him, grabbed his shirt, pulled him to me, and pressed my lips to his. He was startled for a moment before deepening our kiss. I wrapped my arms around his shoulders while one of his arms tightened around my waist. He backed us up towards the wall, bracing one hand above my head. I ran my tongue over his lower lip and he opened his mouth. I got completely lost in kissing him. I'd missed him.

He broke away suddenly and placed his forehead against mine. We both took a moment to breathe and then he moved back and looked at me.

"I need to know what this means?" he asked. I should have talked to him before kissing him. I should have figured out what I wanted to say first. I should have worked out and untangled the mix of emotions in my head.

"I know. So do I," I replied. It was time to be honest with myself and my feelings and stop being so scared. I took a deep breath and stared into his deep brown eyes. "I tried to pretend otherwise, but you were right. I did push you away. I used my contract as an excuse, and then I used everyone finding out about us as an excuse, too. But I wanted you then, I want you now, and I want you for however long you will have me. I want us to be together, as a real couple, and I no longer care what anyone else thinks."

He smiled and moved closer to me again. "Are you sure? Because if you are, there's no getting rid of me now."

"I'm sure."

He leaned in again and kissed me hard, his tongue sweeping into my mouth like he was trying to make up for all the time we'd lost. My hands roamed up and down his back. His lips trailed kisses down my jaw to my neck. I gasped when he sucked on a sensitive spot.

"I didn't think I was into big romantic gestures," I said as his mouth pressed kisses along my collar.

"I hope you're not expecting me to do an interview every time we argue," he said.

"I'm sure you can find other ways to make it up to me," I replied and he squeezed my ass. I grinned up at him as I lifted a leg and hooked it around him, bringing our bodies even closer.

He adjusted one arm so it rested against the wall above us, to steady us.

"Good, because I'm far better at make-up sex than public speaking." He kissed me and I wrapped my arms around his shoulders and neck, holding onto him.

I started to explore with my mouth and tongue, along his jaw and down his neck, getting completely lost in him.

I ground my hips against him, feeling his hard erection through the layers of our clothes. A desperate moan escaped from my mouth. Make-up sex should probably be slow, meaningful, with time for longing touches and exploration, but we didn't have time. We'd also spent over a month hardly talking, always seeing each other at race weekends but never being alone together.

His eager hands roamed over my body, up and under my top, while my fingers went to the button and zipper of his shorts. I yanked the zip and pulled the shorts down to his thighs, taking his boxers with them.

He chuckled at my impatience, but I ignored him and unbuttoned my shorts. He helped, moving back, pulling at my shorts and then my underwear, tugging them down my legs, his fingers brushing against my smooth skin. I shoved my trainers off, kicked my feet out of my clothes and pulled him back up to me, my hands guiding him closer to my body. He rested one arm on the wall above us and snaked his other around my waist again. But he paused, letting his lips hover just above mine.

"Someone's in a hurry," he said in a low, teasing voice.

"We don't have much time, and I'd really like it if you fucked me. Please?"

He responded instantly, lifting my leg to hook around his waist and then kissing me hard. Suddenly, he was there at my entrance, and with one thrust of his hip, he was inside me.

I let out a loud moan. He felt so good.

He was hard and fast and it was exactly what I needed.

"Yes!" I shouted, feeling my body tighten. "More," I half-whispered, half-moaned, my voice not sounding like my own anymore.

"You want more?"

"Yes, yes, yes," I repeated like a prayer. "Please."

"Can you take it?"

"Yes!"

His arm gripped around my waist and my leg tightened around him as he slammed into me. I could feel my muscles coiling, the pressure building, almost tipping over.

"Winter, I'm so close, I can't..."

"Aiden!" I let out a cry as I came undone. He followed me with his own orgasm.

"Fuck," he whispered, leaning his sweating head against mine as we both breathed deeply.

"Yeah," I breathed, agreeing with him.

***

I RETURNED from the bathroom with my Torrin polo straightened out as well as I could get it and back in my navy shorts. I'd run my fingers through my hair and it didn't look too bad. Aiden was back in his clothes, his perfect self, and not looking like he'd just fucked me against a wall. He came up to me and brushed a stray lock of hair out of my face.

"Do I look okay?" I asked.

"Gorgeous as always. Hopefully, the blush on your cheeks will fade by the time you get to the circuit." He gave me one of his cocky grins.

I rolled my eyes.

"I know we're going to try this whole being in a relationship thing," I started, sitting down on the edge of his bed to retie my laces. "But perhaps it's best I leave your hotel through the back and not face any camera crews at the front."

"Yeah, sorry that my interview has created another media storm," he replied, scratching the back of his head.

I laughed. "It's fine. After today's race, I don't care who photographs us. Perhaps I'll visit you in Monaco again and we can walk around holding hands."

"Are you talking dirty to me?" he joked, that annoying grin back on his face.

"Shut up." I hit him playfully as I stood up from his bed.

"How about this? We leave at the same time, but I'll head out the front and distract the photographers while you head out through the back."

"Okay, that should work." I nodded and made to leave, but he grabbed me for a quick kiss. He pulled back and looked nervous for a moment. He looked like he wanted to say something, so I waited, staring up at him.

"I'll see you on the track," he said.

"See you there."

FIFTY-THREE

BRAZIL

SUNDAY - RACE DAY

The last race and his last chance to secure the Championship. In the end, it all came down to one corner. Three cars turned in and only one car came out. His dad once told him never to yield.

WHAT WAS I meant to do now? Pretend like this was another normal race day? The sun beat down on the grid as I stood with Gem and my mum at the side of the track with the usual pre-race fanfare in full swing. VIPs, cameras, and reporters buzzed up and down the grid while the teams continued to work on the cars.

I couldn't get Aiden off my mind and I couldn't keep the smile off my lips every time I thought about what we'd done that morning. I could smell him on me, his cologne and just the scent of him on my skin and in my hair. Gem kept smirking at me and I tried my best to pull myself together. I shouldn't be thinking about him, or us, or our future plans, not right before the last and most important race of the season. The most significant race of my life, and here I was thinking about a man.

"Are you listening to me?" Mum asked.

"What?"

"Think that means she wasn't listening," Gem muttered from beside me.

We both leaned against the barrier, trying to keep out of the way of the pre-race build-up. A few journalists and TV pundits lingered as they passed us by, but none of them stopped to ask me for an interview or comment. It might have something to do with the hard glares Mum threw their way. She stood in front of Gem and me like a bodyguard.

"You were late this morning, you changed our prerace plans, and now you're not listening to me," Mum said.

"I had something to do," I answered and Gem muttered something under her breath. I glared at her. "Mum, I'm sorry. I'm listening now: what did you want to say?"

"I was asking if you needed to speak to Ash or the strategists one last time."

"No, I've got my strategy, and Ash is happy with the car's set-up," I replied, looking over her shoulder to where Aiden stood with his team beside his Silvers car.

Our eyes met for a moment and we held each other's gazes. I smiled and he smiled back. He broke eye contact first as one of his engineers bumped him on the arm. At least I wasn't the only one distracted and not listening.

Mum huffed dramatically and then turned around to see what, or rather who, I was looking at.

"Really?" She turned back to face me. "I could kill him for that interview. He couldn't wait a few hours until after the race." She shook her head.

"Mum, I'm fine. I'm focused." I wasn't.

She folded her arms and found another reporter to glare at.

"Stefan doesn't look happy," Gem commented, tilting her head in his direction. He stood with his engineer next to his car in third position. His forehead creased in a deep frown as he discussed something with his engineer, occasionally gesturing at the car.

"He's never happy." I shrugged. Nothing new there.

"Maybe there's something wrong with his car," Mum said, looking over her shoulder at Stefan. "Michael doesn't look happy either."

"I'm not standing next to Stefan for the national anthem. I will move away from him and I don't care if it causes a scene," I said, sounding childish.

Mum shook her head at me.

"I think the feeling is probably mutual after what you said to him yesterday." Gem laughed.

"He deserved it," Mum said, surprising me. She'd always told me to save my talking for the track and not to get into petty squabbles with other drivers.

"Looks like they're getting ready for the anthem. Better head up there," Gem said as Matias da Silveira walked by in his red race suit, closely followed by Satoru Hayashi, both of them going towards the front of the grid.

"Okay, see you after the race," I said to Mum.

She pulled me into a tight hug. "Whatever happens out there, I'm proud of you," she said, squeezing me even tighter.

"Thanks, Mum." She leaned back and gave me a quick once-over.

"See you on the other side."

I nodded at her and then made my way to the very top of the grid, where race officials had set up an area for the drivers to stand.

I spotted Stefan heading towards the right side, so I went towards the middle. Other drivers were joining the line and a few teammates chatted to each other as they waited. Aiden was still beside his car, talking to one of his teammates. Josh stood next to him, holding a big umbrella over them both.

"Hey, Winter," Benjamin said, taking the spot to my right. "Good luck today."

"Thanks," I replied, smiling back at him. "Did you wear your lucky socks earlier?" I asked him.

"I did, and I've got a good feeling about today's race."

"Really?"

He nodded.

"Maybe I should have borrowed your lucky socks," I said as the music went off and the crowd quietened down.

Someone brushed my left shoulder and I turned to see Aiden take the spot next to me. He gave me a small nod and I held his gaze as the anthem started up. We both looked forward at the same time, with the rise of the music, paying our respects along with everyone else. The anthem seemed endless as I stood beside Aiden, trying not to glance in his direction or think about what his lips on mine felt like earlier.

When the music came to an end, the crowd began to chatter and drivers started to move back towards their cars. I reached out and took Aiden's hand. It was as if my arm moved of its own accord, and my fingers squeezed his. He squeezed them back.

I tugged on his hand and brought him closer to me. In one swift move, I let go of his hand, reached up to his face, and pressed my lips to his. He responded instantly, wrapping an arm around my waist and pulling me closer to him. I could hear the crowd and music, but it sounded far away as my whole world narrowed in on Aiden. All I could think about was his mouth on mine and the way his tongue ran along my lower lip, teasing me. I parted my lips and got completely lost in him.

I didn't need to look to know eyes and cameras were on us. I no longer cared.

When we finally pulled away, I kept my eyes on his.

"Good luck," he said, sounding out of breath.

"You too," I replied, also a little breathless.

"I love you, Winter Jones," he said, and my heart beat hard in my chest.

"I love you too," my voice a whisper.

A moment passed between us and then we separated and went back to our cars and teams. Gem smirked at me with that knowing look while Ash and the rest of the crew got on with their jobs as if nothing had happened. As if kissing Aiden in the middle of the track before the start of the race was a completely normal, everyday occurrence. This could be my future, with no drama or fuss. We could simply be two people who were dating and also happened to race against each other. What would it be like to share a good luck kiss before every single race?

I got ready on autopilot: helmet, gloves, last-minute chat with Ash. Everything I'd worked for came down to this one last moment. Time moved in lurches; one second, everything felt slow, like I could hear every cheer from the crowd, and then everything sped up, and I was in the car making my way around the warm-up lap. As I warmed my tyres up, snaking around the track, I could see Aiden's car in my mirrors. I came back around to the straight and lined my car up in its pole position box. As I waited for every other driver to pull into their spots, I stared forward, watching where the five red lights would go out.

Time slowed again. The wait took forever. Finally, the five lights came on. *One, two, three, four, five.* Then they all went out.

I reacted, pulling off the line and heading straight for the first corner. I kept my eyes on the first turn, trying not to worry about anyone closing in on me. I turned left into the first corner, then right into the second. I continued the first lap in the lead, but Aiden and Stefan stayed with me. I tried not to look in my mirrors and focused on my own driving. Everything I did had to be exact. I couldn't risk losing even a fraction of a second as I continued the first lap.

Heading into the second lap, I could feel the presence of cars at my back. I had to pull forward and get a gap between us. As I went round the first corner again, I saw the edge of a car's nose getting closer to me. I looked in my mirrors to see Stefan trying to overtake on the outside, but I had the racing line, and I pulled ahead coming out of the corner. But he remained close to me as we both went into the next bend. Aiden caught up to us, too. He'd lost his second place to Stefan, but he wasn't letting him keep it.

The three of us drove into the next corner, but only I came out of it.

Stefan and Aiden touched. I watched in my mirrors as they both spun off. I didn't get a clear view of what happened, or who was to blame, but now I had nothing but clear track ahead of me and no one tailing me.

Ash came on the radio.

"Aiden is out," he said.

"Is he okay?" I asked.

"Yes, he's out of the car and heading back to his team."

I breathed a sigh of relief.

"And Stefan?"

"He's down to nineteenth place. His car is damaged. The team is scrambling to see what they can do without bringing him into the pits."

"Okay," I replied, trying to stay focused on my driving.

"I'll keep you updated, but there's nothing you can do about Stefan's position. All you can do is focus on your race."

In order to win the Championship, I needed to win this race and take home the twenty-five points, but I also needed Stefan not to score any points. Mum had worked out the numbers last night. If he scored one single point, he'd take the Championship. One point would mean we'd draw, and then it would come down to who'd won the most races. I'd won four, five if I won this one, and he'd won six. For me to take the Championship, he had to finish outside the top ten and score no points, and that was completely out of my control.

"I will."

I did as Ash said, kept my head down and my mind on the track, the way my car felt, the way the tyres gripped, and the speed down the straight. Everything blurred and came together at the same time. I felt connected to the car, like it became a physical part of my body, an extension around me. The laps began to tick by.

"Update?" I asked Ash over the radio. We kept our communication to a minimum. He only gave me the most important information about my lap times, but he knew exactly what update I wanted.

"Stefan is still outside the top ten," Ash replied.

"Where?"

"Focus on your race, Winter. I'll let you know when you need to know."

I groaned but continued to focus, taking every turn and corner smoothly, trying to perfect every aspect of my racing. My lap times stayed consistent and I pulled out in front with a comfortable gap between myself and the car behind me in second. The laps fell away and my pit stops went to plan.

When I got to the last ten laps, Ash came back onto the radio.

"Stefan is in twelfth; he's gaining on the next car, but remember, he's still carrying damage to his car." Twelfth was outside the points. He'd need to finish tenth to take the Championship.

"If only the chequered flag could fall now!"

"I'll keep you updated."

Ash started counting the laps down. Ten laps to go. Nine to go. Eight, seven, six. I wanted to tell him to quit it as the nerves grew the closer to the finish line I got, but I had a feeling Ash was counting them down more for his own benefit than mine.

"He's moved up to eleventh," Ash said.

"Not the news I was after!"

"We have five laps left. He won't reach Koskinen in tenth in time." I needed to win and I needed every car in the top ten to stay exactly where they were, with no incidents, no car failures, nothing that could give tenth place to Stefan.

"Do you promise?" I asked, but Ash didn't reply. He went back to counting down.

Five laps to go. Four to go. Three, two, one.

I went over the finish line and won the race, but had I won the Championship?

Ash came back on the radio. At first, all that came out of his mouth was an unintelligible roar of noise. I held my breath.

"Stefan finished in eleventh! You did it! World Champion!" he shouted down the radio.

I screamed back at him.

I'd won. I was the new Formula One World Champion.

NOTHING COULD BEAT THIS FEELING, happiness on an adrenalin high. I stood on the top step of the podium, my team cheering me from below, and a crowd forming on the track, all shouting, cheering, and waving flags. The president of the International Motorsport Federation stepped up to my podium, shook my hand and gave me my first-place trophy. I held the trophy up and the crowd cheered again. Looking down, I spotted my parents with my team; Mum and Dad both with tears in their eyes. Gem and Reyna stood beside them, beaming smiles and shouting something with the rest of my team: Ash, the mechanics, the pit crew, engineers and strategists. Michael and Stefan's crew were nowhere to be seen.

The national anthem started to play and the crowd quietened. Benjamin secured second place. He stood to my right, standing a little straighter and prouder for the anthem. Perhaps his lucky socks had worked in the end. Hayashi stood on my left, coming third. He'd battled his way up from tenth on the grid. While waiting to come out onto the podium, I'd seen some of his overtakes on the screen in the cool-down room. I glanced at him as the music played. He grinned down at someone in the crowd just below the podium.

I looked back up and listened to the drone of the anthem. Part of me still couldn't believe I'd done it. All the years of working my way up in different race series, the crashes, the bad cars, the not knowing if I'd ever reach this moment. Now, I'd won the Championship. A single tear escaped and rolled down my cheek.

Movement caught my attention. Someone was pushing their way through the teams crowding below the podiums. A few Torrin members parted and Aiden came through to stand right at the front. He smiled up at me.

The national anthems ended and before I could react, Benjamin grabbed his bottle of champagne and started spraying it at me. Hayashi joined in with his and I tried to get them back with my own bottle. Champagne drenched my hair and rolled down my neck into my race suit. Instead of getting them back, I took my bottle and sprayed the crowd below. More cheers erupted and Benjamin and Hayashi joined me at the rail with their champagne.

I locked eyes with Aiden once more. Instead of continuing with the celebrations, I took a sip of my champagne and handed my drink to a slightly confused Benjamin. He took it and I started to run off the podium area, down the stairs, and out into the crowd where the teams were gathered. I found Aiden in the crowd, sandwiched between one of the Torrin mechanics and a Lawrence team member. I reached for him over the barriers and he pulled me to him.

Our lips met and we kissed in front of a screaming crowd.

Championship Driver Standings

Winter Jones – 276

Stefan Brudes – 275

Aiden Sterling – 274

EPILOGUE
THREE MONTHS LATER

Life was good and he planned on making the most of every second of it.

I TURNED THE PAGE, adjusting the book in my hand. The midday sun warmed the deck. I should have moved into the shade or headed inside the boat, but I'd gotten to a really good part of the book. I was pretty sure the two main characters were about to hook up in a bathroom.

Aiden walked out onto the deck carrying my water bottle. He placed it down beside the lounge chair I was relaxing on. We decided to take a holiday together during the winter break, to get away from it all before the new race season started. The yacht was Aiden's idea. I'd never been that keen on boats, but he'd promised me a relaxing trip with plenty of sunshine and he'd kept his promise. I'd worn a bikini practically every day since the start of the holiday. The weather off the coast of Cape

302

Town was gorgeous: blue skies, light breeze, and warm days and nights.

Aiden grabbed his lounger and set it up right next to mine. He wore a pair of dark swim shorts and I couldn't help but look over the top of my book as he leaned back into his chair, his perfectly toned chest on display. He grinned at me, catching me checking him out. I went back to my book, trying to play it cool.

"What are you reading?" he asked.

"It's a romance between an ice hockey player and a figure skater," I replied, not taking my eyes off the page.

"I see," he said, pulling the book down from my face so he could lean in and kiss me. I parted my mouth and let his tongue sweep across my bottom lip.

I broke the kiss and pushed him back.

"Hey! Stop distracting me! I'm trying to read. This is the only time I can catch up on my reading."

"I had other ideas on what we could catch up on." He grinned again, with the smile that made my mind go blank. He pulled the book out of my hand, shut it, and placed it down on the deck. His lips were back on mine and I forgot about the fictional ice skater and hockey player. His hand ran over my stomach, up over my breasts, to my neck. His fingers tangled in my hair. He groaned as I pulled back from the kiss.

"That line was really cheesy," I said, my voice coming out more breathy than I'd expected.

"It worked, didn't it?" he replied and kissed me again, his fingers moving from my hair down to the bikini tie at the back of my neck.

He'd almost freed the knot when my phone started buzzing, making us both jump. It vibrated against the deck beside my water bottle. I broke the kiss, part of me doing it to annoy Aiden, the other part curious to see who'd messaged me. My parents knew I was on holiday and Dad promised to stop Mum from messaging me and to let me have some downtime. Gem also said she wouldn't get on me about keeping up my training, but she would set me a tough post-holiday training plan afterwards. My new F1 team, Cavallo Rosso, also knew I was away, so I wanted to know who'd contacted me.

I picked up my phone to Aiden's annoyance, smirking at him. Gem had sent me a link to an article and a four-word message.

Gem: Look who's joining F1.

I clicked on the link.

"Oh my God!" I sat up so abruptly that I almost knocked Aiden off his sun lounger.

"What's going on?"

"Georgia Stone is joining the F1 grid next season," I replied, scanning the article. "*The controversial, outspoken racer will be joining F1. Better known for her outbursts than her racing, Georgia will join the Hunter team. The daughter of American tech billionaire Jonathon Stone and ex-supermodel Lilian Stone, the highly critical female driver will be the second woman on the grid next season. She will race alongside team-mate James King, who has a reputation as an F1 party boy.*" I continued reading, getting more irritated by the article as I went on.

"Ugh," I grumbled.

"Am I missing something? I thought you'd be happy. Another woman on the grid. Less of a spotlight on you, right?" he asked, sounding unsure of himself as I glared at him.

"She used to bitch about the W series. She never ran out of funding like me and many of the other W racers, not with her dad to bankroll her." I shook my head and went back to the article on my phone.

"Oh, I see how it is," he said, putting on a serious voice.

I raised an eyebrow at him.

"You've already replaced me. We haven't even started the new season."

"What are you talking about? Replaced you?"

"She's your new rival and I'm old news now," he replied, grabbing my phone out of my hand. He held the power button down until the screen went black.

"Hey!" I reached for it and he moved to place my phone on top of my book. "Look, no one could replace you. You'll always be my first racing rival."

He laughed and pulled me back down so we were both relaxed in our loungers.

"That's good, because the next Championship is mine."

I scoffed. "That's what you—"

He cut me off with a kiss.

GridGossip: Hello, F1 Fans! Welcome to my new account! This season, I will have all the best racing gossip straight from the source. I'm an insider now with exclusive access to the behind-the-scenes of F1. Last season marked a change for the sport, and I don't think it will ever be the same again. I can't wait to share all the secrets! Like, share, and follow!

GLOSSARY

Drivers' Briefing – A meeting of all the drivers and the FIA race director to discuss issues relating to that particular Grand Prix and circuit. Driving standards and safety may also be discussed.

Formation lap – The lap before the start of the race. The cars are driven out onto the track, and then form up on the grid for the start of the race. Sometimes referred to as the warm-up lap or parade lap.

Grid – The formation of each driver's starting position on the track at the beginning of the race.

Hot lap in Qualifying – Hot lap means a fast lap. In Qualifying, drivers on a hot lap are trying to do their fastest lap time around the track. It's expected that other cars on the track that aren't on a hot lap move aside to let the faster cars pass.

Marshal – A course official who oversees the safe running of the race. Marshals observe the spectators to ensure they do not endanger themselves or the drivers. They act as fire wardens, help to remove stranded cars or drivers from the track and use waved flags to signal the condition of the track to drivers.

Out brake – A term used to describe a driver braking too late or too softly and then overrunning a corner. A common mistake made during overtaking moves.

Paddock – An enclosed area behind the pits in which the teams keep their transporters and motor homes.

Pits – An area of track separated from the start/finish straight by a wall, where the cars go for new tyres. Drivers stop at their respective pit garages.

Pole position – The first place on the starting grid.

Practice – On-track sessions on Friday and Saturday mornings when the drivers do laps working on their car's set-up in preparation for Qualifying and the race.

Qualifying – The knock-out session on a Saturday in which the drivers compete to set the best time they can in order to determine the starting grid or starting order for the race. The fastest time secures pole position for Sunday's race. Qualifying is split into three parts: Q1, Q2, and Q3. Each phase is a knockout system, with the slowest five drivers being eliminated in Q1 and Q2, with the remaining ten drivers making it into Q3. The Saturday Qualifying session lasts for a set amount of time, with Q1 lasting eighteen minutes, Q2 lasting fifteen minutes, and Q3 lasting twelve minutes.

Racing line – The optimal path around a racetrack. Sticking to the racing line usually ensures a fast lap time.

Retirement – When a car has to drop out of the race because of an accident or mechanical failure. Sometimes abbreviated to DNF – did not finish.

Rookie – A driver who hasn't participated in an F1 Championship before.

Safety car – A vehicle that is called from the pits to run in front of the leading car in the race in the event of a problem that requires the cars to be slowed. For example, if there is an accident and marshals need to remove a car from the track, the safety car will be deployed to slow the cars down while the marshals are on the track or the edge of the track.

Steward – One of three high-ranking officials at each Grand Prix appointed to make decisions. They will make decisions on whether a driver has broken a rule and what penalty will be applied.

Time penalty – Time penalties can be added after Qualifying or a race has ended. Depending on the amount of time added, drivers can lose their position.

ACKNOWLEDGMENTS

First, I want to thank you, the reader. Thank you for picking up my debut novel! Thank you to the BookTok community. You have changed the publishing world and you gave me the confidence to self-publish.

Thank you to my parents and family for supporting me through the publishing process. Thank you to my grandmother for always telling us stories as children and thank you to my sister, Steph. Thank you for reading many of my early attempts at writing: some of them were truly terrible.

Thank you to my friend, Zeena. Thank you for being such a great and supportive friend and for all the funny videos you send me, especially the cute cat ones. Also, thanks for listening to all my many rants over the years. Sorry, there will probably be more.

Thank you to my friend, Nicky. You've always believed in me and offered me support and encouragement when I needed it the most.

Thank you to the best writing critique group ever! Thank you, Chelsie, for helping me with those scenes I struggled to write. Thank you, Cori, for always picking up on my plot holes and asking the right questions. Thank you, Bethan, for waiting to read the whole MS and for all your helpful feedback.

A big thank you to my editor, Lindsey. Thank you for squeezing me into your schedule last minute and for all your hard work editing this book.

Thank you to my proofreader, Sophie. Thank you for fitting me in last minute, for all your hard work and for the fast turnaround too!

Thank you, Amber and Rebecca, for beta reading and for answering any of my publishing questions. It's been so helpful to know I have indie author friends who have done this before and make me feel less lost during the process.

Thank you, Charly, for your publishing advice and for helping me when I had a massive self-publishing panic.

Thank you, Femke, for naming one of my characters. Bastiaan is going to have a bigger role in the next book and I'm thinking that his close friends call him Bas.

Thank you to all my work colleagues, past and present, but a big thank you to Clare, Jemima, and Tally, for all your support, encouragement and kindness.

Thank you to everyone I've met through BookTok, Bookstagram, BookTube, and to all the girls and guys in the buddy reads Discord chat. I know I'm not the chattiest member, but it's meant so much to be included and have a place to chat about reading and other things like the latest series of Love Island, the Eras Tour and discuss the ups and downs of each F1 race.

And finally, thank you to my cat, Motley, for the distractions, for the zoomies, and for stealing my chair.

ABOUT THE AUTHOR

Holly Rose writes romance and The Rivals is her debut novel. Holly spends her free time with her cat, Motley, hiding in the garden shed. When she's not writing and reading, she's probably listening to Taylor Swift, watching F1, or eating pizza.

instagram.com/hollyrose_writes

tiktok.com/hollyrose_writes

youtube.com/hollyroserose_writes

www.ingramcontent.com/pod-product-compliance
Lightning Source LLC
Chambersburg PA
CBHW030940120726
47906CB00002B/649